W9-DCF-203

LIES THAT BIND

LIES THAT BIND

An Alex Duggins Mystery

Stella Cameron

Severn House Large Print
London & New York

This first large print edition published 2017
in Great Britain and the USA by
SEVERN HOUSE PUBLISHERS LTD of
Eardley House, 4 Uxbridge Street, London W8 7SY
First world regular print edition published 2017 by
Crème de la Crime Ltd, an imprint of
Severn House Publishers Ltd.

British Library Cataloguing in Publication Data
A CIP catalogue record for this title is available from the British Library.

ISBN-13: 9780727893079

Severn House Publishers support the Forest Stewardship Council™
[FSC™], the leading international forest certification organisation. All
our titles that are printed on FSC certified paper carry the FSC logo.

Typeset by Palimpsest Book Production Ltd.,
Falkirk, Stirlingshire, Scotland.
Printed and bound in Great Britain by
T J International, Padstow, Cornwall.

To Jerry.
And for all the dear furry creatures
who have imprinted on me their
innocent hearts.

Prologue

The smart ones appreciated a man who could think for himself.

Sid Gammage would show Gary Podmore how much more useful good old Sid could be, and how much more he could be worth.

If I say it to myself often enough, I'll believe it.

He stood in deep shadows behind the empty security hut by the gates to Podmore Hauling and Storage. He'd been in that yard almost daily in the three years he'd worked for Podmore as a lorry driver. This was only one of a handful of times he had been to the place at night, but from what he'd overheard two men talking about in the toilets the previous week, night shifts could be where he was heading.

If Gary gave Sid what he wanted – what he needed.

Autumn flirted with the first winter bites and he pulled his woolen hat well over his ears. Gary would listen to him, he had to. The way the proposition was put, the words used, would be very important, but Gary was a good man and he had always given Sid a fair shake.

Few lights showed in the yard and the alleys between buildings were depthless black rectangles.

Sid straightened his back. He beat a tattoo on his thighs with the flattened fingers of his gloved hands.

Come on, come on. Must be the cool night that shortened his breath. He felt his heartbeat in his throat. This was different; that's what unnerved him a bit. He'd never stepped outside his comfort zone to push for something – something he had to have, more money, even if he didn't yet know what he'd have to do for it.

Where was everyone? This was Tuesday, the right night according to the arrangements he'd made with Podmore. And the guard – where was he? Even if work had stopped around seven as it supposedly did, there was twenty-four-hour security, wasn't there? Watching for a moving flashlight beam, he strained to hear the crunch of rock beneath heavy work boots – signs of the guard about his rounds.

The man's small maroon truck wasn't beside the guardhouse. Should have noticed that before.

Could be they were cutting some people's hours to trim expenses. Never a good sign, but it was more likely that Gary didn't want any extra eyes around for his night runs. That's what he'd heard the men muttering about, night runs, and how jammy they were to pull down so much money for simple jobs. He wished he knew what kind of business they were doing but he had already decided that if it was something off the books, he was as capable as any man of not seeing or saying anything. The money was all he cared about.

The wind was bloody gale force and grit stung his face. This Northampton area and stops along the M1 in both directions were his territory. He could drive it with his eyes shut. And he'd been reliable all the time he'd worked for Podmore. His record should stand for plenty.

A vehicle turned in at the wide driveway leading to the yard. Headlights rocked over a speed hump and approached smoothly, the engine almost silent. Must be Gary's Mercedes. He could see the passage of some low light across the black sedan's glassy sheen.

Sid felt a rush of blood through his veins and he ran to open the gates, swing them back, first one, then the other. The Mercedes cruised along the block of warehouses and loading bays to the left and slid to a stop.

Stuffing his hands in his jacket pockets, Sid tucked his chin into his upturned collar and walked briskly toward Gary Podmore's car. At the driver's window, he bent to see inside. Gary gave him a salute and grinned while Sid opened the door.

'Evening, Gary.' Everyone in the company used first names. 'I reckon winter will be at us, soon enough.'

'Very likely.' Thanks to his father's hard work, Gary had been to fancy schools and didn't sound like many around here – except for one or two in the offices. 'Let's get inside and find something to warm us up.' The boss stood and slammed the car shut. He clapped Sid on the back, aiming him toward the building that was all offices above a single vehicle maintenance floor.

Inside the building, Gary threw a couple of switches, lighting the metal steps ahead and the overhead catwalk leading to his own office.

3

'I didn't see your van when I got here,' Gary said, moving ahead to open his office door.

Sid followed him into the room. 'Came on the motorbike. It's behind the guard hut.' He came close to mentioning not seeing the guard but thought better of it. 'I like to use it when I get the chance.' And it was cheaper to run.

'Take a pew,' Gary said. 'A beer, or something stronger?'

'Make it a beer.' Sid sat on the edge of a brown leather armchair, one of two facing a big desk. The only window overlooked the yard behind the buildings and in daylight there was a view toward the city. Sid liked seeing it like this, as a blanket of lights in the distance.

'Bitter or a lager, what's your poison?'

'Something darker, if you've got it,' Sid said.

He didn't hear Gary coming until a glass tankard appeared over his shoulder. 'Digfield, of course. Mad Monk is a favorite of mine. I'm joining you. It's been a long day and this is just what I feel like.'

The beer had a good head on it and Sid took a deep, satisfied pull. Instead of going behind his desk, the boss sat in the other leather chair and rested his glass on the knee of a surprisingly rumpled-looking pair of jeans. The man had a way of making you relax. To look at him now, who would think he owned all this?

'You're straightforward, Sid,' Gary said, touching the back of a hand to his blond mustache. 'I like that. I know where I stand with a man like you.'

4

Sid smiled and sat straighter. 'I hope your missus isn't upset with you having an extra appointment tonight.' That sounded like the right tone to have. Friendly but not too familiar – wasn't it?

'I have a lot of evening meetings. Let's get to it. You let me know you wanted to talk to me about extra work. At night, you said. I think you had something particular in mind.'

'I do,' Sid said. And he had to put it just right. 'I heard you have some night runs that go out. It's not being talked about by everyone, nothing like that. Just something I overheard. My mum used to tell my dad to watch what he said out loud 'cause little jugs have big handles. She meant me. Some get the brains and the looks, but I got the ears. Sometimes I wear ear plugs—'

'I see,' Gary said and Sid shut his mouth. When he was nervous he talked too much. 'What made you think I might have something for you? This is work that's important in a different way from the everyday runs. This is my way of paying back for all the good fortune I've had. My work for the larger community of less fortunate people, if you like.'

Charity work? Sid swallowed. He wasn't in a place where he could volunteer for things. 'I see,' he said. His debts were way out of hand. 'Things are always a bit of a push for me with the kids and no help with anything. I'm looking for a way to make extra money and thought it would be nice if I could do something here where I've got my regular job. I do admire you for helping out with people in real need.' He might as well be honest but it wouldn't do not to recognize the man's volunteer works.

'Who talked to you about this?' Gary wasn't smiling. He regarded Sid with hard, unflinching eyes.

He'd expected this. 'Two men,' Sid said, making sure not to flinch himself, or look away. 'I didn't see them, Gary. Honest.'

'The one thing I can't afford is indiscretion. Loyalty isn't an option, it's a requirement. Talk could ruin everything.'

'I haven't said anything except to you. I—'

'I believe you.' Gary puffed up his cheeks and seemed lost in thought for seconds. 'But I need to find out who shot their mouths off. Any ideas?'

'No.' Sid took a swallow of his beer.

'Do something for me. If you hear someone you think might have been one of those men, come straight to me. Can you do that?'

And then Gary would fire them? He wouldn't do anything worse, would he?

'Sid?' Gary's eyes stayed on Sid.

'Of course,' Sid said. He had difficulty swallowing.

'Good.' Gary slipped out of his denim jacket and hooked it on a coatrack. 'I'd offer you more beer but I don't want you over the limit when you've got to drive.' He chuckled.

'Of course not.' The glass in Sid's hands was still half-full. The other man, going back and forth between Mr Nice and something vaguely threatening, unnerved him.

6

Seated again, leaning toward Sid with his hands loosely clasped between his knees, Gary looked very serious. His own beer sat on a table beside him, barely touched. 'Sometimes fate sends us what we need. Do you believe that? I do.'

'I do, too.' But not always fast enough to keep the wolf from the door.

'Good. Tell me about yourself. I know you're married and you have kids but it's hard to keep up with the people who work for me.'

'Of course it is. I'm a widower.' Sal had walked out the first time years ago, after their first child was born, left Sid and their baby, and not a bit of an explanation. Four years later she turned up – with another baby. Sid had wanted her back fiercely and he took in the little one as he would his own. Sal lasted less than two more years before she took off and never came back again. That had been nine years gone now and not another word.

He felt Gary staring at him, waiting for him to say something else. 'It's easier now the kids are older, seventeen, and thirteen.'

'Expensive, though,' Gary said. 'We've got children of our own, so I know. I'm very sorry for your loss.'

'It was a long time ago.' No need to talk about what had really happened.

'How would you feel about driving at night on a regular basis? Fairly long runs, hundred or so miles each way, but straightforward and you'd be working with several other drivers doing the same thing. I'm expanding and I need another good man. The pay is more than good. And if you can find a way to keep up maybe a half-day shift as well, so much the better – and you'll be that much better off.' His smile was pleasant as if he understood Sid was in a tight spot.

Rubbing his forehead, Sid tried to calculate distances, and the times when he'd sleep. If he made enough he might have to get a cheap room somewhere. The boys would manage, they'd been managing since they were little. The three of them pitched in together and they got through. He wanted them to have the education he'd missed. He wanted them to really get somewhere. They were bright and might get scholarships. If not, this could be how he managed it, but that was over and above the debts he had to get rid of.

'Sid?'

He looked up quickly. 'Sorry. Thinking about logistics is all. Yes, I want to hear all about it, and do it. I've a clean driving record and every customer I deal with would put in a good word for me. I was just working out the best way to handle the two shifts. It'll work, though. Yeah, this sounds good, Gary. Thank you.'

'What about the children at night?'

A boss who cared about his workers and their families. How unusual was that? 'I've got a sister. Bit younger than me. Single. She's an artsy sort. Self-publishes the odd children's book and does illustrations for people. Doesn't make a lot, I don't think, but she gets by and she's been good to come and stay for a few days if I've needed help. Sickness or whatever. I think I could work something out with her. Staying free at ours would be a help to her, and . . . yeah, I'll have everything well in hand.' Anyway, the kids were used to carrying on alone if they had to. Cheryl could be unpredictable but he'd have to see what could be worked out and he wasn't about to queer this chance when it looked so good.

A door, it must be the front one downstairs, slammed with enough force to send shock waves up the metal stairs. Gary shuddered. 'Damn it. I thought we shut . . . oh, that'll be Ellis and Nicky. They work on the project for me. Nicky does all the paperwork.'

Sid listened to footsteps on the stairs. 'How many drivers are there in this group?'

'Er, four.' Gary frowned. 'Five with you.'

There was no knock before the door opened. Nicky was a well-padded woman around forty wearing a headscarf over brown curly hair that stuck out over the collar of a bulky woolen coat. Her face was pleasant enough in an ordinary way – too thin perhaps, and with puffy darkness beneath her eyes. She nodded at Gary and stationed herself not far from the door, trainers planted apart and her hands in her coat pockets.

Ellis was not ordinary. Well over six foot and built like a bouncer but without an ounce of fat on all the muscle, he wore his dark hair combed straight back from a broad pockmarked face. He approached Sid with a hand outstretched. 'Ellis,' he said, glancing at Gary who nodded. 'Welcome aboard then. The boss mentioned you. We need the help.'

9

Gary didn't answer. He got up and went behind his desk, took out an envelope and went to tuck it in an inside pocket of his jeans jacket.

'I use another site to coordinate these other runs,' Gary said. He didn't sound relaxed anymore. 'We'll head over there now so you'll know where to go tomorrow. I'd like you to start tomorrow.'

That soon? Before there had been time and opportunity to go home and discuss what he was about with the boys?

'Is that a problem?' Gary snapped at him.

Sid's knees locked. He hadn't expected the complete switch in Gary's manner.

'No problem at all. Are there forms to fill out or anything?'

'Leave all that to us,' Nicky said, not meeting his eyes. 'There's no hurry and I like these things neat and tidy which means I can't hurry the process.' She didn't sound British. Could be Eastern European. Sid noticed she didn't look at him – or either of the others, only at the floor.

He could back out if things got a bit sticky, Sid thought. Intuition, feelings – emotion – had never been encouraged when he was growing up and his coping skills for any situation that was new, and not quite straightforward, were thin.

'You don't have a problem with that, do you, Sid?' Ellis said. His smile wasn't reassuring. 'You come to me if you do, see. The woman doesn't understand the men.' He sniggered and Sid felt a bit sick.

'I don't have any problems.' Damn, he sounded hearty and nothing like himself. 'Would you like me to come earlier than usual in the morning so I can get familiar with what I'll have to do later? It'll save time.'

'Like I've told you, we'll go over that now,' Gary said. 'That's why Nicky and Ellis came in. You come in my car. They'll follow.'

The jumpiness attacking Sid's insides was making it hard for him to concentrate. They'd said there was no hurry for anything, now he had to rush off somewhere else with them.

Gary waved him ahead and out of the office. Nicky followed but Ellis and Gary fell back. They spoke in low voices and Ellis glanced at Sid, kept his eyes trained between his boss and Sid.

He'd as well make sure he wasn't getting in over his head. Now, rather than when it might be too late. 'You'll understand if I get in touch with my kids first, explain what's going on? Just a quick call. Then I'll get home afterwards and talk to my sister. I can be in as early as you like in the morning.'

It couldn't be hot but his shirt stuck to his back and his palms sweated. He prayed his anxiousness didn't show.

'You're with us now,' Gary said. 'We'll get over to the center and get you settled. It's still early.'

'I'm going to need to find somewhere to stay when I can't get home,' Sid said. His breath caught in his throat and he coughed.

'Already taken care of,' Gary said, grinning.

'We've got rooms at the center. Good grub, too. I'll follow you down.'

Sid hesitated, then started down the stairs.

'See you there,' Gary called out to Ellis and Nicky.

'Have you said anything at all to your sister about taking on extra work, Sid? Just so she'll be ready when you contact her?'

He knew he didn't want these people to think he wouldn't be missed other than by his kids who were used to his odd hours. 'She wouldn't be surprised if I asked her for some help,' Sid said over his shoulder, reaching the bottom of the stairs and pushing open the door to the outside. 'She can come if she's needed so no worries there.'

That was another lie, but it didn't matter unless he was getting in over his head.

'Good for you,' Gary said. 'Let's get going. We've got a fair amount to cover before you head out. The most important thing for you to remember is that you are part of a small, tight team now. What we're doing is important. We rely on each other and, first and always, we are loyal. We never talk to anyone else about our business.'

One

Five Weeks Later

The bus from St John's Primary School rolled to a stop in front of The Black Dog, Folly-on-Weir's only pub, the center of adult village life.

Children in red blazers, striped ties skew-whiff at the unbuttoned necks of their white shirts, straggled into sight and hung around to gawk at two police vehicles that had stopped, sirens still intermittently bipping, waiting for the school bus to move out of their way. The instant the bus did pull out, and the police took off again, sweeping up the High Street in the direction of Underhill, the next village, their flashing lights dimmed by sunlight struggling in and out behind scarves of smoky-looking cloud.

Visions of a garish, speeding funeral cortège sent a shiver through Alex Duggins. She turned her back on the scene. For once it was nothing to do with her.

A flotilla of ducks, webbed feet barely clearing the water, flapped along the pond on the village green, grating out their annoyance at the interruption in their afternoon peace.

'Here, Bogie,' Alex called, still distracted by the activity on Folly-on-Weir's main road. They rarely saw police cars, especially with flashing lights, unless . . . Alex whistled to her black and

13

gray terrier. The less she concentrated on what felt like the response to some serious crime, the better.

The ducks flapped and shook their wings furiously. Bogie had taken advantage of her distraction to dash back and forth by the pond, leaping and yipping from time to time.

'You know better than that.' Alex raised her voice and hurried toward him. 'Naughty, naughty boy.'

He planted all four feet and looked back at her as if he couldn't imagine why she would be cross with him.

Frowning darkly, Alex wiggled the leash in the air and Bogie approached her rapidly, belly lowered in his 'uh oh, I'm in trouble' mode.

Sun struggled against shifting drifts of gunmetal cloud scudding along before a strengthening wind. Winter had made its official entry.

'Alex, what's going on?' A commanding voice reached her from behind and she turned to confront Heather Derwinter striding toward her. 'If anyone knows, you do. Why all the fuss?'

Heather, wife of Leonard, of the impressive Derwinter Holdings, reigned as uncrowned queen of Folly and environs, not that she showed her face in the village often unless it was in the Black Dog, Alex's pub, with a noisy group of horsey, well-booted friends.

'Afternoon, Heather,' Alex said, bending to clip on Bogie's leash. 'The only thing going on for me is that this naughty dog still wants to chase birds.'

Heather lifted her blond hair away from the

14

collar of a buttery, tan suede jacket obviously tailored to fit her lovely curves and made from hide as supple as silk. Her cream trousers fitted tightly and without a wrinkle. 'You know what I'm talking about. Honestly, Alex, you do like to play vague. When you do that you only make people more curious and more convinced you know things you're not saying. I saw the police cars, then I saw you while I was waiting for the school bus to drive on. So I pulled over to ask what you know. Did you get any messages from your friend the chief inspector? Or were you the one who called in some horrible cockup on the way to Underhill. That's where they're all going. Or points farther on. Come on, old thing, give a girl a break and tell all. It's usually your job to dredge up some frightfully bloody disaster. And I do mean *bloody.* Where's the body?'

For an instant Alex came close to laughing; Heather could be a caricature of herself. The effect always amused Alex. 'I've got to run, Heather.' She bundled Bogie into her arms, partly because she loved to feel his warm, compact little body against her, and partly to make him a reason for hurrying away. 'This fellow's getting heavy. We shall have to cut down on the filets. See you later.' She grinned and waved and trotted away toward the road. 'It's starting to rain. Better get that scrumptious jacket in the dry. Looks as if we're in for a storm.'

'You'll let me know when you hear something?' Heather cried.

Not if I can help it.

'Alex!'

Heather didn't give up easily. 'Of course,' Alex told her. 'But it isn't anything to do with us. They're just passing through.' That was her own wishful thinking.

'I feel better now,' Heather all but yelled across the green at her. 'If there was anything to worry about, you'd know.'

Alex buried her face in Bogie's back. Her eyes prickled. Must be the gusts that blew straight into her face.

No wind caused her to stiffen, or sent goose-bumps climbing the back of her neck. The sight of a dark blue Lexus sedan driving on the rear bumper of the police car in front of it was responsible for the revolutions in her stomach. She couldn't make herself move. Whatever the reason for the police being here, she wasn't ready to see Detective Chief Inspector O'Reilly so soon after their last encounter. That car could be his.

'Hey, love, I've been looking for you.' A familiar arm surrounded her shoulders and squeezed her closer.

'Tony,' she said, leaning against Tony Harrison but not looking away from the High Street. 'That looks like trouble.'

'It does. But for once it's not our trouble.'

'Of course it's not,' she said, smiling up into his blue eyes and seeing a mirror of the disquiet she felt. 'Is it? Look, people are going to the Dog. They want to find out what's happening.'

His dark blond hair whipped across his forehead. 'They always expect to find out everything there, don't they? They won't be lucky this time.

Come on, I wanted to ask what you thought about something.'

Walking slowly, ignoring widely spaced raindrops, they reached the road and crossed to the grassy patch in front of the pub. The picnic tables and benches were empty, probably because of the cooling weather. As always, colored lights outlining the roofs were on. At night they gave the place a welcoming touch but most of all, they were there because Alex liked them.

'I walked down from the clinic and went in the back,' Tony said. 'Through the kitchens, but your mum said you were on the green. Katie's waiting on her blanket for Bogie.'

Katie was Tony's big, golden, mixed-breed dog who loved Bogie only slightly less than her place in front of the fire in the bar. Tony was the local vet who cared for a large number of pets and farm animals.

'You seem uptight,' he said, rubbing her arm. 'Don't let a couple of police cars frighten you.'

'I'm not frightened.' She looked up at him. 'Yes, I am. Not frightened exactly. On edge. Part of me doesn't want to know what the police are after and part of me does. Tony, do you feel . . . curious? I think I might and that's sick, isn't it? I should just be hoping nobody's hurt.'

'You could allow yourself to be normal, love. I'm curious, too.'

She handed Bogie off to him. 'But not because you feel you ought to be involved somehow? It's not that, is it? Or, you don't . . . Oh, I don't know.'

'Finish what you started to say.'

Alex turned her face against his arm. 'You don't actually want to take part in it? Whatever it is? You don't wish you had some sort of official reason to be included?'

That earned her a frown. 'I'm not sure I know what you mean,' Tony queried.

'Of course you don't. Forget it. I can run on sometimes.'

'Can't we all. Are you free tonight? Or should I say, can you be free tonight?'

'I can. What's up?' Her knees felt a little wobbly. She'd been aware of her own preoccupation and worried he might read it as a withdrawal from him. But she didn't want to change their usual casual, comfortable way of rubbing along together. She repeated, 'What's up?'

'I miss you,' he said, the corners of his mouth jerking upward in more of a grimace than a smile. 'You're here but I'm starting to think . . . I just want us to have some time together. Talking time. Reconnecting time, I suppose. Are you all right with that?'

This was her fault for not paying enough attention to the signals he'd sent – in his quiet way. 'If you say so. What time?' Smiling at him was always the easiest thing in her world.

Tony grinned and the tension went out of his face. 'Good. OK if I pick you up here when I'm finished? Could be a bit late – not before eight, I shouldn't think. I've got a late surgery.'

They crossed the road. The police vehicles had

disappeared over the hill and the red-blazered children were rapidly dispersing in laughing groups.

'Let me pop this fellow inside and we'll talk out here about that other thing I mentioned.'

She'd forgotten there was anything else. 'OK.'

Tony was a big man but he moved with easy, loose grace. His physical strength showed, even in the casual clothes he preferred. A check shirt with well-worn jeans tucked into green Hunter boots looked good on him. Alex never understood why he was so unaware of being attractive. Perhaps widowhood had matured him to a point where he looked for more than the physical in any interaction with women. The thought made her blush. There had never been any reticence in the physical between them.

He went all the way inside the pub with Bogie and returned a couple of minutes later. 'Just letting Lily know he's there,' Tony said of Alex's mum who shouldered responsibility for the Black Dog's inn and restaurant.

'Let's sit,' Tony said, ushering her to a picnic table that still had its umbrella raised. He sat beside her on the bench. 'You won't run out on me tonight, will you?' he said, looking at his clasped hands on the table.

'Why would I do a thing like that?' She might if she could figure out how to do it without feeling like a worm. *Grow up, Alex. Work out what's eating at you.*

He was watching her closely. 'Because we've both – but particularly you – been avoiding each other. We're like a couple of friends who happen to live on the same street. You say, hello. I say, hello. And all that's left is smiles.'

She pulled one of his hands free. 'That's not exactly true, is it, Tony?'

'Well . . .' He had the grace to look slightly sheepish. 'No, not exactly. But we don't talk much at the moment, Alex. We don't get deeply into things, the things we need to get into – sooner or later.'

'How do we know when it's the right time to do that?' She felt a bit squirrely.

'We don't,' he said, looking squarely into her eyes. 'I wanted to ask you about the boy who works in the kitchen here.'

She looked away briefly, regrouping.

'Scoot, you mean?'

He nodded. 'I didn't even notice him until recently.'

'Hugh Rhys took him on. He knows the family, I think.'

Hugh was Alex's manager at the Black Dog.

'That's what I understand,' Tony said. 'Did you know Scoot's got a younger brother, Kyle?'

'No, I didn't. I don't interfere with Hugh's hiring. There's never been a reason to discuss Scoot. He clears tables, loads and unloads the dishwashers, helps with anything that needs doing. He's a good boy and works hard.'

'Still in school?' Tony said.

'Yes, as far as I know. Actually I do know that because he brings books and works with them during his break. He's seventeen, I think.'

'You know the family?'

'I don't,' Alex told him. 'But Scoot is always

very clean and tidy and on time, and he's good around customers. Hugh seems to think a lot of him.'

'Kyle came by to see if I'd let him help out around the surgery,' Tony said. 'Seems a nice kid – not that I know anything about kids. But he's obviously mad about animals and I like the idea of a sort of internship for kids with interests they might want to follow. I think Radhika would enjoy some company now and again, too, and she'd be patient with questions.'

Tony's assistant was a lovely woman of great patience. From India and, despite her small stature, she was easily recognized at any distance by the striking saris she wore.

'Does Kyle want to be a vet then?' Alex asked.

'So he says.' Tony rubbed her hand between his. 'Doesn't care when he comes or if it's just a couple of hours a week. He's really keen to do some volunteer work.'

She looked sideways at him. 'You like the idea of encouraging someone who's actually interested in veterinary medicine, don't you?'

He smiled a little. 'You caught me. Yes. When I was a kid I'd have loved to be around a vet but I didn't know anyone and I didn't have Kyle's gumption to find a clinic and ask for the chance. Once he loosened up he started talking about reading books on vet medicine and how much he'd like to help with the animals – hands-on, he called it.'

'So what's your question?' Alex asked.

'Mostly I wanted to know how the older brother was working out for you. And I'd like

21

your opinion on whether Kyle's too young for this. Do—'

'Oh, Tony!' She interrupted him, laughing. 'Around here the kids are working on farms from a very early age. It would be a decent thing to do. You can keep it on a casual basis. If you're worried, give him a trial and see. Radhika will watch out for him.' Radhika seemed to have an affinity for all people. The villagers loved her and they didn't always accept incomers, particularly exotic ones, too easily. Alex also considered Radhika a good friend.

'Right. That's what I'll do. I'll get back to the clinic and let you face the questions inside.'

Alex wrinkled her nose. 'It's not fair. I should send them all down to you.'

'Wouldn't work.' They both stood and Tony dropped a kiss on her mouth. 'I don't serve beer.'

He strode in the direction of Meadow Lane and his clinic.

Alex risked a glance around the windows but didn't catch any signs of watching faces. Joan Gimblet, Folly-on-Weir's mayor, her brooding son, Martin, of the film star looks and few words, and an older man whom she didn't recognize, left a new black Mercedes parked with two wheels on the lawn and walked, single-file, to the pub.

After holding the door open for the others, Martin turned a gently intense smile on Alex and followed them inside.

Recovering from that smile, she waited a few seconds before entering the building behind them. She wiped her boots on the rough mat by the door, and went inside the bar with a smile on her face. 'Afternoon all,' she answered greetings loudly, shrugging out of her navy blue duffle coat as she went behind the counter.

Hugh Rhys, big, dark and attractive, raised expressive eyebrows but said nothing. Silence had fallen and Alex didn't need to turn around to know the customers had reversed their directions and now faced her again.

'I'll take that for you,' Hugh said, deftly removing the coat from her hands. 'I need to check out back.' And she didn't miss his grin as he left her alone to field questions.

'Right.' She took up a towel to swipe at a perfectly dry counter. 'Who needs help?' The smile would crack her face shortly.

'The usual,' Major Stroud said, rocking on his heels, his smile stretching a trim, gray mustache. 'Bit of excitement in the village, what?' At least he could not have come to the pub to nose around after seeing the police activity. He'd been in much the same spot for several hours.

She poured his whiskey and set the glass down while he peered at coins in his palm as if someone had switched his pence for rand. A few slow blinks later, he let his money clatter on the bar. 'Talk to O'Reilly, did you?'

Dan O'Reilly was Detective Chief Inspector O'Reilly whom Alex had come to know much better than was comfortable – much as she liked the man. Most of the time.

She slid the major's coins into her hand and moved to the register.

'Does that mean you have been talking to the

23

detective?' Stroud said. He had the beginnings of belligerence in his tone. Alex knew the signs of trouble too well.

'I haven't talked to anyone – the police weren't from our local force. Have you tried the new bacon butties? They're gammon and very tasty.'

'S'almost tea time,' the major said, slurring his words. 'Not my kind of fare for that.'

Joan Gimblet walked deliberately between the major and Alex. 'Let me see,' she began, and rolled her eyes, indicating the irascible Stroud behind her. 'I'll have a gin and lime – make it a double – Martin will have his usual half of best bitter, and a pint of Guinness for my brother. I forgot, I don't think you've met Paul.' A sturdy, blond woman, Joan Gimblet enjoyed being mayor. Several strands of pearls rested on her considerable bosom, which in turn rested on the counter. Joan was not tall. She looked around and beckoned to a man who was obviously related to her. He stood talking to Joan's vaguely disconcerting son who certainly didn't resemble his mother in any way.

'Paul Sutcliffe,' Joan said. She lowered her voice and put a finger to her lips. 'He doesn't spread it around but he's been the head at Amblefield School up north for years. Doesn't like the attention that brings. Just retired a few months ago and he's moved in with me now. Paul, this is Alex Duggins who owns the Black Dog. She's our local celebrity.'

Alex winced but kept a bland smile on her face. She had yet to decide how she felt about Joan Gimblet who could be uncomfortably abrasive, or Martin with his watchful dark eyes which frequently seemed trained on Alex.

Paul's complexion had the same florid hue as his sister and his bright blue eyes and full mouth also matched hers. A lot of gray peppered his sleekly combed blond hair and Alex had the thought that Joan's might be like his if she left nature alone. It was rather nice.

He stuck out his hand and shook Alex's firmly. 'Joan's been trying to get me in here for months,' he said. 'She's still old-school. Ladies don't go into pubs on their own. But now I'm her excuse – when Martin isn't available, of course. Nice place. I'll have to make sure Joan brings me often.'

'You'll be very welcome,' Alex said, thinking he looked young to be retired. 'Will you miss teaching?' She pulled the bitter and Joan passed it to her son.

Paul frowned. 'Yes, but not as much as I thought I would. I believe in moving on to new opportunities. You'll have seen the new youth center being built on the acreage not far from the farm. It's finished apart from a few touches. Joan and I will be staying very busy with that.'

The pieces fell together. This was the man who was responsible for pointing out that the youth of the area had no place to congregate where adults could have a part in guiding them, albeit subtly. With the help of Joan and a committee they had assembled, he had pushed the project through. Joan Gimblet lived at Woodway Farm just to the north of the main village and the center was almost complete on several acres of land Joan already owned. Even though she hadn't seen the place, Alex was kept up to date on its progress by the vociferous pros and cons batted about in the bar.

Alex propped crossed arms on the counter. 'I think what you're doing is exciting. We need something like that here. I grew up around Underhill and Folly and there was really nowhere for youngsters to go. How will you fund all this? I've read about the project but not about the financial arrangements. You shouldn't be expected to shoulder all the expenses, Joan. That's very valuable land.'

Paul gave a loud snort of laughter. Alex noted that Joan didn't join him.

'Natural question,' he said, snuffling into a handkerchief. His face remained flushed. 'Good for you. Most people hesitate to ask.'

'Not exactly *comme il faut*,' Joan said, her eyes narrowed. 'Poor form, if you ask me.'

'Not a bit of it,' Paul said before Alex could attempt an exit from what could fairly be called rude. 'I'm getting some backing from the county and I've got some individual financing. Joan's been tireless with businesses, local and much farther afield. People think it will help young people for miles around.'

Through a smooth move to place his bitter on the counter, Martin Gimblet inserted himself between his mother and Paul Sutcliffe who both inched apart to make room.

Alex avoided looking at Martin and turned to Joan. 'You haven't come to me, Joan. I'm hurt.'

Another bark of laughter from Paul bought his

sister – and Alex – a moment to formulate a response.

'You're on my list,' Joan said with a sweet smile that didn't get as far as her eyes. 'I have all the businesses on the High and on Holly Road to visit yet. Pond Street won't be left out either.'

That meant Alex's friends, Harriet and Mary Burke would be seeing Joan. The sisters owned Leaves of Comfort, their tea and bookshop. Alex wished she could be present for the questions the ladies would come up with.

'I look forward to hearing more about it,' Alex said, and she did.

'Have you ever really met Martin?' Coming from Paul rather than Joan, the question was surprising. 'He's our family celebrity in the making. He's an actor but I can claim him as one of my stellar students at Amblefield.'

'My uncle exaggerates,' Martin said, his voice clear, quiet and deep. 'I'm still a student. Theater. Oxford. A year in. Wasted two years of my life and Ma's money on anthropology. Taking a gap year, actually, and doing some regional theater. You're in the arts, aren't you, when you're not tending bar?' His smile was disarming and made of his face something very charming.

'Graphic arts,' Alex told him easily. 'I've been out of the swim of the commercial stuff for several years now, but I still like to paint when I can.'

'Hey, Alex.' Kev Winslet was gamekeeper at the Derwinter estate and a regular at the Dog. 'What's all the fuss about, then? One of those white vans went up the High a bit after the other stuff. What do they call those?' Beefy and too fond of his beer, Kev liked to be in the center of anything notable in Folly.

She straightened. 'SOCO, you mean?' and immediately regretted her response.

'That's right,' Kev said. 'I told 'em you'd be the one to know. What's that for, then?'

'Scene of the Crime Officer, I think,' she said, turning her back to deal with Joan's double gin and lime.

'And they don't come unless there's something really bad, do they?' Kev persisted.

'I wouldn't know.' Alex set the gin in front of Joan. She had already poured Paul's Guinness. 'There you are,' she told them. All three were looking at Kev Winslet.

'C'mon, Alex,' the man said, guffawing. 'You know. It'd mean someone died before they brought in one of them.'

Hugh tapped her shoulder and put his mouth by her ear. 'Doc James just called. Says to give you the heads up. They found a woman's body in some woods at Underhill. Sounds very messy.'

Two

One of the benefits, or more often the drawbacks, of your father being the local GP was that you usually got any really bad news before anyone else.

Tony rested a gloved hand on the small gray

tabby he'd just spayed and caught the expression in his assistant Radhika's soft, dark eyes across the operating table. They stared at each other over their masks in full understanding. Tony's dad, Doc James, had been taking care of the local people since before Tony remembered, or so it seemed. He and Radhika had just listened to Doc over the speakerphone letting them know that a body had been found hidden in some trees near the neighboring village of Underhill. The police were treating the death as a murder.

'Shoot,' Tony said quietly, watching rain splatter the window. 'Here we go again. Not in Folly but too close for comfort.'

'Try not to worry,' Radhika said quietly. 'These horrible things happen but praise be this time it doesn't involve you and Alex. It doesn't, Tony.'

'No,' he said. 'Of course not. Perhaps it's an accidental death. Dad could have been getting ahead of himself talking about murder.'

'I expect so. I will finish here. You will want to go to Alex.'

'Yes, she needs to know before the police visit the Dog – which they will.' He could not hide feelings for Alex from Radhika, probably not from anyone who knew them. 'The boy, Kyle, he's coming after school tomorrow. Will that work for you? I'll be in later but I thought he could spend time with the Georges' poodle until one of them can get here to pick him up. He'll be groggy for a while after his dental. Poor old thing does like a lot of attention.' The Georges owned Folly's bakery.

'Oh, yes. That will be wonderful and most

helpful.' Radhika laughed. 'If he is truly eager, he will be welcome here. Perhaps we will help another to follow in your steps, Tony.'

He went to his crowded office in a front room and stepped over one of three animal crates to get to his desk. This was the recovery overflow as well as an occasional extra waiting area for pre-surgery patients. The cottage pleased him as a clinic and hospital. People who brought their pets seemed quickly at home among chintz-covered chairs, diamond-paned windows, and with the sound of the tiny stream that ran past a few feet from the cottage.

Alex didn't always carry her mobile when she was working so he called the pub number.

Hugh Rhys answered, 'Black Dog. How can I help you?'

'This is Tony. Is Alex around?'

'She's in the kitchen,' Hugh said. He cleared his throat. 'It's been a bit hectic here.'

'OK, listen. A body's been found in some wood to the north of Underhill. It's isolated back there, just fields and the odd spinney – like the one where they found a woman's body. Dad couldn't tell me anymore. But he thought we ought to know and he was right.'

Hugh let out a long sigh. 'We know.' Hugh had dropped his voice to a pitch barely audible over the hubbub in the bar. 'Your dad gave us the news. My first thought was, not again. If I were a fanciful man I'd start talking about living on cursed ground.'

'Well, don't,' Tony said. 'I'm worried the police will eventually get to the Dog and start asking questions. It won't matter that Alex can't answer them, they'll ask anyway and if we're really unlucky it'll be O'Reilly and Lamb. Lamb would start in about too many unnatural deaths in a small area. Even if this one is near Underhill. Most people think of it as an extension of Folly-on-Weir.'

'Aye,' Hugh said. 'That's what I'm thinking. I'd hoped we'd seen the last of that lot. I'd better tell Alex what you say about the police. Are you coming over?'

'Yes, of course.' He wanted to say more, to warn Hugh not to make too big a deal out of the death, but he stopped himself. 'I'll be on my way shortly.'

If Lily didn't stop pacing back and forth across the kitchen and around the central worktop, Alex didn't know if she could stay calm much longer. Lily moved piles of thick white plates from one counter to another, opened refrigerator doors and closed them again without looking inside.

'Scoot,' Alex said to the older of the two Gammage boys, 'sit down, please. Explain what's the matter. Has someone done something to you? Hurt you?'

'No.' Tall and blond, all color had left the boy's face. He glanced repeatedly at the back door.

Alex said, 'Speak to me. I can't help you if I don't know what's wrong.' It came out much louder than she'd intended. 'Please, Scoot. Why are you watching the door?'

Someone knocked that door, rapidly, sharply, and Scoot, carrying a book under his arm, raced to open up and let another boy in. This must be Kyle. Rather than a book, he had a battered skateboard under his arm. A tow-headed, skinny boy, he didn't look a lot like his brother except for the present panicky look in his eyes and a body held like a bundle of sticks that could break apart if you touched them.

Lily gave a refrigerator door a mighty slam. 'What is it? Tell us quickly. I've got to go and check some guests into the inn.'

'I found someone dead in our woods,' Kyle said, in a voice that was starting to break. He spoke to his brother rather than Lily. 'Scoot, we gotta go somewhere and decide what to do.'

'You found that body?' Alex said. 'You poor kid. Come on in properly. A cup of tea is what you need. And something to eat.'

The boy shook his head. 'She was all twisted up, Scoot. Her face was blue – kind of black – and her eyes looked like they'd pop right out of her head any second. They looked like they were full of blood. I couldn't feel anything in her wrist, but I remembered how they put their fingers on the neck on telly. But there was a cut there. All the way around. Like someone put a thin wire or something around it and pulled it tight. Something was coming out of her mouth. They'd pulled her scarf over the cut. I put it back so she wouldn't look so bad. There were bruises on her neck, too, and her hand was bloody; all the nails torn down – the other hand was underneath her. The smell was awful. I never saw anyone dead before.'

Scoot clenched and unclenched his hands at his

sides. 'It's not your fault that happened to her. We don't have to worry about it.'

'I went to the Polka Dot to make that call to you.'

'You got a call from Kyle, Scoot?' Alex said. 'That's what upset you?'

He didn't seem to hear her.

'Alex?' Hugh hurried into the kitchen. 'What's going on?'

'We're fine.' They weren't fine. Children should never be as afraid as Scoot and Kyle were now.

'Tony called about what the police went to Underhill for,' Hugh said.

She nodded, yes. 'But we already know about it. Kyle here found the body and called the police. I can manage fine with the boys. Mum, calm down and go see to the people checking in. Hugh, we can't leave the bar unattended.'

He hesitated before turning back.

'Did anyone in the Polka Dot hear what you said?' Scoot asked. The Polka Dot was the corner grocery shop in Underhill. In addition to limited food, they carried everything from wax candles to hairnets, hair grips, mostly-new trainers and boxes of chocolates that didn't look quite right when you opened them. Those who foolishly bought the latter and complained were told the film of white on the chocolates was 'special.'

Kyle had not answered. He stared at Scoot and shifted from foot to foot.

'Did they?' Scoot kept his voice down. 'Did they hear what you said on the phone, Kyle?'

'Mum,' Alex said, 'I'll handle this till you can get back.' Her mum almost ran into the passageway leading to the restaurant and inn.

'The police came,' Kyle said. 'They made me go back there. To the woods. They were nice enough but I was scared. No, not scared, just a bit worried. After I showed them the body, they told me to wait in the cottage and they'd come to ask questions when Dad gets home.' His eyes definitely teared up.

His eyes were green and faintly almond shaped. When Alex realized she knew eyes so similar to his from another child, she barely held back a gasp. They were quite like her own eyes, and the wretched expression in his must have been in her own more often than she wanted to examine.

She grabbed two mugs and filled them from a tea urn. She added milk and a lot of sugar and gave one to each boy. 'This will buck you up,' she said.

'What did you say to the police?' Scoot asked. 'You told them Dad's away, didn't you? You said we're on our own?'

'No! What do you take me for? They'd bring in Social Services.' He clapped a hand over his mouth.

'You could have called me without going to the shop.' Scoot looked beaten. He wouldn't look at Alex.

'I didn't want to stay there with – you know. Anyway, I lost my phone.'

'Where?' Scoot looked stricken. 'We gotta find it!'

34

'If you need another phone we'll get you one,' Alex said, prepared to offer anything that would calm these kids down.

The boys had fallen silent, as if afraid they might say something in front of Alex that they wanted to keep secret.

Lily returned. 'Drink that tea,' she said firmly. 'Everything's OK.'

'It's not,' Scoot said. 'We don't want the police to find out anything about us. About Kyle and me, that is. We haven't done anything wrong but we can't have them interfering with us . . . with the way things are now, anyway. We don't need anyone. It's nothing to do with us that a person got killed.'

Within half an hour, Tony was walking toward the center of the village.

The November air snapped cold about his face and head. How quickly this year had rushed by and what changes it had brought his way.

Would Alex find some excuse to beg out of getting together this evening? Would this murder, although it was nothing to do with them, be another reason why they would not look at their own lives yet? All he hoped for was a fresh start for what he had begun to see as dwindling closeness between them.

Katie was still at the Black Dog with Bogie. The two of them would stay there all the time if they could get away with it. By now the Burke sisters would be at their table by the fire, completing the nightly tableau they made with the dogs and one of the sisters' two cats, Max, who traveled there in a small, tartan, canvas-covered shopping cart.

The thought of risking almost everything he cared about with Alex trapped air in his lungs. He parted his lips but breathing didn't get any easier.

He smelled clematis, its last vanilla scented blooms of the year. The trellis over a cottage doorway on his left carried the woody vine he saw each day as he passed, usually on his way to walk Katie. Even in the saturated darkness, creamy blossoms popped, like stars in a black sky. The sky itself was overcast tonight, sporadic showers of heavy raindrops still falling.

Was he content with his life here? Was it enough to practice animal medicine and exist in the confines of a Cotswold village? It was as long as he had Alex. At the beginning he hadn't been sure he wanted to risk getting too close to a woman again, but he had become close – very close – to Alex.

He must be breathing or he'd have passed out by now but he couldn't remember taking in any air. If Alex didn't feel the way he did, what then? What if he was wrong in thinking she shared his feelings and hopes? What if she wanted to back away from him, to give them some space, or however she put it?

A sudden smile surprised him. He couldn't believe Alex would walk away from him for good. Regardless of her hesitation to commit – and he did know how she had carefully deflected any of his advances toward a permanent future together – regardless, he believed their lives were bound together. Her expression had showed she knew he felt very serious about what was on his mind.

God, he hoped he was right.

'Tony, wait there!' Like a materializing thought, Alex ran to meet him. She lowered her voice. 'Let's walk back the way you came. This won't take long. It can't. You know what's happened, don't you?'

'Of course, Dad called both of us.'

He could feel the height of her agitation.

She slowed down. 'Just listen. Mum and I need you to back us up. It's Scoot and his brother. Kyle found the body. He's with us now but he's not doing so well.'

'Hell.' Tony stopped walking and looked at her. 'That's rotten for—'

'Yes, it is. Listen, please, Tony. Those boys are living alone in their cottage. We could have helped them before this if we'd only known. Hugh thought they might be on their own a lot but never mentioned it. He should have. He thought he could appoint himself their watchdog but he doesn't understand everything that goes into keeping an eye on children. Look, it's too complicated to explain everything. If the police get wind of this, Lily's going to say she's the brothers' go-to person while their dad's working. It won't be a lie because that's what she's going to set up. I'll help. Please back us up if you're asked.'

'Why not just tell the truth?'

'Scoot's terrified they'll bring in Social Services. He doesn't know if they'd let them stay like that. Hugh and Mum don't, either. Neither do I. It's too much of a risk. We've got to cover, at least until their dad gets back. Kyle's pretending to be tough but he's shocked and scared.'

He rested his hands on her shoulders. 'This could be more than any of us can handle, love. You're doing exactly what I'd expect you to do. I'll back you up, of course I will, but keep in mind that we may all regret getting involved.'

She was quiet, her face turned up to his and the glitter of tears, or some strong emotion in her eyes. 'I know. All I'm asking is for you to say what I've told you. This is something I have to do. I believe in them and I understand some of what they're feeling. You won't be involved and—'

'I don't give a rat's arse about being involved! I do care what happens to the kids, but most of all I want you and Lily far away from . . . There's another angle. Remember that it's more than a good idea for us to keep our distance from another murder in the area.' He held up a hand to stop the torrent of argument he could feel coming. 'Just tell me what you have to do. I'll get the rest later. Why does this have to be decided in such a hurry?'

'It's been decided.' She felt stiff against him. 'Scoot just stood there, staring. Then he asked when the police had said they were coming by the cottage to question Kyle. Apparently they intend to go this evening when the dad's there, only he's not going to be. You should have seen Scoot's face. All he said was, "They'll take you away if they find out, Kyle." And Kyle looked gutted.

38

'When the police show up at an empty cottage, they won't take long to find out Scoot's got a job with us. It'll make them mad and they'll come to see if he's at the Dog. Tony—'

'I understand, love. Really I do. Don't worry – if I'm asked, I'll back all of you up. It's not like the boys are well known around here – they live in Underhill, not even Underhill really. And they keep to themselves. Do you know how many people know they're in that cottage on their own?'

'Until tonight, nobody. It's Kyle who has me the most worried. Scoot was furious with himself for letting the truth out in front of us, but he's older and not quite so vulnerable. Apparently the boys and their dad are used to getting along without help. I didn't ask about their mother but he said they were fine, had always been fine. Just the three of them. Each time he mentioned the three of them I could see him closing up like he was keeping something secret inside. Kyle just went deeper into himself. But I could have been building up something that wasn't there. I'd better get back. Give me a few minutes before you come. The police may not show up at all tonight. We can hope. Once we're closed we'll have to decide what to do next.'

She turned and ran again, slipping in and out of darkness when she passed cottage lights. Then she was out of sight as she must have dodged down the side of the pub.

Tony reached the Black Dog and pushed his way into the warmth flowing back from inside. He heard Hugh's laugh over the evening hum that would only get louder.

The comfortable familiarity stopped him. He stood still, listening, thinking. His life was good. Was it too good? Was he risking everything by wanting even more?

Cold air hit him as the door opened again. A uniformed policewoman came in and Tony immediately connected her with what Alex had told him.

'Good evening,' she said, her accent local. 'Do you come here often enough to know the regulars?'

Her brusque approach irritated him. 'Yes, I suppose I do, but I'm not here as often as some. I imagine most people in the village are acquainted with just about everyone else who lives around here.' He wanted to get rid of her but couldn't think how.

A tall, slim woman, she was attractive with sharp features, her blonde hair pulled back under her hat and wound into a braided bun at her nape.

'Constable Miller,' she said offering her hand.

Tony accepted a firm shake, glanced at the identification she showed and tried to decide if he could ask about the death near Underhill. Surely that would be normal. 'Tony Harrison,' he said. 'I'm the local vet. A lot of activity around here today. Police activity, I mean. I hope it's nothing serious.'

She was busy writing his name in a notebook. 'I may want to talk to you later, Dr Harrison. Do you know where I'd find Alex Duggins or Hugh Rhys?'

40

In other words, she would be asking the questions around here. 'Go on into the bar. Just wait at the counter.' He didn't feel like elaborating further. The more he said, the more likely he was to say too much.

Officer Miller walked confidently into the bar and Tony wanted to follow her but knew it would be a mistake.

Once inside the crowded room he went over to the Burke sisters' table to greet them and accept some fuss from Katie and Bogie. The dogs were smart enough to think that since he'd just arrived, he probably intended to stay so they need not take evasive action to avoid being hauled home. The orange tabby, Max, his remaining eye closed, his chin sunk on his chest in an attitude of bliss, curled on Mary's lap. The dogs hadn't taken long to accept that if they wanted to share the sisters' space, it meant tolerating Max. Or perhaps they realized he could inflict some pain if annoyed.

Harriet and Mary's cheeks were pink from the fire's heat. Mary wore one of her usual Spanish style combs above her bun of fine white hair. Harriet's hair was a short silvery nimbus around her face.

'Ladies,' Tony said, 'how are you? Winter's in a hurry this year. Make sure you don't forget your mufflers.'

They both laughed, Mary's eyes squeezing shut behind impossibly thick glasses. 'How about a sherry for each of you? Harvey's Bristol Cream?' He kept an eye on the policewoman who talked to Hugh and scribbled in her notebook.

With a quick glance at each other the sisters turned deeper shades of pink and made weakly declining gestures.

'I'll get them,' Tony said, concealing his grin. These two very intelligent women were a village treasure and they did love a little sherry, in addition to their halves of shandy.

Taking his time, he approached the bar, greeting familiar faces, but paying attention to Officer Miller. While he watched, Hugh led her behind the counter and toward the kitchens behind the walls of bottles.

Minutes passed before Alex took Hugh's place to serve and pulled two beers before she looked directly at Tony. 'What will you have?'

'Half of Ambler,' he said, indifferent to drinking anything at all tonight. 'I see Kev Winslet's spreading myths with Major Stroud. What's going on out back?'

'Hugh's in charge,' she said tightly. 'I hope he won't make a mess of things. Mum had to get back to the inn yet again.'

'Hugh's capable,' he said, sensing some under-current of discord. 'He's always seemed good with young people.'

'Hasn't he, though?' Their eyes met but Alex looked away. 'The policewoman said she'd let me know when she wanted to talk to me. I think that was my order to stay away until summoned.'

'I spoke with her briefly when she came in,' Tony said. 'All business. She doesn't seem like someone who would have kids eating out of her hand very easily.'

'I didn't like the way she spoke to all of us. I

would rather she hadn't walked in on the boys but Hugh didn't have any choice but to tell her they're here. I hope she thinks we keep a sharp eye out for them when their dad's away.'

Tony didn't feel encouraged but he kept that to himself. 'So she's talking to Hugh?'

'She said she had to see the boys. And she wasn't impressed at the suggestion that they needed to go and do their homework.'

'Damn.' Tony looked into the foam on his beer and took a long swallow, thinking hard. 'They're not supposed to talk to minors without an adult, are they? A parent or something?'

Alex shook her head slowly. 'I don't think so. I should have stayed.'

'You wouldn't be any different from Hugh. The officer knows the rules. She won't get into anything important if it can't be used as evidence.' He set down his glass. 'Well, she hasn't told me to get lost yet. I'm the one who spends time with Kyle, so—'

'Since when?'

'Since tomorrow when he starts volunteering at the clinic. All I can do is try to get away with it. I'm not standing by while some officious . . . I'll see if I can pull a convincing act as stand-in guardian.'

Smiling slightly, Alex leaned toward him. 'Let's not raise her hackles. I don't think she's fond of men.'

'Nothing to lose then,' he grinned. 'Wish me luck.'

Three

Detective Chief Inspector Dan O'Reilly trudged along a muddy gravel track studded with weeds and vines. He shone a high-powered torch on the ground in front of him, cursing mentally with every plodding step he took. Why the hell hadn't he brought his muck boots? Why had he taken the bloody things out of his car and left them behind in the first place?

You were going to work on the garden at the house, only you were called out before you could even get started.

He couldn't get a decent impression of the fields back here behind Underhill by torchlight but he had to make the effort. He could have been at it a couple of hours ago while there was still some daylight, if he hadn't had to wait around for the police surgeon to show up. He had paced outside the white tent, behind him now and lighted up from inside like an oversized Chinese lantern filled with ghostly figures, only to have Dr Molly Lewis complain about the mess that had been made of the crime scene when she did arrive. She wasn't her usual humorous self and Dan didn't push her. He had left and minutes later got a right bollocking from his boss because she had called him and vented.

Never mind the game of pass-the-parcel, this

was the age-old copper pastime of pass-the-blame – to anyone farther down the food chain than you. Dan O'Reilly didn't usually play that one but this time he had a list of inept culprits to skin.

The sound of an incoming Skype call came from his mobile and he dug it out of an inside jacket pocket. His heart dropped a beat. Calum was the only one he Skyped with but they always made a date ahead of time.

He answered and turned to face the direction he'd come from so he'd be able to see if anyone approached. 'Hey, there, boyo.'

'Hello Dad.' Calum wasn't wearing his usual grin. 'Why is it dark there? Where are you?'

His boy looked like him. The longer they were apart, the more he noticed the similarities. Calum's hair was curlier than Dan's but it was just as dark, as were his eyes.

'Dad? Are you sitting with the lights off?'

'No. Sorry. I'm outside. Still working. You know how that goes.' Immediately he regretted the comment. If he hadn't spent so much time working, he might still be married and have his wife and son with him, although possibly not. Things hadn't been easy between him and Corinne for several years before the disaster that forced them apart – or drove her to divorce Dan.

'I wish I could come and stay with you, Dad,' Calum said. He was just twelve now and prided himself on being grown up, the man of the house since Dan hadn't been with them. 'I wouldn't be any trouble. It would be good to go back to school with my same friends again.'

The request, the way Calum had obviously thought it through, scrambled Dan's thoughts. He knew Calum missed him and looked forward to his visits, but he had never expected this.

'I thought you liked living in Ireland,' Dan said. 'You and your mam couldn't wait to get back there.'

'Nobody asked me if I wanted to come.' Calum frowned and Dan thought he saw a sheen in the boy's eyes. 'I was born here but I grew up there. I only used to come here for visits and that was OK.'

Dan could feel the sticky fingers of a bad mistake getting ready to grab him. 'Doesn't your mam like living in Ireland?' He shut his mouth before he could add that during the last five years of their marriage she'd talked of little else but going back there.

'She loves it, Dad. And it wasn't so bad before *he* butted in. They're going to get married, so they say, and we'll all be happy together, Mam says, only I don't want him. Mam says I only imagine Bran doesn't like me and I'll get over it. But I won't, Dad. Honest, I won't. Can I come and live with you?'

Shocked, Dan realized how tightly he was gripping the phone and eased up a bit. 'We all have to slow down and talk about it,' he said. He missed this boy so much.

'So you don't want me, then.' It was a flat statement.

'Come on, Calum, you know that's not true.' He made himself smile. 'Of course I want you. But your mam's not just going to let you go.

46

Maybe we can try for a redrawing of the visitation rights. You were only nine when . . . before. Now you're older and not so vulnerable. Shall we see if we can arrange for you to come here sometimes – for longer – instead of me going there?' After the attack on Corinne and Calum while Dan was working into the night on a case, Corinne hadn't had much difficulty getting complete custody and ensuring Dan had to go to Ireland when he wanted to see his son.

'Bran's got two boys,' Calum said quietly. 'They're OK but I don't like it when we're all together. They're older and Bran talks to them like I'm not there.'

'Your mam will never give you up,' Dan said with dread building in his belly. He'd give anything to have Calum with him but the odds were stacked against that legally, at least until Calum reached maturity.

'I want to come,' Calum said with the stubborn thrust of the chin that Dan knew so well.

'And I want you to come.' The instant he said it he knew his mistake, even if it was true.

'Yay, Dad,' Calum whooped. 'You'll work it out. You've always been able to work things out.'

I couldn't work anything out when I felt Corinne slipping away, or stop her from taking you back to Ireland. The image of the man who had broken into their house that night, the flash of his knife blade, rushed back. Dan put his fingers to the scar on his jaw. He'd got back from working late in time to save his family from a knife-wielding mad man, but not before too much mental damage

47

had been done. Rarely a day passed when he didn't contemplate what would have happened if he'd been another fifteen minutes, or even five, getting home.

'Son, hang in there while we see what we can do, OK?'

'But, Dad—'

'Whatever we do has to be done right. You understand that.'

Calum sniffed. He didn't respond.

'Look, I'll talk all this through with your mother to find out where things stand, OK? You and I will have our usual call at the weekend, though.'

'All right,' Calum said. 'It's your turn to phone.' He hung up, leaving Dan with the eerie Skype blips and a turquoise screen.

What he couldn't do was rush into this. He had to think first – a lot. For all he knew, Calum would change his mind in a week and not want to leave his mother.

Calum had never wanted to be taken away from his father. Dredging it all up ripped Dan apart.

So Corinne was getting married again. Well, Dan was glad for that and he hoped this time it would work out for her.

He turned back and gave his torch beam a few desultory swipes across the apology for a track around the field. His hands were cold although the palms were clammy. There was a great deal to consider before he talked to Calum again.

Keeping his mind on the woman lying dead back there had to be his focus. Years of training had taught him to compartmentalize – most of the time.

'Hold up, guv.' His partner, Detective Sergeant Bill Lamb loped up behind him. 'Isn't this a waste of time? Why are we doing it anyway? Crime scene can get out here at first light. They can tape everything off properly tonight, too, and make sure we've got officers on watch.'

'For God's sake stop passing the buck.' Bill was unfortunate enough to play into Dan's current negative line of thinking. 'You're right, though. But I'm better out here doing scut work than back there blowing my top and having to regret it later. I see you've got your boots.'

'It's a wise thing to expect muddy fields when it's been raining, guv.'

'Don't tell me the obvious. Did I miss any revelations about the deceased?'

'After you left I got crowded out by the techs. I could hardly see what was going on in there. Why were so many people inside the second cordon?'

'Rhetorical questions about anything could put me over the edge, my lad,' Dan said. 'Did Molly say anything other than she doesn't have a clue how long the body's been there? Won't even guess on time of death? It could have been stran- gulation, or not, and anything else she felt like saying she couldn't say?'

'Right on, guv. Doc Molly didn't give us a dickey-bird. Nothing. No getting away from what happened to the deceased's neck though. Whatever they used doesn't seem to be there.'

'That's no surprise. Anything useful from missing persons yet?'

'Negative,' Bill said, kicking up gravel. 'They've taken fingerprints so we'll see what Holmes turns up. Looks like kids run dirt bikes around and around out here, by the way. Doubt if there'll be any useful tire or footprints in this slop.'

Dan straightened. Moisture had squeezed between his shoelaces. 'Bloody wet, always wet when you think it's going to be dry. Damn weather forecast. I want every inch of this gone over. You're right, though, it'll have to wait for the morning, but first light and I expect 'em out here, boyo.

'Unless our corpse moved itself into those trees, someone else has been here. We'll find something.'

'I saw the marks, guv. I reckon she was dragged just far enough to be among the trees. D'you reckon she was killed here?'

'Who knows? Bloody advance guard tramped over everything,' Dan said. 'That or someone was holding Highland Fling practice while the murder was committed.'

A uniform slogged toward them. 'Sir, Dr Lewis says to tell you she's leaving. They'll be moving the body.'

'Is that it, then?' Bill asked, sounding as surprised as Dan felt. There should have been enough to keep the crime scene teams there considerably longer. 'Did they find any ID on the body?' Bill added.

'No, sir. No bag or wallet, either. But she had an envelope of money – unmarked envelope – and drugs in her pockets. Looked like smack, and maybe roofies.'

Dan stepped around Bill. 'How much? Of each?'

'Didn't see, sir. Doc said it. I think she bagged everything straightaway.'

'Right,' Dan said. 'Good man.' And to Bill he muttered, 'She's in a hell of a hurry.'

After a short conversation with Dr Molly Lewis, he and Bill slogged out of the field by way of a broken-down style and found their way beside a lone cottage set away from any others and with no lights inside.

'That's the Gammage place. Doesn't look as if anyone's home,' Dan said.

He knocked the door several times before giving up. Drawn curtains covered all the windows but he peered through the letterbox, shone his torch over as much of a tiny hall as he could reach with its beam. 'Can't see anything. Where is the boy who found the body? This is his place, right? I thought he and his father were supposed to wait here for an officer to question them.'

He knocked the door again.

'Don't have the foggiest where the kid is,' Bill said. 'Constable Miller is following that up. She'll report in when she's got something. The boy is Kyle Gammage. Thirteen. He ran to a shop to call for help. He probably didn't want to be back there on his own.'

'Bloody disorganized, all of it,' Dan said. 'Another mess in our favorite locale. At least it isn't Folly itself, though.'

He felt Bill looking at him but pretended he didn't. His partner would be thinking of the other cases they'd dealt with in Folly-on-Weir . . . and about some of the people they'd become involved with.

Rain started falling again. Big, hard drops that slammed the top of his head and trickled through his hair to his scalp. 'We're out of here,' he told Bill. 'Meeting first thing. Spread the word that I want everyone together at nine sharp.'

'Yes, guv,' Bill said. 'Will we have to set up locally, d'you think?'

'I damn well hope not. That bloody parish hall in Folly is a nightmare but this place is too small to have anything we can use.'

'It seems to work better to be in the middle of everything for these rural jobs, though.' Bill coughed. 'We know the drill to getting things up and running around here.' A handkerchief flashed white when he used one to wipe his face.

'You mean that's what worked better for the Folly cases. I suppose it did. But maybe we'll get lucky and clear this one fast. This is a filthy night.'

The Gammages' cottage stood at the back of a field between the one where the body had been found and the village itself. What was visible of the area was unkempt. Stones and roots found the toes of unsuspecting feet and long grass wrapped itself around trouser legs, soaking to the skin.

'Molly wasn't talkative tonight,' Bill remarked as they walked. 'She must have some idea what quantities of drugs were found.'

'And whether there were ten fifties or fifty

thousand pounds in that envelope,' Dan responded. He didn't add what Bill would already know, that Molly probably tossed down a stiff one before she got to Underhill. She had her own driver and sat in the back where she had plenty of privacy. Her days were long and mostly grim. The job could be getting to her.

Eventually a lane led to the High Street, the same one that ran all the way through Underhill, up hills and down again for the five miles into Folly-on-Weir. All the official vehicles were parked in a row outside a hodgepodge of tiny shops.

'Look at this place,' Dan said, waiting to get into his car. 'How many pairs of eyes are watching us do you think? All these dark windows don't mean the whole village is empty. House to house early in the morning.'

Once the windshield wipers did their job, Bill drove away, ducking to peer through the mostly clear spots. 'They need proper lights here,' he said. 'Damn dangerous.'

'Probably lucky they've got any at all,' Dan replied, buckling his seatbelt. 'I don't suppose much money trickles this far down.'

Ten miles the other side of Folly, Bill's mobile rang. He worked it out of an inside jacket pocket and grunted acknowledgement.

'Let's have it then,' he said into the phone after a moment, and Dan looked at him. He'd sat straighter and was looking left and right while he drove with one hand. 'That was a mistake, Miller. You know the rules. I'm looking for somewhere to turn around. Where are you now?

Just a minute.' He swung off onto a track where mud sprayed as high as the windows, then wheeled around to retrace their route. 'OK, Miller, go on. But first, don't ask another question – of anyone – until the DCI and I get there. Now, where exactly are you holding this disaster in the making?'

'What is it?' Dan said.

Bill drove faster, listening, and eyeing Dan frequently. He muted the phone and said, 'Rather you than me. This is the lovely Miller, the one with a crush on you.' He returned to the constable on the phone. 'Shit, Miller! The guv might as well hear it straight from the horse's mouth,' and handed the mobile to Dan who noted his partner's owl eyes, and his lascivious grin.

Four

'At least you could have invited Constable Miller to wait in the bar, Tony,' Alex said. 'It's tipping down out there.'

'She's a big girl,' Tony commented. He did look a bit uncomfortable 'She'll find her way out of the rain and while she's at it, maybe she'll think over what she just did and get advice from someone with experience. She must know she can't come in here and start firing questions at a couple of kids without making sure there's a parent or their representative present.

'Anyway, how long do you think it would take

Kev Winslet to start talking to her out there? Or the major?'

'We may not have long here before that woman comes back so we'd better decide what to do next,' Hugh said. 'Their dad isn't available. We have to be prepared—'

'We don't talk about our dad.' Kyle turned on his older brother who stood with crossed arms clamping a book to his chest. 'Scoot, what are we going to do. They know Dad's not here?'

'I didn't mean to say anything,' Scoot said, his voice barely audible. 'I panicked. If we can't stop the police from poking around, they might have someone come in and say we can't be on our own at our place. I don't know what they might do with us then.'

Scoot was almost as tall as Tony, with thick blond hair that curled over his collar, and an appealing, sharp-boned face. An open face filled with anxiety as he looked at his brother.

Dressed in a faded, wet, red T-shirt and jeans cut off at the knee, Kyle hitched at the skateboard under his arm. He stood, straight-backed but visibly trembling.

'That policewoman will come back,' Scoot said. 'We've got to have a plan.' As if he'd forgotten they weren't alone, he caught his brother by the arm. 'We mind our own business. No one has any right to interfere. Let's go. We'll figure out where while we pick up some things from home.'

Alex wanted to hold the boy and tell him everything would be OK. She grimaced, thinking how popular that was likely to be.

Lily came into the kitchen in time to hear what Scoot said. 'Hugh,' she said, 'would you go back out front and hold down the fort, please? And for goodness' sake don't give a hint there's anything going on.'

'You aren't alone in this,' she told the boys, and pushed Scoot, a head taller than she was and much heavier, backward into a chair. 'Sit there and listen. And you, Kyle, don't even think about leaving.'

Alex and Tony looked at each other with raised eyebrows.

'Your dad goes away regularly, right?' Lily said.

Neither boy said a word.

'Well, does he?'

'Not too often,' Scoot muttered. 'Only on longer hauls. Kyle and I manage just fine. Dad checks in with us and we're careful. We go to school and now I come here to work, too. We both get our homework done. We keep up the cottage and wash our clothes. We've got money for food.'

'Mum, stop me if you need to,' Alex said. 'Kyle, they're going to insist on questioning you about . . . well, about what you found this afternoon. That's fine. Not fine, but it isn't anything to do with your life with Scoot and your dad.'

'No,' Kyle said, and Scoot mumbled agreement.

'You know my mum. And Tony and me – and Hugh. We want to help you, just till your dad gets back.' She saw Tony look down and shake his head. *Too bad.* 'Mum keeps an eye out for you if your dad has to be gone overnight. You stay with her. That's what we'll tell anyone who asks. Are you all right with that?'

'Just for as long as the police are around,' Lily said. 'Or until your dad gets back. When does he get back?'

'You're only going to say this, right?' Scoot asked, ignoring her question. 'It's not for real. We're OK at our cottage, so you'll just pretend for the cops.'

'They'll be all over the area where you live,' Alex said. 'It's close to where you found the lady, Kyle?'

He nodded. 'She was in the field behind our cottage – in those woods there. Come on, Scoot, let's go home. We can do our own thing.'

Tony shoved away from the counter he'd been leaning on. 'That means you want to run, Kyle. Don't do it. You won't get anywhere and you'll bring trouble down on yourself. It's your business. We can't stop you from doing whatever you want to. But you'd be better off just waiting for the police to come and talk to you rather than having them run you down because you're trying to get away. You haven't done anything wrong, but running makes you look as if you've got something to hide. This death is nothing to do with you. Think about it but do it quickly. All we have to do is get you through the questioning. The police won't be interested in you after that.

'And don't forget your volunteer work with the animals. You start after school tomorrow. I know I'm looking forward to having you.'

Scoot and Kyle hung on Tony's words, eventually nodding, yes. 'OK,' Scoot said. He looked to Kyle who was far too pale but he nodded again.

'And you come to me tonight when you leave here,' Lily said. 'Straight across the High Street here. Corner Cottage. You'll be comfortable there and you come and go whenever you want. I wouldn't do this if I didn't think it's unfair to upend people's lives when they're working hard just to get along and stay together. We'll make sure you pick up some things from home – just to get you through till your dad can take over.'

Pink patches stained her cheeks. Alex watched her mother and was forcefully hit with what she should have been aware of from the start of all this. Lily had brought up a daughter on her own and things must have been stressful sometimes. Money was tight and there had been times when managing at all took a toll. Some of the teasing and downright mean bullying she'd had aimed at her she would never forget, although she no longer felt sad for the child she had been.

Alex didn't know who her father had been. Whenever she had asked, Lily became silent. She never answered the question. Lily had always meant the world to Alex and she couldn't bear to see her hurt so she had stopped asking in the end.

'Where should we be now,' Kyle said suddenly. 'The cops said they wanted to talk to me with my dad at our place, and I didn't tell them he was out on a job and wouldn't be back for a bit. What will they say about that? About me not telling them? I wish Dad would come home,' he finished very quietly.

'I bet you do.' Tony clamped a hand on the back of the boy's neck. 'And he will. But till he does you've got plenty of friends here so trust us. And if the police mention that you said you and your dad would be at the cottage, tell the truth. You wanted to see your brother.'

Lily smiled at the boys but Alex could almost feel her tension. How often had it seemed almost impossible to keep things together when she'd been a young, single mother?

'That woman copper will get permission to come back in here,' Scoot said. 'She's bound to move on from what Kyle saw and ask where Dad is.'

'But we know where he is,' Alex said, forcing a smile. 'He's working to keep his family. And Lily and I are looking after you when it's necessary. They can't argue with that unless you boys say otherwise.'

'We won't,' Kyle said firmly.

Scoot nodded emphatically.

'You should go out there and clear tables, bring in some empties,' Tony told Scoot, as if he'd been keeping a pub all his life. 'Kyle, take Scoot's book and chair and get over there in the corner. You're waiting till he gets off. Shove the skateboard by the door. Alex, go out and help Hugh. Look normal, everyone.'

Scoot left with a tray and cloth but Kyle hadn't quite made it into the corner with his chair before a loud knock came at the kitchen door. 'Sit,' Tony hissed, and waited a few seconds before opening the door.

Five

Alex hadn't been prepared to meet the direct gaze of Dan O'Reilly, although she shouldn't have been surprised either.

'May we come in?' Dan said. He looked past Tony to Alex and his expression softened. 'It seems it's our fate to come together regularly in less than happy circumstances. How are you?'

'Fine, thanks,' Alex said. 'How about you?'

Detective Sergeant Bill Lamb followed O'Reilly in and once more Alex couldn't look away from his light blue, unblinking eyes. He continued to have his thick, sandy hair cut in a longish crew cut.

'Good to see you both,' Tony said. 'Nasty business in Underhill.'

'We might have known you two would be involved somehow,' Lamb said. 'Do you know who the dead woman was?'

Dan's mouth moved as if he intended to say something, but he closed it again and didn't look happy.

'Why would we?' Alex said. 'It hasn't come out yet, has it? Not publically.'

'Are you off duty, Dan?' Lily asked and actually sounded affable when she must be on edge. 'A drink?'

60

'Thanks, Lily, but no.'

'Watch out for the skateboard,' Lily said, raising her voice as Constable Miller came in and almost caught the end of the board with the toe of a shoe. She stood behind the door and kept her eyes down.

'Sandwiches.' Hugh stuck his head around the partition between bar and kitchen. He gave the detectives a disinterested nod. 'Two rounds of ham and cheese. In that covered tray on the counter by the fridges. I've got to get back.'

Alex put the sandwiches on a plate and ran them out to the bar.

'How's it going?' Hugh asked.

'The way you'd expect. You could cut the atmosphere with a knife. Lamb already got a dig in. Quick, what's Mr Gammage's first name?'

Hugh frowned. 'Shoot . . . Is it Sean? No, Sid, that's it. Don't volunteer information unless they ask for it.'

She sucked in a big breath. 'We're all tiptoeing around. I hope we don't make a mistake.'

'I hope we *aren't* making a mistake,' Hugh came back. 'A big one.'

Alex returned to the others in time to hear Dan ask to talk with Kyle who looked terrified.

'Nothing to worry about, son,' the chief inspector said, smiling, his dark eyes warm and encouraging. 'You did the right thing calling us when you did. How do you feel? Bit shocky?'

'I suppose so.' Kyle swallowed loudly.

'Don't blame you. Is your dad on his way? He'll want to be with you while we go over this.'

Prickling climbed up Alex's neck to her scalp.

61

She was used to the reaction to stress – or premonition of unpleasantness – but didn't like it any better than she ever had. They could all be in a sticky spot shortly.

'I thought you were staying at my mum's tonight,' Alex said. 'Isn't Sid out on an overnight run?'

Kyle's eyes got huge. 'Yes,' he whispered.

'They'll be going over to Corner Cottage shortly, Dan,' Lily said, as if she was enjoying a visit from old friends. 'They've got to finish homework. And school's early in the morning.'

'We'll do our best to get through this quickly,' Dan O'Reilly said, affably enough. 'Bill. Use the front door to take Officer Miller into the pub. I don't want to feed the chatter and have them thinking there's a big conflab going on out here. Sit together at a table with enough chairs for someone to join you. Have your notebook out, Constable, in case someone says something useful. Remember, Bill, you've got a lot of old friends in Folly.' He chuckled.

Lamb, his expression blank, put his hat on and went back into the rain with Miller who left while casting an odd look at Dan O'Reilly. Alex frowned but Dan didn't seem to notice anything.

Lily pulled a loaf of brown bread from a sliding rack under a counter. She started making more sandwiches which Alex doubted they'd use before they had to be thrown out.

'You must be Scoot.' Dan grinned at the boy when he came into the kitchen with a loaded tray. 'I've got a son about your Kyle's age. He lives with his mother in Ireland most of the time

62

and I miss him. Your dad must find it hard when he has to leave you.'

'We manage,' Scoot said promptly. 'We've got everything organized.'

They continued the polite back and forth but Alex had stopped listening. This was the first time she'd had a peek inside Dan O'Reilly's private life. She took it he was divorced or separated from his wife. The pleasure his son brought him was obvious.

Dan was comfortable around the boys, Alex thought. He didn't wear a hat and his damp dark hair curled more than it did when it was dry. She wondered what he did with his off hours. A good-looking, interesting man never had to be alone if he didn't want to be.

'Alex?' Tony said.

She glanced at him and smiled. 'Sorry. I was doing some wool gathering.'

Tony had caught her staring at Dan and he didn't smooth out a frown quickly enough. 'Since Kyle volunteers for me at the clinic and his dad approves of that, I'm wondering if I could stand in for Sid. What do you think?'

'How old are you, son?' Dan asked Scoot.

'Seventeen,' Scoot said promptly. 'My birthday's in a couple of months, a bit more.'

'No other adult relatives?'

'No,' Scoot said. He looked uncomfortable with that last answer. And he gave Kyle a hard look.

If there were any other relatives, they weren't popular with Scoot.

'Hugh will tell you I'm a good worker,' Scoot

63

said in a rush. 'And Alex and Lily. They all know us really well so they can be here for us.'

Dan pulled a bag of sweets from a trouser pocket and offered it to each boy. They both took one of the detective's signature favorite sherbet lemons and all three sucked on the sticky yellow sweets.

'This is only to get a feel for what you saw in those woods, Kyle. You aren't involved but we'd be grateful for anything you can share with us. Tony, if we think it's getting too deep, we'll stop but I can't see that happening. OK?'

'Absolutely,' Tony said. He'd shed his Barbour jacket and looked relaxed in his sweater and jeans, and his inevitable Hunter boots. In these parts people didn't go slopping about in the mud without their wellies, unless they were Dan O'Reilly, evidently, whose shoes were caked with still-drying slime.

He took out his notebook but once it was open, set it on the worktop. He took off his trench coat and looked around but Lily quickly hung it behind the door to the back car park.

'Kyle, would you feel more comfortable if we went into . . . the restaurant? Do you have diners, Lily?'

'We're not serving dinner tonight,' she said, busy stacking the freshly made sandwiches on a second tray. 'Bar food only.'

'This is routine,' Dan told Scoot. 'We interview witnesses individually.'

With Kyle in the lead, Dan, Tony and Alex trooped along behind him. Lily had shaken her head, no, when Alex indicated she should go,

64

too. Probably a good idea to keep things low key. And she might think it was a good idea not to leave Scoot alone even though he was already loading the empties into a dishwasher.

In the restaurant they settled at a round oak table in a back corner. Alex quickly cleared tapestry place mats, cutlery, glasses and serviettes to another table and sat down.

'This is my fault,' Kyle said abruptly and rushed on: 'If I'd been where I was supposed to be I wouldn't have found her. I wish I hadn't. Who does things like that to people?' He rubbed at his neck. 'I hate him whoever he was.' A clammy-looking sheen coated his pale face.

The windows on two sides of the table reflected back the image of them sitting together, leaning forward across the table. Alex was tempted to close the drapes over the windows but pushed the thought aside. No one would hear what they said even if they were right outside.

'Kyle,' Dan said quietly. 'What do you mean, if you'd been where you were supposed to be.'

'I'd have been on the bus home with the other kids and I wouldn't have been in that field playing around. But I'd rather be alone. I don't like all the pushing and shoving with the others. I ducked out of last period and got a regular bus that goes by the school. I took my dirt bike out back to ride around the field. Scoot and I built some radical jumps. He's a lot better than me so I have to practice more.'

'Let's move on,' Dan said.

Lily arrived pushing a trolley loaded with a teapot, cups and saucers, a jug of milk and sugar.

She plopped a plate of sausage rolls and another of sandwiches on the table together with some lemon curd tarts and left Alex to deal with the tea. Before she left, she drew the heavy damask curtains over the window. 'Cozier,' she said shortly.

'What time did you get to the field?'

'About 2, or it could have been earlier. I was going to ride for a while before . . . before coming to wait for Scoot until we could go to Lily's cottage to finish up homework. Then we'll spend the night there because Dad won't be home. He's working really hard because we've got a lot of expenses coming up. Dad wants Scoot and me to stay in school so we'll do better later on. We want that, too. Everything costs so much – that's what Dad says.'

Dan had accepted a cup of tea and leaned back, holding the saucer against his chest. 'It's always good to have plans. And your dad's right, everything is very expensive. You might not want to slough off school in the afternoons too often though, not if you want to do well in school.'

'I know.' Kyle looked abashed. 'Look what's happened because I did.'

'You found the lady, how?'

'I found her. She was there, is all. I walked my bike around to a break in the fence between the fields and went in. Then I started riding but it was really wet and slow. I went around a couple of times but then I got off because I decided I'd give it up today. I thought I saw something blue in the trees so I left my bike and went to see.' He swallowed. 'She was dead. Her face was all weird and blue – purple, I suppose.'

66

'How did you know she was dead for sure?'

Kyle looked at Dan as if he might be short of a lot of brain cells. 'Her eyes were open and popping out. Instead of white around the outside, they were bright red. And her nose had bled all over her mouth. Stuff was coming out of there – sick, I think. Her pulse wasn't beating. Someone killed her with a wire or something, didn't they? Pulled it tight around her neck.'

If Alex never heard this story again it would be too soon.

'You looked at her neck?' Dan said, looking puzzled.

'To feel . . . like I see on the telly. To feel for a pulse. There wasn't one, I'd already tried her wrist. Her hand looked like she didn't give up easy. The cut on her neck was under her scarf. I put the scarf back so it would be like it was left. She had on cool trainers – Nike Air Max. Bright blue. That must be what I saw first.'

Dan had brought his notebook, and scribbled a few words.

'Did you ever see this person before?' Dan asked.

Kyle had a sausage roll halfway to his mouth. 'I don't think so but you couldn't tell much with her face all weird like that. I don't think so.'

'Did you touch anything but her neck and the scarf.'

'No!' Kyle made a horrified face. 'I tried to see if she was alive, but I knew she wasn't. Then I ran to the shop – The Polka Dot – and phoned the police. Then Scoot. Lily heard and said I should come here.'

'Did you see anyone else around the area of the woods or fields?'

With a mouthful of sausage roll, Kyle had time to think and he appeared to think deeply. He swallowed and said, 'Only a bit later. It was before you came.'

Alex couldn't miss Dan's straightening back. 'Male or female?'

'I don't know. Everyone looks the same in a big coat with a hood and all the rain coming down so you can't see so good.'

'What time do you think you saw this person?'

Kyle turned a dull red. 'I don't know. Later.'

'Later than what? Later than when you found the body? Or later after you'd what?'

Kyle's blush deepened until it looked painful. 'I went back home. I wanted my phone so I looked for it. I knew I wouldn't find it because I lost it a couple of days ago, but I hoped I'd just find it. I saw someone through the window.'

Dan said, 'Which window?'

Alex came close to interrupting. Was this normal, this battering with questions?

'The one upstairs. In the front. That's Scoot's and my room. You have to bend down to see out because it's low and sticks out from the roof. I thought something moved so I looked. I saw someone running with their head down.'

'Toward the field or toward the street?'

Kyle rubbed his eyes. 'I don't know. I was scared.'

'What did you do?' Dan put a hand on the boy's shoulder. 'It's all right. It's not easy to

68

remember things that happen to us when we're bothered.'

'I sat in the corner away from the window. They couldn't have seen me from down there but I didn't think of that. I just wanted to be safe.'

'OK,' Dan said, patting Kyle's shoulder now. 'Have some tea. We'll go on with this later.'

'Tomorrow?' Kyle said with hope in his eyes.

'Can't wait that long, son,' Dan said with a twitch of his lips. 'Just until you've had more tea and things to eat. I could use this tea myself.' He glanced at Tony and Alex.

'Good tea,' Tony said and picked up a sandwich. He looked around and rescued the serviettes Alex had put on another table.

Alex followed suit with some food. She was ravenous. 'This has been an awful day for you, Kyle,' she said. 'It's a good thing you had friends to come to.' Was that too obvious, she wondered?

'Did you go to look for your phone before you went to the shop?' Dan said.

Kyle's color rose again. Alex prayed he wouldn't deny it if that was what he'd done.

'Yes,' he said quietly. 'I wanted to find it and talk to Scoot. I wanted my dad.' He sounded so young and when his gaze moved to Alex she gave him a wink of encouragement.

'And the person you saw, going whichever way, was gone by then? Before you called from the shop.'

'Yes.'

'Was he or she carrying anything you noticed?'

69

'No. Had on a big hooded slicker. A black one.'

Dan made a short note. 'Do you think the direction they went might come back to you?'

For a while Kyle didn't answer. He seemed to be deep in thought again, but in the end he dropped his head forward and sniffed. Alex pulled a tissue from her pocket.

'It's been a hard day,' Dan said. 'Take it slowly. Sometimes it all gets muddled up when we're in a strange situation.' There were times when he sounded more Irish than others – this was one of those times.

'He stood across from the cottage for a long time, staring at it, before he took off,' Kyle said. 'I wasn't afraid.'

Which said just how afraid he had been more clearly than an admission.

'He went across in front of the cottage and that way, I think.' He pointed in the direction of what would be Folly from Underhill. 'Over the fields, I suppose. There's several ways to get on the road again going that way. Probably lots of them.'

'He stared at your cottage for a long time,' Dan said. 'What does that mean? A minute? Five minutes?'

'Five, maybe,' Kyle said. 'It seemed like forever. We don't see people back there.'

'Why do you think he was doing that?'

'To scare me,' Kyle said promptly. 'Like he was telling me he knew I was in there and he could come in if he wanted to.'

Alex glanced at Tony and he shook his head

70

slightly. Did that mean what Kyle described gave him the creeps as it did her?

'So it sounds like he followed you from the body?' Dan said, leaning back in his chair, expressionless.

He was deliberately scaring Kyle, putting ideas in his head that might shake loose more. The boy didn't answer but his face was ashen.

'He could have watched you look at the body, then come after you to see where you went.'

Alex wanted to tell Dan to stop but if she did, she was likely to be sent away and never included again. She would become too much of a liability to him and then she couldn't try to support Kyle.

'Sir?' A policeman appeared at the opening to the kitchen passageway.

Dan beckoned him forward. 'Come on in, er . . .'

'Wallace, sir.' This officer, boyish looking and Asian, bore stripes on his uniform sleeves. 'Could I have a word, sir?'

Dan excused himself and joined Wallace in the passageway. The two men spoke so low that their voices were barely a murmur.

'How are you doing?' Tony asked Kyle. 'We shouldn't say too much but remember that a lot of what the police tell you, or ask you, is to see if you get unsettled. And they want to shake more information loose if there's anything you've forgotten or are holding back.'

Kyle hung on Tony's words. The trust there made Alex smile a little. But she wasn't amused by Dan's toughness. He didn't have to as much as raise his voice to put some nasty ideas in Kyle's head.

'The chief inspector's a softy, really,' she said. 'Sometimes he puts on a mean manner to shake you up.'

Tony gave her a look of disbelief. Perhaps she had laid it on a bit thick. 'We're here for you,' she told Kyle, hoping to dig herself out of an unfortunate slip. 'You don't have to worry.'

Within minutes Dan came back and took his seat, put a gray plastic envelope on the table. 'Describe the body for me again,' he said to Kyle.

Alex managed to only half-hear the ghastly repetition.

'And you're sure of the time when you found it?' Dan said.

Kyle worked his chair backward a little and held his hands between his knees. 'Yes.' He looked at the ceiling and said, much more quietly, 'No. I left school after first period this morning.'

'OK,' Dan said. 'We'll talk about why you did that a bit later. Does Scoot know?'

A miserable shake of Kyle's head.

Dan laced his fingers behind his neck. 'And you took your bike out soon after you got home?'

'Yes.'

'And found the body.'

'Yes.'

'When was the last time you were back there with your bike?'

'Two nights ago.' Kyle pushed at his hair until it stood straight up in the front. 'We use bike lights.' His fair skin was crimson and sweaty.

'Other kids use that track, though?'

'Just us,' Kyle said. 'People stay away.'

72

'Do you know why that is?'

Without warning, Kyle leaned way forward, crossed his forearms on the edge of the table and rested his forehead. 'We're different,' he said clearly. 'We don't have a mom but mostly, Dad likes us to keep to ourselves so he doesn't welcome other people coming around.'

'He scares them off?'

Kyle let out a long breath. 'I suppose so. They think we're weird and poor. They don't know anything about us. We like things the way they are.' He looked up, sat back. His cheeks were still stained red.

'That's it for now, then,' Dan said. 'If you're not at your cottage I can find you here?'

'Or at Corner Cottage,' Alex said. 'He'll be there tonight.'

'I'm sure you'll usually find him at school in the daytime,' Tony said, winking at Kyle. 'And he does volunteer work for me. Between Scoot and the rest of us, we'll know where he is.'

Dan looked thoughtful. 'Kyle's army,' he said. 'Looks like you're well protected. It's best to keep your own counsel, son. If you've got anything to share, come straight to me.' He took out a card and gave it to Kyle. 'Best way to keep out of trouble – more trouble.'

Now wasn't the time but when it was appropriate Alex intended to tell Dan O'Reilly what she thought of his methods when he interviewed already frightened boys.

Six

That evening after Tony took Scoot and Kyle to get clean clothes and supplies from their home, the boys went to Lily's. Her spare bedroom had only one bed, but she made up another with an airbed on the floor and both Scoot and Kyle seemed relieved to be at Corner Cottage. From what Alex and Tony had heard, Lily was about as close to a granny as those kids would get.

After the boys were settled with school books at a table in the tiny dining room at Lily's, she told Alex she'd take the rest of the night off and Alex knew the reason. Her mum had gone into protective mode.

At the Black Dog once more, Tony expected to find a police presence but O'Reilly, Lamb and Miller had left. 'I don't know if I'm relieved or not,' he said to Alex. 'I was hoping to winkle some details of the investigation out of Dan. If he's in the mood he occasionally shares a few pithy bits. Usually when he thinks we might be holding out on something he'd like to know.'

He got one of Alex's intense green looks from beneath her eyelashes. He wasn't sure what it meant but decided he'd find out if and when she wanted to share what was going on in her head.

Tony sensed he was being watched and looked

directly at the Burke sisters. They had spent hours at the Dog today but appeared bright-eyed and as if they were popping to tell him something.

'Flashing red lights off your starboard bow,' Tony said.

Alex glanced to her right. 'Harriet and Mary,' she said. 'Very funny. Looks as if they've got empty glasses. I doubt if they've ordered more sherry for themselves. They've had tea, though.'

'I'll get 'em some sherry,' Tony said and made for the counter and Hugh.

Alex, determinedly smiling, went to join Harriet, Mary and the menagerie. 'I thought you'd have gone home a long time ago,' she said.

Mary fixed Alex with a steely stare through her Coke bottle lenses. 'Why, because old fuddy duddies like us should be in bed by now? We have to make sure you and Tony are all right. We saw the police coming and going. They think they're so subtle. About as subtle as tea bags.'

Harriet joined Alex in laughing. 'I thought tea bags were tasteless, you've always said,' Harriet commented.

'Exactly. Not subtle at all. Obvious rubbish.'

'Tony's gone to get you both a sherry,' Alex said. She sat down where she could see the whole bar and rested her elbows on the table. 'Anyone interesting been in since we left?' Bogie planted his front paws and nose on her leg.

'A reporter quite soon after you'd gone,' Harriet said. 'She managed to corner the police while they were still here but I don't think she got much out of them. They're all gone now. We got a nice enough nod from Dan but some phone message came through and they were away as if they'd sprouted wings. I think he'd have come to talk to us otherwise.'

'What did you do with Lily and those boys?' Mary asked. 'You all disappeared at the same time.'

Alex covered a smile. 'Nothing gets past you, does it?' She scratched Bogie's neck while he craned around to lick kisses on her wrist.

She got blank looks from the women. Harriet said, 'We only saw the younger boy for a moment. Is Scoot, the one who works here, is he the younger one's brother? They don't look much alike.'

'How did you see Kyle?' Alex said, pulling her chair well under the table and leaning close to Harriet.

'Mmm.' Harriet raised her brows and looked at her hands in her lap. 'I saw him with Scoot when I went to the door to watch the dogs go out. I never leave them outside on their own. The boys were talking near the back corner. Scoot had that big-brother look about him. He wasn't happy. He looked concerned about something.'

'So you just decided they must be related?'

'Yes. And now I know I was right.'

Alex sighed. 'Please would you avoid mentioning anything . . .' She paused. It was always best to stay as close to the truth as possible when coming up with a fabrication. Her mother had taught her that.

'What is it?' Mary stiffened. The cat stirred

irritably on her lap. 'You're worried about something.'

'The boys' family is having a hard time,' Alex said, noticing that both Tony and Hugh had gone into the kitchen. 'We're helping them out but it wouldn't do for that to be public knowledge. People need their pride intact.'

Mary looked over her shoulder and Harriet leaned to see the bar herself.

'If we can help, just say so,' Harriet said. 'But it doesn't have to mean anything if Tony and Hugh sneak off to the kitchen and leave the bar unattended.'

Alex narrowed her eyes at the woman. 'In other words, you think that looks like something to be concerned about?'

She didn't get an answer. What had made them leave?

Juste Vidal, the French divinity student who had helped out at the Dog for the past couple of years would be in the next day. Alex was relieved. If things remained as unsettled as they were, they might ask Juste to increase his hours.

'Will you excuse me?' Alex got up – to Bogie's disappointment. 'I think I'd better go and keep an eye on things.'

'Don't worry,' Mary said, and patted Alex's hand on the table. 'Whatever this is, it'll work out. We've all seen much worse.'

Alex couldn't be sure of that yet.

Seven

'I say we put one of these up on each door and in a couple of the windows,' Tony told Hugh. 'There's nothing to be gained from waiting till tomorrow.' He looked closely at the posters in his hands.

'We could gain a bit of time to let the boys calm down before the whole village starts talking about it,' Hugh responded. 'We're already sitting on a powder keg with them.'

'Is this a private club or can anyone join?' Alex said, standing with one foot still on the bar side of the dividing wall with the kitchen. 'Good thing Juste's coming in tomorrow. We can't start looking like a do-it-yourself operation.'

Tony could tell she wasn't in as much of a careless frame of mind as the words suggested. 'Sorry,' he said. 'Take a look at these. A police officer brought them to the back door. He said he'd been told not to raise any fuss by going through the bar. He also said they want these put up tonight and handed to people as they leave.'

'Who is it?' Alex said, looking carefully at the woman pictured on the flyer. 'This is an E-fit, isn't it? Done from the dead woman. Why would they do that so quickly? She was only found today.'

There was no answer for her question.

Alex glanced back at the bar, put the flyer on a kitchen counter and went out to take care of customers.

'I'd better get out there,' Hugh said, but Alex appeared again before he could go.

'Do you think the woman was killed longer ago than we assumed?' she said, dropping her voice. 'The police can check the whole country to see if anyone's put in a missing person's report matching her. If they haven't it could be they have nothing at all to go on.'

She took up the flyer again. 'This is one of those "pleasant" faces. Unremarkable. How horrible to think she was dead when this was done.'

'Why don't I think about things like the reason for the early flyer?' Tony said. 'Probably because you're a natural crime fighter and I have to learn as I go along. There's a thought, who would have guessed we were going to turn into investigators?'

'Who would've thought we were going to turn into Murder Central here in little old Folly?' Hugh said. He didn't look amused, not that he had often been in a light mood since the last crime spree they had suffered through.

'This one wasn't in Folly,' Tony said.

'Don't think the press won't point out that we're cheek to jowl with Underhill,' Hugh retorted. 'They probably think of Underhill as our suburb.'

'What does it matter?' Alex said, irritated. 'We have a killer on the loose.'

'Probably not,' Hugh said. 'He's most likely to have moved on.'

Shouts of laughter came from the bar. Tony didn't feel like checking the source. 'Let me take sherry to Harriet and Mary,' he said. 'While I'm at it, I'll take a few flyers and get them up.'

Alex leaned her temple against the wall. 'This may not be a popular suggestion, but I think we ought to track down Sid Gammage. Kyle, particularly, is more upset than is good for him.'

She was probably right but Tony wasn't ready to jump on that bandwagon, not when they'd already said – or more or less said they would help the boys keep their situation quiet. The father was a long-distance lorry driver. It was unlikely he'd welcome calls. If the police decided they had to make contact, they would make the decision.

'OK,' said Alex, clearly reading his reaction, or lack of one. 'I can tell you don't agree. We'll wait, but not too long.'

Smiling, Tony went with her into the bar and she poured two glasses of Harvey's Bristol Cream.

He carried them to the table near the fireplace. 'Is it true they found the body near the Gammages' cottage?' Mary asked.

'Yes.' Tony didn't intend to encourage discussion.

Another roar of mirth went up, apparently in a response to a 'how long can you hang your spoon on your nose' contest. Tony shook his head. Harmless enough, he supposed.

He put two flyers on the table.

Mary picked hers up and took it close to her

80

nose, but Harriet turned her head sideways. 'Is that what she looks like?' she asked.

'The woman who died, yes,' Tony said. 'The police brought them by.'

'So no one's reported her missing, or not yet,' Harriet said. 'And none of our visiting clever clogs have the faintest who she is.'

'I've seen her,' Mary said.

Given that Mary barely saw at all, that sounded unlikely.

Harriet picked up the second flyer and studied it. 'When?' she said. 'She looks dead.'

'She is dead,' Mary said tartly.

Tony struggled with a reflexive laugh. He cleared his throat several times. 'Where do you think you saw her, Mary?' he asked.

Alex joined him. She heard the question and looked from Mary to the dead woman's picture.

'She bought a bag of Bath buns,' Mary said. 'And a bottle of Vimto to take away.'

All three of them stared at her.

'About three weeks ago,' Mary said, frowning. 'I remember thinking the Vimto didn't go with the buns.'

'Used to be a health drink,' Harriet said. 'Before they put all the fizz in it. Probably better for you than most things, though, and tasty.'

'Might not be her, I suppose,' Mary said, peering more closely at the flyer. 'She had a scarf over her head, I think.'

Alex got a sickening reminder of the scarf Kyle talked about. 'Think about it,' she told Mary. 'If you decide you should, call it in. You could always ask for Dan O'Reilly if you'd be more comfortable.'

He was surprised Alex didn't take over the task of contacting the police, but he was glad. She needed to step back from this one, not that it would be easy given their involvement with Scoot and Kyle.

'We'll take the dogs off your hands,' Alex said. 'Tony and I are making an early night of it.'

Blinking, Tony gave her a hard look and she looked suddenly overheated. 'We've got things to discuss.'

She clipped leashes on Katie and Bogie. 'See you tomorrow.'

For once the ladies didn't have any quick comebacks.

A drive up the winding road from Folly-on-Weir had taken them to the Dimple, a shallow valley just over the hill crest where both Alex, at Lime Tree Lodge, and Tony at his unnamed house amid it's sumptuous gardens, had lived for several years. Barely visible against a steel dark sky, Tinsdale Tower, the folly from which Folly-on-Weir got its name, made a jagged black blur. The Tooth, as locals called it.

Tony and Alex lived only minutes apart. Often, they shared lifts. But to Tony's despair, Alex liked to ride a bike back and forth to the village when the weather was good enough to leave her Range Rover behind. She'd crashed her first one but replaced it quickly. Clipped into a basket, Bogie rode in front of her to skim down and labor up the hill with him holding up his nose to the wind, ears flapping, and resembling a car bonnet ornament or sailing ship's figurehead.

The silences, broken only by the sound of the windscreen wipers, had grown too long.

'Shall we talk at my house?' Tony asked when it was almost time to take a turnoff.

In a lot of ways, she preferred his place. It was cozier, smaller, even though it was still too big. 'Let's go to mine,' she said. That way if things went really badly, he would be the one who had to leave. Tidier, especially since he'd insist on driving her home from his house if she decided to leave.

'OK.' He turned off into the driveway that ran between stone gateposts topped with glowering griffons, downward to the front of her large two-story block of a yellow stone house. 'Katie thinks this is her home, too.'

If she were honest, she'd admit – aloud – that the sometimes affair, sometimes slightly uncomfortable friendship they had carried on for so long without any commitment was of her making. She had a failed marriage behind her, and the loss of a baby girl at birth. Tony's marriage had failed, then his wife died and he returned from Australia a widower. They were not shining examples of people who were good at making intimate relationships work.

That was an excuse.

'Here we go.' Tony turned off the engine and hopped from the vehicle. Alex threw up the hood on her coat, got out and slammed her door before he could come around to let her out.

Why did she do that? She always raced to let

herself out of whatever they were driving before he could help her. They both knew it.

The dogs caught up with her as she unlocked the front door. They tore inside toward the back of the house and Alex's favorite spot, the formerly dark little study she'd had opened up by adding a conservatory onto the side of the house and removing the adjoining wall except for a heavy carved wooden molding at ceiling level. Alex had kept an old black iron fireplace in one corner. When this was lit it made the room alive as well as cozy.

The noise of rain on the conservatory roof echoed into the room and got louder when she opened the sliding doors between the two areas. This was what she had wanted, to feel the outside in all its changing seasons and times of day, coming into the house. When she flipped on low lights in pots of plants and troughs along the conservatory windows, the effect became eerie or magical, depending on her mood. Tonight it unsettled her and she turned back into the room.

She had felt Tony walk into what he referred to as her 'den' behind her. 'Shall I light the fire?' she said. 'It's that kind of night.'

'I'll do it.' And he knelt to pile up pieces of kindling and balance small split logs on top.

Flames curled over the fireback sending lighted embers up the chimney.

'I always light the fire,' Tony said, sounding as if his mind was in more than one place. 'You always ask if you should light it, but—'

'You do it,' she interrupted. 'Sounds like a

84

habit, doesn't it? Like things we say and do because they've become automatic. Like me hurrying to get out of the Land Rover before you can open my door.'

He stood up slowly, held the mantel with both hands and stared down into the fire. 'Yes, exactly like that.'

'I'm not sure,' Alex said. 'Any ideas?'

'Ooh, you're inviting me into dangerous waters.'

'You're a good swimmer, aren't you?'

'I doubt if I'd survive a really strong riptide, but here goes. You may be afraid of giving up any of your independence so you behave like a bra-burner when you feel danger approaching.'

She sputtered with laughter. 'That's priceless. It sounds so unlike you to say something like that.'

His smile was slight enough not to count. 'Am I close?'

'Probably.' Of course he was close. She took off her coat. 'OK, you've got it right. Don't you feel nervous about finding yourself in another failed relationship? I've never had a friend like you. No matter what happens to me I know you'll support me. You'll take my side.' Taking advantage of an opportunity to catch her breath, Alex went into the hall to hang up the coat.

When she returned, Tony hadn't moved except to concentrate on the floor.

The dogs were on alert. Lying on a carpet in front of the hearth, both of their heads were raised, their eyes and ears tuned in to the atmosphere.

'I'm tempted to say we shouldn't do this in

front of the children,' Alex said, waving a hand toward Katie and Bogie.

'Alex, I wish I could find some humor in this and I hope we can find a comfortable place in our hearts and heads that includes both of us.'

'I did make sure we came together to talk tonight, Tony.' She pressed damp palms against her jeans. 'Why don't I know the right things to tell you?'

He offered her his hand and she slid her fingers into his palm. 'What's the worst thing you think could come out of this?' he asked. 'Be completely honest.'

The thumping in her chest ought to be visible. 'OK. That you'll say you want us to step back from one another.' Swallowing was an almost painful effort.

He pulled her a little closer. 'I don't think I could do that, but we've got issues. Even while we rely on each other and trust each other, there's something in the way of us moving forward.'

What did she want to ask him, to tell him?

Looking sideways at her, he studied her face. With one hand, he wound a curl behind her ear and rested a thumb at the corner of her mouth. 'It wouldn't be easy,' he said. 'But if you don't want me so involved in your life, that's the way I'll make it be. I thought I was going to say something quite different from that but it isn't the time after all.'

She was messing this up, but she was also doing the best she could. 'I couldn't stand it if you weren't here, Tony. I know I'm behaving like a teenager with arrested social development, but I am trying.'

'Yes.' His little smile wasn't convincing. 'But do you know – no, do you have any idea what you want for us? Tell me to back off. Tell me I'm sucking all the oxygen and you want more for yourself. I can take it – not so much, but I'll hold it together.'

Lightning crackling with flashes of brilliance through the conservatory roof made her jump. Thunder followed in seconds, and a rainfall that pelted the glass roof and sent a near waterfall swilling sideways over the windows. Lights in the troughs inside turned the slashing sheets blue.

Alex pulled Tony to face her. She gripped handfuls of his sweater at the waist. 'I arranged the dramatic effects,' she said, but he didn't look amused. 'I don't want you to back off. There's plenty of oxygen for both of us. I want you, Tony. I'll make sure I do better than I have lately. I've been distant and I've missed you but I wasn't sure what to do, or if I should do anything. I'm just not ready to make any commitments – that's assuming you want them any more than I do.'

With his forearms on her shoulders he stood quite still and made no comment.

In other words, it was her turn to do some of the work. 'If you don't like this, say so. I'll keep it simple. You are my friend and my lover and that's what I want. I have issues I haven't worked out yet and until I do, I'm not fit to offer more. I hope—'

'Enough,' Tony said. 'You've said everything I need to know for now. If and when you think I can help you with those issues, let me know. And I'll return the favor because sometimes I get tired of keeping up the friendly, easy-going, perfectly balanced country vet façade. I think I'm a bit of a mess in some ways. I know I don't always let you know what I'm really thinking. If that scares you, I'd better get out of here and see you tomorrow – if you want to see me.'

'Tony, do you suppose we could hang around together tonight and take each day as it comes?'

Eight

He was the youngest, but for Scoot's sake he had to hold it all inside. Scoot was the one who followed the rules and never got into any trouble. If something got messed up enough to make their dad mad, it was Scoot who looked scared although it was usually Kyle who was the culprit.

He had to be the strong one.

They were in big trouble now and it was his fault. Not because he'd found that body but because he was sure something had gone really wrong for their dad and he had let people know he and Scoot were alone. He'd got mad at Scoot at the Black Dog for talking about their dad but he only did that because he, Kyle, came barging into that kitchen and giving stuff away. It didn't make sense that Dad had left them for weeks

88

now. And who put the money through the letterbox while they were asleep? Dad wouldn't tell them and he didn't say why it was all happening. He'd told them not to try to call him or the place where he worked. This was the most alone he ever remembered feeling.

The little bedroom in Lily's cottage was really dark. Even if he knelt on the bed and peered between the curtains, the world looked black through the shiny coat of rain on the windows.

Scoot said he should sleep on the airbed because it was closer to the door, but he didn't want to say why that mattered. Kyle knew. They'd always had this thing about it being safer for Scoot to be closest to anyone who came in because he was bigger and stronger and should be between Kyle and any danger.

'I'm not afraid,' Kyle mouthed into the darkness.

Lily had put a night light in the room but once she'd left and they'd been in bed, Scoot took it out. Light made you easier to find if someone came to get you.

When he got into bed it had felt like winter. It was winter. He'd shivered. Now he was too hot and threw off the covers. His scalp was damp and his hair stuck to it and to his forehead. The bump bump he heard deep in his ears was his heart. He'd heard it before, almost every night when they were alone at their own cottage. But this time they weren't alone and he felt even more scared.

He didn't want to close his eyes because then he saw the dead lady's face, and her hand. Her hand seemed to open and close, to dig into the dirt.

Dad wouldn't like it that they weren't at home. He'd worry someone nosey would interfere and say it wasn't right for them to be there alone.

His eyes prickled. His pajamas were old and thin, and they were way too short for his arms and legs. Over his back the material was wet. It didn't seem right to take them off here in case Lily came to check on them. She was a nice lady. All these people were nice to them and he thought they might mean it that they wanted to help.

Dad wouldn't like it.

He kept his eyes open, staring into the blackness that felt as if it might come down and wrap him up, and take away the air, and make him so hot he'd want to scream.

Grow up, Kyle. I've got to be tougher than Scoot, for his sake. Scoot's the best. He tries to take care of us both.

'You awake?' Scoot said quietly. 'I can hear you.'

'Uh huh.'

'You OK?'

'Yeah.'

He listened to Scoot listening to him. If they talked it would all get worse. They didn't need to say the things they were thinking.

'It's OK for us to be here,' Scoot said.

'Of course it is, dope.'

'Just in case, I don't think we should tell Dad we left home. It could worry him.'

Kyle knew what Scoot was really thinking. 'OK. When we talk to him we won't say. We'll

90

go home tomorrow anyway. What do we do if the police say they've got to phone Dad?'

'They can't!'

'But what if they ask for his number?'

Scoot was quiet for a long time, then he said, 'We don't have his number because we can't call when he's driving. If it gets impossible to stop them insisting, we could tell them Dad works for Podmore's but he gets in trouble if anyone phones there.'

'They'll do it anyway,' Kyle told him. 'The police aren't afraid of anyone. And if we said that, they'd only think we were trying to stop them getting in touch – and we would be.'

'Yeah. I gotta go to the bathroom.'

He wished Scoot wouldn't leave him. 'OK.'

The airbed made funny squeaking sounds when Scoot pushed his way from beneath his covers. He opened the door carefully and a slice of light cut into the room, across the airbed, across Kyle's bed.

Scoot slid onto the landing and Kyle didn't hear anything, not even a door opening and closing.

His eyes felt glued open. He faced the light from the door. A whirring sound turned his stomach and he held still. It whirred and stopped. Whirred and stopped.

Sheesh, Scoot's phone on vibrate under his pillow. This late? He scrambled to the floor and pulled out the mobile, pressed the button to answer. 'Yes,' he murmured. He should have looked to see who it was but now he was afraid to take the phone from his ear.

91

'Yes,' he repeated and screwed up his eyes at the weird little shriek his voice made.

'Kyle?'

'Yes.' The pulse beat all over him now. He felt it in his hands and feet. 'Dad. We were afraid you weren't going to call. I lost my mobile,' he finished and gritted his teeth. Best to get it out.

'Don't worry about that. Just listen, son. We don't have long. And you won't be able to call me back on this number even if you want to. After we talk, it won't work again.'

'What's wrong, Dad?' Kyle whispered.

'Why are you talking like that?'

'I don't know.'

'Where's Scoot?'

'In the loo.'

'Did you get any money the day before yesterday.'

Kyle took a shaky breath. 'It was last week.'

'No.' His dad's voice got hard. 'That was another time. Day before yesterday.'

'No.'

His dad muttered and cussed under his breath the way he did when he was angry because things weren't going so well.

'Dad, when are you coming home?'

'Please listen to me, Kyle. There's very little time and it's getting shorter every second. I'll deal with getting money to you. The rent's been paid. And the gas and electricity. Have you got enough food for now?'

'Yes. Plenty.'

Scoot came back in and sank onto his bed,

listening. Even in the semi-darkness Kyle could see how his brother stared at him.

'Everything's OK here, Dad. We're doing everything you said.' He saw Scoot nod approval.

'Good boys,' Dad said. 'Stay away from other people. Go to school and go home. Don't answer the door. If someone comes at night stay locked in until it's time for the bus.'

Kyle felt light-headed. 'Why? Why are you saying all that? Who would come after us?' He tried not to think of the figure in the black slicker, face hidden by the hood although Kyle had known he was being watched.

Had to be a man. He had a thick body. Not really tall but big in his heavy rain gear.

Had he killed the lady? Should he tell his dad about finding the body? He covered the mouth-piece and whispered to Scoot. 'Do I tell Dad about the murder or—?'

'No! Not now. We gotta think.'

'You OK, son?'

'Yeah, I said so.'

'Would you feel better if I tried to get Aunty Cheryl to come and stay with you?'

'No!' He answered so loudly he covered his mouth and listened for Lily to come. More quietly, he added, 'No, Dad, please don't do that. She's weird.'

All Sid Gammage said was, 'OK.' He cleared his throat. 'I can't get home yet. I'm sorry, but I just can't. When I do I won't be leaving again. I'll get work close to home. Or we'll move if we have to. Is Scoot back?'

Kyle said, 'Yes,' and gave up the phone. He

lay down and pulled the covers up to his chin. Now he was cold again.

'I understand, Dad,' Scoot said. 'Trust us to look after things here. OK, Kyle will tell me what you want us to do. When will you call again . . .?'

Kyle could see sweat shining on Scoot's face and his own stomach turned again and again.

'Why would anyone try to get in . . . Dad?' After a few seconds, he slid the phone back under his pillow. 'He's in trouble,' he said and Kyle could hear how close Scoot was to buckling.

'You can't know that. We've got each other and soon we'll have Dad back—'

'A man said something I couldn't hear but he sounded angry. Dad started to talk but the phone went off.'

Nine

Alex had left her car just off the High Street in Underhill – behind the closed feed and seed outfit. She walked rapidly through the village, away from parked police cars, and began working her way around through lanes toward the area where she expected to find the site of the murder and the Gammages' cottage. She must be careful to keep her distance from the copse where the body was found. It would still be an active crime scene and she didn't want it getting back to O'Reilly and Lamb that she'd been seen anywhere near the area, or worse yet, walk into them.

She wore her hooded duffle coat with black leggings tucked inside her wellies.

In the mud, the boots made noises like marching suction cups. Rain had started again but this time it was the fine, misty kind that settled on her wool coat in a web of glittering specks. It also crept into the roll-neck of her jumper and down her neck.

This was one more late morning when a pewter sky lounged heavily on a bank of only slightly lighter-colored mist and the hills and fields, the trees, what rooftops there were in the distance, all were a smudged charcoal rendering in shades of gray.

Alex didn't know what she hoped to find but from what she'd heard so far, this wasn't a simple, chance murder. What would Tony say about what she was doing? He never expected her to clear her decisions with him, probably in part because he knew she would not suffer being overlooked by anyone, even if there was a possibility she might be in love with them.

She did love Tony and she knew he loved her, but love and life were never simple and needed to be approached carefully from every possible direction.

Alex wanted love but she didn't dare to believe love could be a gift tossed into her lap the way it seemed to have been. And that frightened her. She could never, ever, let go of her love for Tony without knowing how much she had lost. Last night and early this morning . . . later, she would allow herself to live it all again when she didn't have to be on alert like this.

Concentration was her essential today. First thing, while Tony slept on, she'd driven to Lily's cottage to pick up the boys – both with dark circles under their eyes and so much silence she hadn't bothered to ask how they were.

She had forgotten Scoot had his bike at the Dog and rode back and forth. He took off on his own. At first Kyle had insisted that he would walk to his usual bus stop, but she had prevailed and driven him to school, stopping a distance away to let him catch up with a group of kids and finish the walk to school. She hadn't left without seeing how Kyle stepped off the pavement when a boy landed a sharp kick on his ankle.

Some things never seemed to change but she hoped Kyle would learn that he could change the way he dealt with them. Bullies lived for the reactions of their victims and the approval of other bullies and bullies in hiding. Alex felt the old rush of confusion and disgust.

The two boys had said they'd make their own way back to Corner Cottage later. Scoot would ride to work at the Dog first, but Alex intended to find Kyle after school and get him to Folly. She thought he would go to the cottage he called home until she tracked him down and persuaded him to go with her. She would have to find a way to contact Sid Gammage or they would all be without a boat and up a river they didn't fancy wading in.

I'm getting in too deep. It's the boys, I want

to take care of them and I don't know how to keep the balance right. Help is what they need, somebody well-meaning to look out for them, not a stand-in mother.

Being hard on herself might be noble, Alex thought, but it wasn't necessarily constructive. She trudged on, doing her best to keep her face down and not look around her too often. Tony would not be pleased to know what she was doing, but he was different from her, more willing to let things play out and hope the end would be good. She might have been like him if she didn't have a horrible hunch disaster was waiting in the wings for the careless. No, she told herself, that didn't mean she considered Tony careless, they were simply different.

When she'd decided to come here today, it hadn't been as arbitrary as it might seem. She had built a sickening possibility around the murder so close to the Gammage cottage. Alex hunched over as she walked.

Her phone vibrated in her pocket, startling her, and she looked at the caller readout. Naturally, it was Tony. 'Hi,' she said. 'You slept well,' and she laughed a little although she hoped it sounded less false to him than it did to her. 'It was good, having you there with me.'

'More than good for me,' he said, his voice rough and sleepy. 'I wanted to hold you when I woke up. I can't believe I slept so long. I'll have to get my skates on.'

She smiled. 'When I woke up, you were holding me, Tony. I won't say what you were holding, but I liked it. I decided I wanted to drive Kyle to school. Mum wrote him a note for the attendance office. Scoot rides his bike. Nice boys, but they're troubled. I think you were probably right when you suggested we were biting off more than we can chew. But we're going to manage somehow. I think you feel the tension, too,'

He didn't answer at once but she didn't prompt him.

'It isn't hard to care about them,' he said finally. 'What worries me is that you'll throw your heart into saving them – and I don't doubt they're in some sort of trouble, the whole family, I mean – but I don't want you broken-up by this – or anything else.'

'I'm not weak,' she told him. 'Trust me to be sensible.' Even if that wasn't her history . . .

Tony yawned, coughed and apologized. 'I hope Kyle won't back out of coming to the clinic this afternoon. He could think I wouldn't want him with all this going on.'

'No,' Alex said. 'I've reminded him where to get off the bus for your clinic.' She didn't say she expected Kyle to do a bunk and intended to round him up if he did. 'Tony, I want to say something?'

'Anything, sweetheart.'

Sometimes he was too calm, too reasonable. 'I think it's important not to say anything that could link Sid and the boys to this death – to anyone. It could get back to the police and make trouble we don't need.'

'Where did that come from?' Tony asked. 'Why would there be a link?' She could hear how puzzled he was.

'You know me – a worrier. I had a horrible thought that the woman's murder could be something to do with Sid being away for so long. What if it is and giving the idea to the police might be dangerous? To the boys or their dad?'

There was a lengthy silence before Tony spoke. 'What if they're already in danger and the police should be thinking about that?'

'I've considered that. We've got to talk to Sid. Are you with me on this? I'm sure the boys are hearing from him, or they have a number for him. Or we can ask them if we can get hold of him through his work. That sounds obvious but if it really was, why wouldn't they have mentioned telling him about the murder.'

'The killing doesn't have anything to do with them, except for Kyle finding the body so close to their cottage,' Tony said. 'They may have told Sid, but they obviously fear outside interference in their lives more than anything.

'I've got to get to the clinic. We do have to decide how to play this. The main thing is not to make intrigue where there isn't any. I tend to think this family is going through hard times and nothing more complicated than that. Scoot and Kyle have been told to keep to themselves and they're expecting their dad to be upset when he finds out their situation has been shared. It still seems reasonable that this tragedy with the death is nothing to do with them.

'I suggest we keep a close eye on the boys but consider having a word with Dan O'Reilly.'

'OK,' she said uncertainly. 'Yes, that's what we'll do. We'll decide a bit later.'

'Good.' He sounded relieved. 'Where are our girls?'

She forced a little laugh. 'Where do you think? They're propping up the bar for morning biscuits, like the social dogs they are.'

The Gammage cottage must be the one she saw in the next field with several rundown outbuildings behind.

Tony was chuckling about the dogs.

'I'd better get back,' Alex said, feeling only slightly guilty at the deception. 'I'll hope to see you by the time doggy daycare lets out.'

That brought more laughter but Alex said, 'Bye,' and switched off.

The cottage looked dilapidated but the area was kept tidy. Patchy grass around the cottage had been mowed but needed cutting again. The rest of the land which must once have been part of a small farm had lost most of its form under a heavy covering of the bleached and broken remains of abandoned crops overlaid with prize specimen weeds, brambles, bushes, waving grasses and the occasional conifer. Fruit trees, their branches bare now, stood in their original ordered lines.

Alex walked on, looking ahead but with frequent glances toward the cottage. She had not mentioned her suspicion that Kyle might repeat the truancy of yesterday to Tony, and most definitely not to Lily who was already visibly anxious.

A few hundred yards from the Gammages' cottage, showing clearly through almost leafless trees, stood a white tent Alex would rather not

100

find familiar. Even at a considerable distance she could see sagging crime scene tapes flapping in a cordon around the tent, and activity in and out of its entrance.

More tape stretched across a gap in the hedgerow where a wooden stile stood and ahead she could see other lengths of waving blue and white plastic streamers where the police had closed off the whole field.

Alex rubbed at her crossed arms.

The hedgerow grew higher in spots. She looked ahead to find a patch that promised a good hideout but in the first place she came to the hedge was too thin to give much cover. She was luckier with the next and carefully made a wider gap to see through. The weather and poor light helped her feel more confident she wouldn't be seen.

Not that there was much that she hadn't already seen. There were no signs of any plain-clothes police but now she had a clear view of a white SOCO vehicle parked at the back of the copse. These people also didn't want to be watched while they trundled back and forth with brown paper bags closed over whatever finds they hoped would help catch a killer.

Alex got her creepy sensation and looked behind her, expecting to find someone standing there. There wasn't, but she shuddered remembering how often murderers returned to their crime scenes. It excited them and for some it recreated the sexual thrill that many of them needed as much as an addict needed a fix.

The thought was enough to send her back the way she had come, slipping along as rapidly as the mud underfoot and the increasingly heavy rain would allow.

She drew level with the Gammage cottage and ducked down, staring at a small window over a side door. For a second she had thought she saw a light. She didn't see it now. The heavy racing of her heart and the sweat on her back brought a wave of sickness.

A reflection from somewhere must have caught the glass. And she wasn't living up to her mostly unflappable reputation.

What would look like a light in that window without being a light? There surely wasn't any sun.

The door opened.

Alex held her breath and scratched her face on sticks in the hedge. Yes, it had opened but just a very narrow crack and there it stayed.

She felt suddenly hot. If Kyle Gammage had skipped away from school the moment he was sure she'd driven away, he was in big trouble. He and Scoot had Alex, Tony and the others all worrying about them, and taking risks that could spell trouble for them eventually. Not one of them expected accolades, but a little trust shouldn't be too much to hope for.

The door opened wider but it was an adult figure, not Scoot or Kyle, who slid out, back to the wall, and shut the cottage again. This was a man, husky but of average height, and wearing a dark-colored coat with a hood. Inside the hood, a scarf covered the lower half of his face.

Alex dropped almost to her knees. He was coming toward her, straight toward her. She looked back and forth along the lane. Running and hoping to get the attention of the police could be her only option. First they had been too close, now they seemed miles away. But they weren't.

The man dodged to the first outbuilding beside the cottage and went inside.

Relief made her so wobbly she almost sat in the mud. He hadn't come this way because he'd seen her. But what was he doing – looking for something to steal? Looking for something he expected to find there – something he knew was there?

Was this Sid? She had no way of knowing since she didn't think she'd ever seen him. Even if she had, she was too far away to see this man clearly.

A crime in progress or not? If not, why was the man there?

That depended on who he was.

Contacting the police could bring everything down on their heads.

Not contacting the police could bring everything down on their heads.

Ten

'O'Reilly.' He answered a call with the press of a button on the dashboard.

The pause that followed was too long.

'O'Reilly here,' he said again, making an effort to warm up his tone.

Again the pause.

'Who are you trying to reach?' he said, not so warmly.

The third time might not be a charm for a crank caller. He steered into the flow on a roundabout that would feed him off toward Folly-on-Weir and reached to cut off the call. He had dealing with Constable Miller in his mind. That had to be delicately handled and there hadn't been time last night.

'Dan, it's Alex.' She cleared her throat, possibly as an excuse for her unnaturally tiny voice.

'Hello, Alex.' Bill Lamb's eyes were boring into the side of his head. Perhaps not boring, but definitely aimed in that direction. 'What can I do for you?'

'Tell me I'm overreacting, probably.'

He'd like to take it off speaker, but that would only be awkward afterward. 'What is this in relation to?' he asked very formally.

'Um, the recent thing in Underhill.'

He narrowed his eyes. 'What thing would that be?'

'A woman was found dead there, I believe. Allegedly.'

'Good girl, you're learning the accepted lingo. Just as well since you seem to be involved – to a greater or lesser degree – in these unpleasant events, surrounding one, um, case after another. What's got your attention this time?'

'Have you already made up your mind you don't want to talk to me about this, should I contact someone else?'

He smiled to himself. 'If you'd rather do that I'll understand.'

104

'You make the decision.'

'She can be a witch,' Bill Lamb whispered. 'I keep warning you. When will you believe me?'

Dan gave him a one-sided smile. 'I do believe you but I also believe in seeing how far I can push people,' he whispered back. For all to hear he said, 'You might as well tell me, Alex.'

'OK, here goes.' She coughed. 'Everything that happened yesterday is public knowledge to the entire community and probably many more people by now. A woman was murdered in a copse behind the village of Underhill.'

When she stopped speaking, he said, 'Mmm,' and steered onto the road leading directly into Folly-on-Weir. 'I'm sure you recall that we do already know that.'

'I'll come clean,' Alex said. 'Curiosity overtook me and I came to the area behind Underhill to see where the body was found. I walked through the lanes around the field where the murder took place, or where it supposedly took place.'

'The truth shall set you free,' Dan said.

'After it pisses you off,' Bill added.

Dan gave him a look but Alex's laughter distracted him. He liked to hear her laugh, and he liked it that she didn't take offence at the minor coarseness.

'Was that all?' Dan asked Alex.

'No.' She continued to speak softly but he decided not to comment on it. 'I'm still there.'

Dan frowned. 'Where?'

'In the lanes. A man came out of the Gammages' cottage. He went into an outbuilding, er, on the left as you look at it from the village.'

'South west?'

'I don't know.'

Bill let out a loud breath and crossed his arms.

'There are lots of people like me,' Alex said. 'I can't tell which direction things are.'

Dan considered that. 'If you say so. Must be inconvenient. Did you recognize him?'

'No. He was too far away but I doubt if I know him.'

Dan put his foot down a little harder. 'When he left, did he head toward the village?'

'He hasn't left.'

Dan accelerated hard. 'Is there any chance he can see you?'

'I don't think so.'

'For god's sake, woman, either it's possible or it's not.'

'I suppose anything's possible.'

Bill was matching his own frown. 'If you attempted to leave, could you be sure this man wouldn't see you go?' Dan asked.

'No.' This was almost inaudible. 'The hedgerow is low in a lot of places.'

He made up his mind. 'Stay where you are until you see a uniformed officer, or more than one, coming for you. Have you got that?'

'Yes,' she murmured. 'Thank you and I'm sorry about this.'

'Hang up.' All he wanted was to get to her.

Eleven

Crouching, sodden, her calves cramping, Alex waited, putting a wet hand above her eyes to ward off the rain each time she checked for the police.

She was no stranger to embarrassment but this might turn out to be the ultimate humiliation.

So what, she was a big girl. All she should think about was getting out of here in one piece and avoiding repeat performances. How many times had she been told she was rash?

Once again she peered through the hedge. No movement.

Heavy, squishy footsteps all but sent her flailing all the way into the bushes. She straightened a little and looked to her left. A police constable, well decked out for the weather, came toward her. A second one jogged to catch up with him.

The second officer was a woman and, unfortunately, Alex recognized Officer Miller. Rain dripped from the bill of her hat but she didn't as much as blink as she bore down on Alex.

Damn it all.

'Afternoon, miss,' the first officer said. 'Let's get you out of here. I'm Constable Burrows and this is Constable Miller.'

'Come with us, please,' Miller said, bending to grip her elbow and haul her to her feet. 'Watch where you step.'

Alex managed not to laugh. There was no good place to walk. 'Thanks, Officer Miller,' she said, making a move to remove her arm from the other woman's grip.

'Let's make sure you get there safely,' Miller said tonelessly and kept a firm hold on Alex's elbow.

She glanced at Burrows who raised his eyebrows and studiously looked away.

In silence except for the spatter of rain on oilskins, they walked back the way Alex had come, rather more smartly than she found comfortable since her legs were a lot shorter than Miller's.

At least Burrows didn't take hold of her other arm and make her feel like a felon.

How could it take so much longer to walk back than it had on the way in? And when they were racing along?

At last they took an alley between shops fronting on the High Street and hurried through to the pavement. A police car was parked a few yards away. Miller slowed her pace as they passed two women whose faces were familiar, and Burrows opened the back door of the car.

'Are you sure about this?' he asked his partner who already had a hand on the top of Alex's head to guide her into a seat.

'Out of the rain this way,' Miller said while Alex glared up at the woman's smirk. 'Buckle in, please?' She continued to keep the door slightly open and stand in the gap as if Alex were a flight risk.

'She must have her own vehicle,' Alex heard Burrows say. 'She could wait there.'

'And risk her driving off?'

So that would be the excuse for this nastiness. Alex pushed down the hood of her coat and undid the toggles. After the race to get her here, she was hot.

'Here they come,' Miller said.

A Lexus, dark blue naturally, cruised in to park behind the marked car and Dan O'Reilly made a rapid exit with Lamb only seconds behind.

Dan drew level with Alex and relief crossed his face.

'I put her in here rather than her own car to make sure she didn't try to leave the scene, sir,' Miller said, virtually standing at attention. 'She tried to pull away from me back there. Not very hard, it's true. But nevertheless.'

Standing behind Dan, Bill Lamb covered the bottom half of his face and Alex had a sneaking suspicion he was amused by all this.

'No problems here, sir,' Burrows said, shifting from foot to foot. Drops fell from the rim of his helmet. 'Four others are watching the property in question. They haven't made contact so I'd say there's no sign of the subject yet.'

'Thank you, Burrows.' He reached past Miller and opened the door wide to offer Alex his hand. 'Where's your vehicle?'

Alex accepted the hand and he helped her out of the police car. 'At the other end of the village,' she said, wrinkling her nose. She was a nuisance to him and this after promising herself she would never be that again. 'Easy walk.'

'I'd like to talk to you,' Dan said. 'You'd be more comfortable in my car, if that's OK.'

Alex told herself she was showing her better nature by not sneering at Constable Miller. 'Yes, thank you.'

'Lock the door till we get back.' He handed her gently into the Lexus and smiled. 'Better give someone a call so they don't get worried about you.'

Bill fell in beside him and they walked off toward the alley with Burrows and Miller in single file behind them.

Settling back in her seat, Alex realized the six or seven people on the pavement, pretending they weren't getting soaked, or giving her curious looks, probably comprised the biggest crowd she'd ever seen in Underhill.

She gave them a merry wave and a regal incline of the head, settled back and closed her eyes.

Sometimes, she thought, you just had to fake it.

Twelve

Doc James waited until Tony went outside the pub again before joining Lily at one of the windows in the bar. 'What did she say when she called?' He put two shots of brandy on the table nearby and pulled out a chair. 'Please sit down and drink this, Lily.'

She reacted as if she had only just noticed he was there. 'Tony's really worried. Alex told him she had to have an interview with the police about some man in a field. Then she said she'd get back as soon as she could. That was hours ago. Two hours, anyway.'

The pub patrons were subdued. It would be hard to miss either Lily's or Tony's agitation. Doc was impressed that no one had asked what was going on – yet. Unless Heather Derwinter, a rare customer, had asked Mary and Harriet Burke anything. Heather had come in, looked around and gone to the sisters' table.

Martin Gimblet, the mayor's son, sat alone at a small table just inside the door and his head turned sharply each time it opened. Doc couldn't help wondering if he was one more piece of extra custom who had heard fresh whispers on the village grapevine and come to see whatever there might be to see.

Lily sat down and he joined her, taking a sip of a brandy. She stared at the glass and finally drank from it.

'I try not to interfere with my son's reactions or decisions but I'm wondering if I should risk it now.'

That got Lily's full attention. 'And do what, James?'

'Remind him of how slow the police can be sometimes, especially if a few things come along that take their attention before they get to your issue. And mention that Alex might not be happy to find him pacing up and down outside – obviously waiting and fretting.'

She pointed to his glass. 'Drink that down then and go out there.' Her expression was so serious he chided himself for putting more negatives into her head. 'Do it, James. All either of them needs – or you and I – is for something else to blow up around here.'

He gave her a smile, swallowed half of the brandy and went outside.

Tony was, as expected, pacing the grassy verge outside the Dog and listing first one side and then the other and he reversed directions and leaned to stare along the road into the gathering gloom.

He didn't greet Doc.

Not a good sign.

Doc considered using an abbreviated version of what he'd told Lily.

'If I call her and she's being interviewed . . . forget that, they probably take your phone away first,' said Tony. 'I should track Dan down—'

'Come inside before she shows up. If she finds you pacing around out here she'll either feel guilty, which you wouldn't want, or she'll get royally mad and tell you off.' If that was the wrong approach, so be it.

Tony stood still and faced Doc. 'You're right. Don't you ever get bored with being right?' He strode into the pub and Doc followed at his own pace.

Before the door could swing shut behind him, he held it open for Martin Gimblet who was on his way out. He looked at Doc but his eyes lowered as he pushed an envelope into his hand. Gimblet didn't say a word but while Doc was watching the man's departing back, he saw Alex's Range Rover swing past into the back parking lot.

To give or not to give Tony a heads-up? He got into the bar in time to see his son turning from Lily to head for the counter. The smile on his face didn't wipe away all of the strain but it was an improvement.

Alex walked into the bar from the kitchens and started talking to Hugh. She patted Juste's arm and met Tony just before he could walk behind the counter. One look at his face and she kept on walking until she reached the snug and shut herself inside.

Thirteen

The fire in the bar hadn't warmed through to the snug yet which meant it had been allowed to go out – possibly for several hours.

Alex slid open the hatch to the bar and waved to Hugh. 'The fire's alight now, isn't it?' she asked him when he arrived.

He put his hands on his hips. 'Yes. And all I'm going to say beside that is that things haven't been good around here since early afternoon.'

'Right.' She closed the hatch more sharply than she'd intended. Things hadn't been good around here? He had no idea how horrible they'd become as her afternoon progressed.

A tall shape appeared outside the glass-paneled door and after a single rap, Tony came in. He met her eyes but with no particular expression on his face. Why didn't he get mad the way other people did. He was obviously furious with her.

She sat on one of the banquets that ran around the snug, crossed her legs and studied the mud splatters on her trousers. She'd taken off her wellies and left them at the kitchen door.

'Are you all right?' Tony asked.

'No, I bloody well am not all right. I'm angry with myself for making a dumb decision and putting myself in a position to be more embarrassed than I ever remember.'

'Would you like a cup of tea?'

Damn his reasonable manner; his control over his emotions. 'No. A double vodka tonic might be just the thing, though.'

'You don't like vodka.'

'How the hell do you know whether I like it or not? You've never seen me have any. It's a good drink – you should have one, too, it might let you relax into being human.'

Tony went silently to slide open the hatch to the bar. Juste arrived quickly, his green eyes deeply concerned behind steel-framed glasses.

'Two double vodka tonics, please,' Tony said and waited there while Juste went to get the drinks and brought them back without a word.

Tony put a note on the counter but Juste tried to hand it back. 'On the house,' he said.

'Thank you, but on me this evening, Juste.' When he was offered his change he waved it away. 'Have something yourself. How are the studies going?'

'Well, thank you,' he said in his female-killing French accent. 'Soon I will hope to be a curate.'

114

'Great,' Tony said and closed the hatch again. He carried the glasses to the table in front of Alex. He sat beside her. She sipped her drink but didn't look at him. 'Perhaps I should have got the whole bottle,' he said. It didn't sound funny even to him.

'Things happen to people,' she said. 'Situations they don't expect. Going to Underhill was a mistake but it seemed right at the time. I can tell you got anxious when I was gone a long time but I didn't have any control over that.'

'I didn't say anything.'

'You didn't have to. You smiled but everything else about you was knotted up. You were angry with me, Tony.' She did look at him then. 'I don't need to answer to you, or anyone anymore.'

'Yeah.' He drank down the vodka and went for another.

She came up behind him and put a hand on his back. 'I'm sorry. I'm being horrible.'

Juste Vidal came to serve him again and Tony asked for two more double vodka tonics, even though he knew they wouldn't drink much of them.

'What happened?' He gave Alex one glass and kissed her cheek. 'Come on. Sit down again and don't be sorry– or not too sorry. You read me too well. I was scared when I didn't hear anything more and you didn't come back.'

'Tony,' she said quietly, leaning against his arm, 'you won't believe what I managed to pull off this afternoon.'

She told him about watching the cottage and calling Dan about what she saw and when it was time to talk about Miller and Burrows, she could have hugged Tony for not laughing at the ridiculous picture it made.

'When I see Dan I'm going to thank him for sending out the troops,' he said. 'Sounds as if Miller's taken a dislike to you. I wonder why that is.'

'I told you yesterday evening that she doesn't seem to like men,' Alex mused. 'Could be she doesn't like women either but for different reasons. Women could seem like competition. She's very ambitious, I think.'

Tony sipped at his second vodka tonic, tiny sips. He wasn't a big drinker and he could say, honestly, that he didn't like vodka.

'I actually felt like a cigarette,' he said. 'If I had any, I would have.'

'You don't smoke.' She leaned to see his face. 'You've never smoked.'

He put an arm around her shoulders. 'I did for a bit in Australia.'

'After Penny died?'

He had not expected her to say that. 'Yes. It gave me something to hold in my hands and fiddle with. I didn't like it any more than I do vodka.'

Her smile warmed him. 'Kyle came to the clinic this afternoon. He's a very nice kid but he's unhappy. Radhika took to him right away. Someone brought in an abandoned kitten. Tiny girl. Maybe two weeks. Unless her mother belongs to someone who knows she gave birth and goes looking for a missing kitten, the baby will have to be hand-raised.'

116

'Poor little thing. Isn't there a list of a few people who foster cats and kittens?'

'Mm,' Tony nodded. 'There is. It's a pity.'

Alex looked stricken. 'Is the kitten going to die?'

'No. But Kyle thinks hand-raising a kitten would be first-rate experience. You should see him with her. He fed her with a syringe the way he was shown, and wrapped her up in a warm towel. Then he sat on the floor comforting the Georges' poodle with the kitten asleep on his shoulder. When I left he looked as if he'd be asleep with them shortly. Radhika will pick up the proper bottle to feed the cat with – and the milk replacement.'

'He's such a nice boy, Tony. Too grown up in some ways but a child in others. I think it's lovely for him to work with the animals.'

'Finish your story about this afternoon. How was the interview at the station?'

'Short,' she told him, closing her eyes. 'It was the search of the fields and the Gammage place that took so long.'

'And?'

'Oh, Tony, I feel ridiculous. They've dusted for fingerprints but . . . This is hard, I'm sure I saw a man there, but they didn't find him. Not a trace. I still had to go to the station. It's a formality. People there pretended not to stare at me, but they stared and tried not to laugh. Even Bill tried to be nice about it. That made the whole thing even worse.'

There was no way to commiserate without sounding condescending, or amused. 'They'll still have to follow it up,' he said at last. 'That killer hasn't been caught. You'd have been wrong not to call in what you saw. You must have seen something.' He finished strongly, congratulating himself for his brilliance.

The way she watched his face made him uncomfortable. 'I told Kyle I don't think he'll be allowed to keep Naruto.'

'Naruto?'

'Naruto the dragon-slayer. The abandoned kitten.'

Fourteen

'Why didn't you tell him?' Bill set down his third mug of coffee.

Empty.

The super had just left Dan's office and Bill put his elbows on the desk, and steepled his fingers against his mouth.

'What he doesn't know, he can't allow to slip out when he makes his damn public announcement. That man loves the sound of his own voice and he likes the idea of his face on the telly even more. How many coffees have you drunk – from my private coffee maker – since you arrived this morning?'

Bill ignored the question. 'That tosser just gave us a right bollocking, guv. We haven't made any progress, he says. We're useless. We're making him look bad. And you let him blather on like that? He really believes we've got bugger all but we've got plenty – especially considering what a short time we've been at it – and we should have fed him something. A few crumbs.'

Dan leaned forward to stand up. 'Holy . . . I don't believe it.' He pushed his chair back, sat again, and thumped his feet on the desk. 'I put on the same shoes I took off last night. Without cleaning them. Look at these shoes.'

'I'd rather not, thanks.'

'Your support in my time of need will not be forgotten. And the last time I checked, I make the final decisions around here. You feed me every gem that worms its way into your tiny brain and I keep any bits I deem worthy. The rest I toss in my circular file. Your criticism of how I deal with the super is duly noted and filed with the bits I just mentioned.

'How do you think my chances look for getting someone to clean up these shoes?'

Bill pushed himself back in his chair. 'You must be joking.'

'Do I look as if I'm joking? There's got to be some eager young beaver anxious to make points.' He took off the shoes, went to the door and opened it onto the squad room. There was an immediate flurry of activity. 'Rather than send some of you to paddle in the mud yesterday, I went myself,' he announced and waited for the noise to die down. 'A pint and a kind word for the dedicated person who can get the mud off these shoes. You don't want the man who represents your department walking around like this.'

119

There were swallowed chuckles, throats cleared and heads went down in record time.

'I'll take them for you, sir.'

The long slender hand that unhooked the shoes from his fingers belonged to Officer Miller, who had been waiting for him to call her in for a 'chat.'

He had no choice but to watch her leave the squad room, shoes in hand. Before she was out of earshot the catcalls went up and a sing-song rendering of the old pub favorite, 'Hello, Hello, Who's Your Lady Friend?'

Shaking his head, Dan retreated to his office and closed the door again. 'Cretins,' he said.

'You do know she wants your body, guv?'

'Ah, sure she does. All the women do.' He sat down again. 'I can't help being a fanny magnet.'

'Jillian Miller thinks you're a dish. She cries herself to sleep every night with your name on her lips. Why do you think she tried – and succeeded – in making Alex's life a misery yesterday? Because Miller's heard the talk around the station about you being soft on Alex.'

'If I had time . . .' Dan let the threat trail away. 'So, it's the blue trainers, right? And the fact I didn't mention the color to the super? So far only Kyle said anything about either the shoes or what color they were. And don't fool yourself that one good discrepancy makes "plenty" of evidence.'

Bill's light blue eyes didn't change expression, as usual. 'Welcome back to the front burner. Anything rather than discuss your love life.'

120

'I don't have one,' Dan said, but he thought of walking Alex to her Range Rover last night, the light lemony scent of her, her arm in his hand when she stumbled – probably because she was embarrassed. He might have to cut Miller's pint to a half.

Bill leaned forward again. 'We'll come back to that. Yes, it's the blue trainers. It wouldn't be dangerous if the boss did talk about them, would it? A few nutters would call in about all the women they'd seen in bright blue Nike Air Max but apart from reminding one maniac of what he already knows, there's no foul.'

Detective Constable LeJuan Harding – otherwise known as Balls, supposedly because he was tough, and he played a mean game of squash – stuck his handsome, Idris Elba lookalike face around the door. 'Apologies for the agro, guv, but this came for you.' He proffered a folded piece of notebook paper. 'From what I've heard, you better round up some heaters to take with you.'

He whisked out of the office again and could be heard whistling on his way.

'Cheeky sod read your note,' Bill said. 'Now they all know what's in it.'

'Not much,' Dan said, reading and refolding the note. 'We'll be operating out of the parish hall in Folly-on-Weir until this one's done. Less distractions there and past results have been better. The locals are always so useful.'

'He means Alex and Tony,' Bill said with a disgusted sneer. 'And the old tea shop ladies. Are we ever going to live all that down?'

'Forget it. Let's get moving. Detective Constable Harding is overdue for an introduction to the finer points of this job. Tell him to collect those heaters. He's going to need them.'

Grumbling, Bill got up. 'What are you going to tell the super about the blue trainers?'

'I'll tell you what I won't be telling him, or not yet,' Dan said, standing up and feeling his socked feet slip on the plastic mat under his desk. 'So far we've kept any details from the masses and I want it to stay that way as long as possible, for Kyle Gammage's sake as much as anything. The fact that we didn't find trainers, or any shoes, with the body is on a need-to-know only basis.'

Fifteen

At mid-morning Tony and Alex left Folly in her Range Rover. They had decided on going to Broadway rather than remaining in the village where everywhere they turned they ran into someone primed with questions about the murder.

At least there was a chance in Broadway of finding a spot where they could be anonymous, or at least, hidden.

The A429 became the A424 and very soon the A44 and Tony slid sideways against the window. He closed his eyes which she took to mean he'd rather not talk. Good. She wanted to try for some more peaceful time to relax her mind, just in case her resolve wasn't as strong as she thought it was.

She felt as much as saw the flicker of his eyelashes at the edge of her vision. 'Just tell me not to talk,' Alex said, smiling to herself. 'You don't have to pretend to be asleep to shut me up.'

'Resting my eyes, that's all.'

'Fish Hill coming up.' When she came to Broadway she always made sure she entered by the route that took her up or down Fish Hill. 'I used to think the name was because it was so steep and crooked, people's cars must fishtail in winter.'

'Very logical conclusion,' he said, sounding more amused than sleepy or in need of resting his eyes.

The steep, scarp face of the Cotswolds rose above the old town with its pretty greens between the road and rows of old stone houses so beautiful that the removal of cars and people would leave what could be mistaken for a painting.

Broadway Tower where William Morris had once stayed with friends, stood against threatening purplish skies atop a high hill. Among his friends to follow him to Broadway were Henry James and Sir John Sargent. Eventually the American painter Francis Millet became so besotted with the town that he made his home there.

'Want to walk up to the tower?' Tony said.

She sighed. 'If the rest of the world had gone away I'd love to. But soon, huh? When you live in a place you don't seem to get out to the sights. We have some fabulous sights.'

'On a fine day when we can supposedly see twelve counties from the tower, that'll be the time to go.'

Alex ducked to peer up toward the tower. 'The sky is pretty melodramatic. It wouldn't snow yet, would it?'

'Nothing surprises me here. But that isn't a snow sky. Can we take the dogs into the Broadway Deli?'

'If we can manage to get them through to the garden at the back, I should think.'

'We can do it,' Tony said. 'They're both clean and I can pass Katie off as an overweight Dorgy.'

She snorted. 'Wrong color, three times too big . . . good luck. But we'll try.'

'Bet if you were the Queen they'd let you. We could swap and I'll take Bogie.'

Alex made a face at him and, after a bit of a search, squeezed triumphantly into a parking spot on the High Street. 'Bogie's a carnival-color Yorkshire Terrier.'

Snickering, they gathered the dogs and crossed the road in front of the lovely old Olive Branch Guest House. Olive trees flanked the front door. 'I've stayed there,' Alex said. 'It snowed and my ride couldn't pick me up to go home. Too bad they got here the next morning – I didn't want to leave at all.'

'Don't tempt fate,' Tony said. 'Those clouds are thick and still. This is the calm. Hope it lasts till we get out of here again and we don't get hit by a major thunderstorm.'

'Look at this,' Alex said, drawn to crates of

fruit and vegetables ranged on sloping displays outside the Broadway Deli. 'I want everything. The colors! Pomegranates, star fruit and the apples. Smell them. I have to come here just for my produce.'

'This Dorgy's getting heavy,' Tony said. 'I'll smell the goodies on my way through the shop.'

Chatter and laughter met them inside a foody's wonderland. Exclamations followed customers along loaded cases and counters and they didn't stop when Tony and Alex slipped through the indoor café and into the gardens beyond.

The dogs went immediately and silently under the table. 'They're pros,' Alex said. 'Don't tell them there are dogs at most tables, inside and out. I like these two right where they are.'

They sat under a green umbrella at a silvered gray wood table. 'Looks like winter, doesn't it,' Tony said. Thick lawns were deep green and smelled of a recent mowing, but the trees had lost most of their leaves.

It was early, but they each ordered a glass of red wine with lunch. Alex decided they would be in Broadway long enough before she had to get behind the wheel again.

'Now,' said Alex. 'The pleasantries are over. We've got an issue or two to deal with.'

'We got an invitation.' Tony put an envelope in front of her. It was addressed to Tony and Alex and she glanced up at him. 'That's a first. Something addressed to both of us.'

'Martin Gimblet gave it to my dad to pass on.'

She wanted to tell him it could wait until they'd

talked of other things but curiosity got the better of her. 'When did this happen?'

'Last night. About the time you got back to the Dog.'

'You opened it.'

He shrugged. 'It's addressed to me, too.'

A single sheet of heavy velum slid smoothly from its matching envelope. 'It's from Joan Gimblet,' Alex said, and read aloud, '"The youth center is as good as finished. You'll remember you were invited to come for a visit. Late tomorrow afternoon would be convenient. Please let us know if you need to postpone this".'

'Cripes,' Alex added. 'That's a bit abrupt. I think the Mayor of Folly-on-Weir considers herself our local queen. She's talking about this afternoon. Don't think I can make that.'

'I know I can't,' Tony said. 'For my sins, I'm due at Derwinters.'

'Good. I'll leave it to you to deal with, then.'

Tony looked surprised. 'I thought you'd give them a call. The invitation is addressed to you.'

'And to you, and you're the one it was given to. Joan would much prefer to hear from you.' She gave him a sweet smile.

'I'm not good at that sort of thing,' he said and quickly added, 'but I'll give Joan a call and put it off,' as he saw the glint in Alex's eye.

She put her mind to her rehearsed script. 'I'll put up a notice about the kitten for you,' she said. 'A big one in a window with a picture of her. Someone will grab her in no time. The sooner she has a permanent home, the better.'

Alex's quiche and Tony's ham ciabatta arrived.

She spread a napkin in her lap and looked up at him. 'What's the matter?'

'Don't you think Kyle's had a hard enough time without saying he can't have something he's fallen in love with? A warm, snuggling kitten who will give him purpose, a living thing to think about rather than dwelling on everything that's wrong in his life? A cat gets to know his or her person quickly. Just like children, they know the hands they can trust.'

Alex realized her mouth was open. She closed it and swallowed hard. 'That's low,' she said, watching him through narrowed eyes. 'I wouldn't have believed you capable of such an attempt at blatant manipulation. You should be ashamed.'

He raised his glass, took a deep swallow and returned her gaze across the rim. 'I learned from the best,' he said. 'And I see nothing wrong with a little pulling on heartstrings in a good cause. I meant every word, by the way. They've never had a pet.'

She felt a weight on her knees and looked under the table to see Katie's nose resting there. Her eyes looked larger, sadder and more pleading than usual. Alex rubbed a wet nose.

'The timing is horrible, Tony. The boys can't even be in their own home at the moment. Virtually not at all after my hallucination yesterday.'

'You really believe you didn't see a man on the property after all?'

Did she? 'They didn't find anyone and I don't know how he could have left without being seen. But, no, I don't really believe I imagined him.'

'Neither do I.' He ate some of his lunch, munching and thinking, his eyebrows drawn now. 'You are not fanciful. Scoot and Kyle are scared. Very scared.'

'We already knew that.' Her quiche was brie based, which she loved.

'More scared than they were at first, I mean. I know a couple of the teachers at their school and I'm tempted to ask one of them if they're seeing any changes in behavior.'

She put down her fork. 'That sounds tempting. But is there a chance it could do more harm than good?'

Tony tipped his wine back and forth in the glass. 'Doesn't matter what we think of doing – everything seems like a grenade with the pin halfway out. We keep skating around it but it's Sid we really need to make contact with.'

He was right, but she felt the pin edge farther out of the grenade. 'In a way it's not right to let this go on without finding and talking to their dad. He needs to get back to Folly and look after his boys. They are fiercely loyal to him. But that's a double-edged sword. They need him right now, but what if we mess up the life they've built by interfering?'

'Yes, I know. I'm thinking your thoughts. Should I find out where Sid works? I could call and try to talk to him. I know he's on the road most of the time but there has to be an employer and a home base.'

There was the other possibility she couldn't seem to put aside. But if she went in that direction there might be no turning back. 'It's in the papers. Not with any mention of the boys but the murder, and the usual sarky comments about reduced life expectancy in Folly and parts around it are all over place. How could Sid not have seen it? And the police announcement on the telly last night. At least he didn't mention my fiasco.'

'Some people don't keep up with the news,' Tony said.

'And sometimes a person has a reason to feign ignorance.'

'My mobile,' Tony said, pulling out the phone from a trouser pocket. It vibrated in his hand. 'Just a sec.' He looked serious enough to bring her to the edge of her chair.

'Tony,' he said, and listened. He spread a hand across his eyes and braced his head on the elbow. 'You're kidding. That ticks me off, Hugh.'

Alex hissed, 'What is it?'

'OK. Yeah. See you.'

'What?' She all but popped out of her chair. 'Why is Hugh calling you?'

'Said he couldn't get through to you.'

She searched her pockets. 'Shoot, I left it in the car. That was brilliant.'

'The police are moving into Folly. Back into the parish hall. Coppers have been at the Dog placing standing orders for coffee and biscuits and all the usual. They march in there like we're supposed to greet them as old friends. Or returning heroes. What a laugh – I don't think.'

Three women passed them on their way to another table. The one in the middle said, 'I don't think I'd live there, do you?'

Alex almost hid her face. 'They're talking about Folly,' she said quietly.

'You don't know that,' Tony said with a reassuring smile. 'We can't let ourselves get paranoid.'

Crossing her arms on the table, Alex said, 'I've got an idea I don't like very much. Have you ever seen Sid Gammage?'

'Nope,' Tony said. 'Have you?'

'I may have but I can't be sure.'

Tony gripped her forearm. 'Why would you keep something like that quiet – if you thought it was important, that is?'

'Because it's more conjecture than fact. And I'm a bit touchy about being laughed at – at least, after yesterday. I need a photo of Sid. It doesn't have to be that good, just something to give me an idea of his build and coloring.

'Tony, couldn't it have been Sid at the Gammage cottage yesterday? He might have a way of slipping out of there without being seen. Couldn't Sid have been quietly checking up on his kids over the last couple of days without letting them know he was there because they could make it hard for him to leave again?

'What if he saw a woman skulking around close to his home and he got rid of her so she wouldn't let on she'd seen him? Or there was a struggle and it was all an accident?'

Tony turned up his coat collar as if he were cold. 'You think garroting someone could be accidental?'

Sixteen

'One thing hasn't changed around here,' Bill Lamb said. 'It still smells of baked radiator dust.'

Dan slid a box of files he'd brought from the station onto the metal desk they had shipped in for him. On previous visits to Folly-on-Weir's decrepit parish hall, Dan had sat at a trestle table that wobbled. At least the battered thing he'd commandeered this time had drawers that locked.

'And the windows still rattle, guv.' Bill looked sour.

'Nothing has changed,' Dan said. 'Get this lot moving around. A sweep of this place, including the gallery, just in case. And I don't mean with a broom.'

'Just in case of what?'

'Get it done.' He checked the hall but didn't see what he was looking for. 'Where's Harding?'

'He asked to get his bearings in the area, guv. I didn't see any harm in it. He said he'll do some door-to-door. Give him a chance to meet people and see if anyone's reacting to the super's telly performance last night. Reckon it was on too late for most around here.'

Dan's eyes ached and he pressed them with finger and thumb. 'Harding's meeting people? Does he think he's the new face of this investigation? I told him to deal with checking that all the computers and phones and whatnot work.'

131

'Don't know what time he got here this morning, but when I arrived around ten he was chatting up the mayor and everything was done . . . except the grumbling from the rest of them.'

'Well, that's something.' Dan started unloading the box into a file drawer. 'What did the mayor want?'

'Just making a royal visit to welcome us,' Bill said. 'If we need anything, just call.'

'Good to know. She could let us know where to find the perp so we can get out of here.'

'Coffee will be here from the Dog. Biscuits and so on, too.'

'How'd you manage that?'

'I didn't. Balls did. He went there for his lunch. Reckons the place isn't bad.' Bill smirked.

'Nervy sod.' Dan couldn't help smiling. 'He'll probably have the whole village wrapped around his fingers in no time. Alex will see through him but she'll find it funny.'

'Listen to you. You'd think you had intimate knowledge of the way the lady's mind works. The preliminary report came in on the autopsy,' Bill finished hurriedly. 'Estimated time of death at least twenty-four hours before she was found. The body had been through rigor mortis. Moved after death. Blow to the back of the head – didn't kill her. Earth in nose and mouth. Possible choking incapacitated her further. Strangulation finished her off. Her hyoid was fractured.'

'Hyoid.' Dan said, narrowing his eyes. 'Between the lower mandible – the jaw – and the thyroid. The type of injury she has is only usually seen in hanging or strangulation.'

132

'I know.' Bill puffed up his cheeks. 'Charming. She must have run into an old friend. Why the level of violence, you wonder. Overkill, excuse the pun.'

'From the state of her hands, she resisted. She looked pretty sturdy, too. Don't forget the drugs and money on the body.' Dan took the report from Bill and scanned paragraphs. He stabbed a finger into the paper. 'Drugs are small stuff – small quantities, that is. And a couple of hundred in twenties. Maybe the killer left it because he was mad it wasn't more. Or to show disdain. Any sign of sexual activity? Mmm, no. Toxicology will take a while but it'll tell us if she was using and how much. Age approximately late thirties. And no one ready to give us a name yet?'

'Dozens of 'em but none of them fit the situation. We've got officers running them down.'

'No one says they've seen someone who matches the description?'

'Not really, guv.'

'Hello,' a man called from the doorway. 'All right if I come in?'

'Come ahead, sir,' Dan called. He'd take any diversion. 'What can we do for you?' He was aware he wouldn't normally be dealing with drop-in complaints or whatever, but what the hell, nothing was ever normal around here.

'This is probably an overreaction,' the man said. 'I'm Paul Sutcliffe, by the way. Joan Gimblet, the mayor, is my sister and I live with her at Woodway Farm.'

'Take a seat.'

Sutcliffe scraped a metal chair across the floor and sat near the desk. Bill stood, feet braced apart, arms crossed.

'Boards up?' Dan thought to ask. 'E-fit and the site are about all we've got to go on yet.'

'Done,' Bill said.

'Fully screened-off area, please.'

Bill raised a brow. 'Will do, guv.'

Dan returned his attention to the pleasant-looking man with graying blond hair and mustache to match. He was above medium height, well-built and his age wasn't easy to guess.

'You were going to tell me something,' Dan said.

'Damned awkward,' Sutcliffe said, thrusting his chin forward as if to ease the fit of his shirt collar. 'A boy, Weston Bell his name is, showed up at Woodway about a week and a half ago. Scholarship fella from my old school up north. I was head there. Retired at the end of the last school year. He said he was hiking, rambling or some such nonsense, but he didn't have a bag or pack or anything with him. I'm afraid we got browned off with him in the end and he left a couple of days ago. At school he was one of those awkward, clinging types and I can tell you, Detective Chief Inspector, my sister and I didn't fancy encouraging him any longer. Smarmy when he was trying to get his own way.'

After a period when Sutcliffe contemplated the distance above him, he continued. 'Felt a bit sorry for the little blighter. Gave him a few pounds and drove him into Morton-in-Marsh for

134

a train. He was on his way back up north to see another of his old masters.

'I don't mind admitting, I was a bit disturbed by the whole thing. He would be about sixteen now – from what I remembered. This morning I called this other master and Weston Bell hasn't showed up there. I realize it may be early to worry but I thought I'd give a preliminary report anyway. He didn't have a mobile but I had asked him to ring through to us when he got there. We haven't heard a word from him. Am I wrong to be here?'

Now Dan remembered why he detested dealing with the public. They all, to a man and woman, wanted instant reassurance and he couldn't or shouldn't always give it. 'No, Mr Sutcliffe. Thank you for being diligent. If you'd go over to the lady officer at the end of that row and tell her what you told me, we'll be sure to keep an eye on things for you. He has a family he could have gone to?'

'I think there was a grandmother or even someone overseas who's a relative. Don't know anything about them. If there hadn't been that repulsive killing in the area I probably wouldn't have given any of this a second thought.'

'He should probably go in to the station, guv,' Bill said – correctly, of course.

'Golly, I don't want to make a fuss out of nothing. It's just that if you hear about someone running across a boy, you know – well, no, I don't know why you might. But I should like to know he's safe.'

Dan dithered between sending him on to the

135

station and telling him they'd keep an ear out for anyone of the description he'd given being reported missing. 'What's the boy's name, again?'

'Bell. Weston Bell.'

Not exactly a downmarket name. Dan wrote it down. 'Just go over to the constable and leave a description, would you? We'll be sure to let you know if we hear anything.'

Sutcliffe did as he was asked.

'I bet half the village thinks they know someone who got knocked off now,' Bill said.

While Bill set off to dispatch a team to check the building for anything untoward, Dan continued emptying his cardboard box. Folding screens were being assembled to cut off the operations part of the room from potential prying eyes. Calum had sent a text to let him know he'd be calling later and Dan anticipated hearing his son's voice with a mixture of pleasure and concern.

Rain battered the windows as they'd all expected. A constable made the rounds using a pole with a hook on the end to close the panels that swung down to open.

Water began to fly through the front door and Dan reached it in time to see Harriet and Mary Burke making their slow way toward the steps. Mary's walker kept their progress sedate. He grabbed up an umbrella from a dusty stand and went outside, opening the brolly as he reached the ladies and holding it over them.

'Detective Chief Inspector,' Harriet said, 'you are always such a gentleman.'

Mary only muttered something he rather thought might be unflattering.

'Dan to you, Harriet,' he said. 'We're old friends, remember. Unless I've got to go back to Miss Burke.'

'Dan,' said Harriet, waving the idea of formality aside. Mary gave him her version of a pleased smile that always resembled a grimace.

'We'll make sure you have a lift home,' he said.

Mary gave an unvarnished grimace. 'Not in one of those,' she said, pointing to a marked police car. 'We'd never live it down.'

'Oh, I don't know—' Harriet began.

'I do,' her sister snapped.

'Not to worry. My car is anonymous. You walked all the way here – too far for you.'

'Rubbish,' Mary said. 'Good for us, except for the rain. I've got to tell you something. I should have done it earlier. I saw that woman in the paper – the one who was murdered. Before she was murdered, of course.'

Seventeen

Tony had needed to get back to the clinic. Alex dropped him off before returning to the Dog. She went in through the kitchen from the parking lot with Bogie under her arm, to be greeted by raucous noise from the bar.

She should have been pleased to see the place crammed with customers; she was glad, but she would have been even more thrilled if she didn't suspect the arrival of the police to set up shop

137

in the parish hall was the probable reason for the hubbub.

Lily hurried through from the restaurant and slapped a hand to her chest when she saw Alex. 'Thank goodness. I've got something for you to look at but it'll have to wait a bit. You know the police are back at—'

'Hugh called,' Alex interrupted. 'I can't believe we're going through this again.'

'Give me a tick,' Lily said. 'I'll find you when it calms down the other side. I found something. I'm not quite sure what it is or what we ought to do with it, but I know it could be important.' Off she went in her immaculate black dress and matching shoes with sensible heels. Lily didn't have to do much to look lovely and Alex was glad she had Doc James to keep unwelcome attention mostly at bay.

But what had her mother found? Alex felt like running after her and making her deal with this now. To flap something of interest in front of her face, only to tell her she'd have to find out what it was later, was unbearable.

'There you are at last,' Hugh said, striding into the kitchen with an overflowing tray of empty glasses and dishes. 'Thank God Juste's got some extra time. He's a life saver.'

So much for tracking her mother down. 'He's training to be a soul saver,' Alex couldn't help quipping. 'Do you think he'll be able to moonlight as a bartender when he's a curate?'

'We need you out front,' Hugh said, clearly not in a joking mood. 'Liz is here, too. She'll load the dishwashers for us. I want you to see what's causing the racket. A woman's death isn't cause for a carnival atmosphere but that's what we've got. It's ridiculous. And frankly, I'm getting bloody angry. Have they all forgotten what's happened?'

She followed him, recognizing the volume of female laughter that overpowered the men.

A bevy of the young women, one or two from the village but most others from surrounding, more spectacular holdings, and decked out in impeccable equestrian gear, were gathered with two men Alex had never seen before. She was surprised at Martin Gimblet being with the group but it was good to see him with some of his own age group.

They didn't need the roaring fire. The crush would have made enough heat on its own. Alex noted that whereas the women all drank beer, wine or the spirits of their choice, both men – laughing as enthusiastically as the women – held Coke bottles.

Alex raised an enquiring brow at Hugh. 'Sometimes I think we've got far too many hale and hearty people with not enough to do in this village, and parts nearby,' he said. 'And they've got too much money.'

Hugh had become so much an ordinary man of the local scene that most people didn't think about his being rich, which he clearly was. Little by little Alex learned personal snippets about him but they were very small, insignificant snippets. Although he had an interesting love life behind him. Alex and Tony knew vague details but would never dare mention it.

'Who are the men,' she asked. 'Heather and her pals are hanging on them.'

'Couple of detectives from what I can gather. Heather Derwinter and Daisy Cottingham are holding forth. I think Heather sees herself as an expert on local crime. She definitely doesn't allow her marital status to get in the way of regular flirtation. Kev Winslet's in with a couple of mates from the Derwinter estate. They think they're pumping that plod in uniform at the corner table. The major is wandering, ever so unobtrusively, from group to group, seeing what he can pick up and pass on. Martin Gimblet came in with them then migrated to more interesting material. Seems more sociable these days. At least, I think he'd like to be.'

Alex sighed. 'As long as they're all enjoying themselves.' She smiled at the way Daisy Cottingham, eligible daughter of a minor notable Alex had heard of but never met, had one hand hooked beneath the elbow of an outrageously stunning black man whom she assumed was one of the detectives.

'I wonder if the gentlemen are gleaning anything useful?' she said. 'They've got an audience hanging on their every word. It's easy to forget how quickly information, and baseless gossip, find their way around Folly. You can't be sure who knows what. I would have thought Heather and Daisy were a bit out of the general stream of things, but who knows?

'I'd better play the charming landlady.' Alex walked to the group and waited for a pause after gusty laughter. 'Afternoon. Can I get anyone a refill?'

'This is our landlady,' Heather said with relish. 'Alex Duggins. Just tell Juste to give us another round of the same, darling.'

'Be my pleasure,' Alex said. She held out a hand to the less flamboyant detective. 'Thank you for coming in, ah . . .'

'Detective Constable Trafford, Barry. They've pulled in a few of us extra like to give us some experience in the . . . out in . . .'

'The sticks,' Alex finished for him with a mischievous grin. 'I warn you, country bumpkins can be a canny lot. Best to get on their right side.'

Officer Trafford was Scandinavian fair with blue eyes, high cheekbones, a firm chin, and an athletic built. His tweed jacket with suede at the elbows suited him, as did the tan cashmere jumper he wore underneath with well-fitting twill trousers. Had he been exposed to sun and wind occasionally, he could have slipped easily into the role of gentleman farmer. Alex decided he was young and rather nice – and that he didn't really enjoy Daisy Cottingham's clinging attention.

Working his way to stand beside her, Martin Gimblet spoke softly so that she had to lean close to hear. Instantly she decided that had been the plan. He put a hand lightly on her back. 'Will you let me get you a drink, Alex?' he said. He had a disarming mouth and eyes that made it difficult to look away. 'All you do is work. Sit with me and tell me your life story.'

She forced a laugh. 'And bore you to death? No way. Let's do that another time, Martin. This is one of those days.'

He didn't quite hide his disappointment but he did give a gentle smile and back away.

Now the man into whose slightly slanted dark and indulgent eyes Heather stared was another matter from the man with him. He hung on every word, obviously gleaning any stray details. He saw Alex was looking at him and shot out a hand, 'LeJuan Harding,' he said. 'Detective Constable. Interesting case here. This is a short pause for me before I continue meeting the local people. You've got a great pub.'

Officer Harding of the close-cropped hair, the mind-stopping glances and indescribable smile, wore self-confidence almost too comfortably. He shook Alex's hand firmly, but not with an attempt at crushing bones to impress. Perhaps the most interesting thing about him was his build; probably 6′3″ or more, some active rugby forwards didn't have his muscle mass or attitude of readiness to spring and sprint.

He came toward her, easing them both out of the jolly circle. 'I do believe you will know this man if you see him again, Ms Duggins,' he said in a soft, rumbling voice.

'It's Alex,' she said, frowning. 'What man?'

'This one,' he said with a chuckle that ended in that lovely smile. 'Me. You are, as they say, taking stock of me. I assure you I am what I say I am. A simple policeman hoping to glean help to take back to my boss. Details to add to his growing pile. I believe you know my boss.'

In her head Alex heard Sade singing that famous line, 'He's a smooth operator,' although she couldn't have remembered the rest of the words.

What woman was immune to a practiced charmer, even if only for an instant – or a few instants. 'Who is your boss?' she asked with businesslike seriousness, dropping her arm from his grip.

'Detective Chief Inspector O'Reilly,' Harding said. 'Didn't I hear the two of you go back a long way?'

This was one of the ambitious ones who would use anything available to his advantage. 'Nice man,' she said. 'We have known each other for a while. And he sent you here to ask me questions about his current case?' Her emphasis on 'his' was very slight.

His eyes narrowed a little more. 'No, no, I'm merely letting you know I'm familiarizing myself with the precinct and keeping my ears open for anything helpful. Heather told me you have been involved in several major cases here.'

'Did she?' Alex tilted her head to one side and gave a small smile. 'I think you've already let me know you're aware of that.'

He grinned easily. 'Whoops, caught. I suppose I did. You're formidable Ms Duggins. Not easy to capture in my web of charming small talk.'

'Why would you want to? I always find the direct approach works best. Do you like our village?'

'I do.' He glanced toward the windows. 'I grew up in the city and I haven't spent time in the countryside, but I'm getting to like it – in small doses.'

She laughed with him before they both fell silent.

'Nasty case,' she said finally. 'Seems like an odd one, too. Any closer to an ID of the victim?'

'No. But it's only been a couple of days. We pore over any missing persons reports, but so far there's been nothing even similar.'

The easy way he discussed the case surprised her. Was he trying to gauge just how close she was to Dan and how much he might have told her?

'Didn't I hear the victim died a day or so before the body was found?'

Harding tilted his head. 'That wouldn't be something I could discuss.'

'I'd have thought the money and drugs on the body would lead to something concrete.' She closed her mouth. Probably half the people in the village knew what had been found on the body but that didn't mean he was aware that they did. And neither would he know that most of them had information about potential time of death being well before the corpse was found.

He looked down and shrugged but didn't pursue what she'd said. Damn her careless mouth. That wasn't like her. She hoped he hadn't noticed that she shouldn't be aware of so many details.

Harding kept his voice down. 'Funny about her shoes being missing.'

The ground felt firmer once more. 'I didn't see

the superintendent's telly bit. Did he mention shoes?'

'Trainers. I think it was in the papers.'

'I haven't had a chance to read about it yet.' She had, but if the shoes were mentioned, she didn't remember. 'I'd better let you get to your work and get to my own. Nice to meet you, detective constable.'

'Before you go,' he said, a serious frown changing his face drastically. 'You have the ears and eyes of Folly, don't you?'

She let her body relax. 'You might say that. It goes with my job, I suppose.'

'Sometimes what we hear turns into noise – nothing but noise,' he said. 'Is it possible, it probably isn't but I should ask, is it possible someone has made a remark about the case, said something you didn't hear from a regular source? You must hear so much in here. But there's only so much public knowledge, so if you heard a comment that sounded – I don't know – like inside information, you'd notice wouldn't you? You seem like that kind of person. In fact, I know you are and that's a compliment based on your reputation.'

There were things she and Tony should talk to the police about, but now and here weren't appropriate. When they thought the time was right, they would ask Dan's opinion, although she continued to hope everything would blow over before they had to.

'Thanks for the compliment,' she said. 'I'll let you know if I hear something suitable. Excuse me, my mum is going to lose her arm if I don't go to her.'

145

Harding followed the direction of Alex's attention and saw Lily, waving almost frantically. 'Mums usually get their way,' he said, and turned into the group again.

As soon as Alex went toward her, Lily stepped outside into a half-hearted shower and Alex followed her.

'What a crowd,' she said. 'It's a good job we don't have a guillotine on and green.'

'What do you mean, for goodness sake?' Lily hurried across the road behind her and went into the front garden of Corner Cottage. Lightning shot across the still purplish sky and Lily jumped.

'Just making a joke for goodness' sake,' Alex said. 'If they held executions in the village it looks as if we could supply our own ghouls to hang around and watch. Maybe do a spot of knitting at the same time. They do love all this unpleasantness.'

Lily nodded vaguely. She rustled paper in her pocket. 'I found this a couple of hours ago. It was on the floor in the upstairs hallway. I think one of the boys dropped it.'

'What is it?' Alex's throat had tightened. 'It can't be that bad.'

Thunder rolled and the shower became a downpour.

'I don't know what it is. Not for sure. Come inside quickly.'

They went into the cottage and stayed by the door. Lily held out a crumpled sheet of paper from a composition book, folded in half but wrinkled like a concertina where she had held it in her fist.

Alex did her best to smooth it flat. 'Was it like this when you found it?'

'No. I should have been more careful but I'm nervous. It's all phone numbers. There's nine of them. That's a lot and not one of them gives the name of the person with the number.'

'You don't know what it is, Mum. Good heavens. Just a page from a notebook with numbers written on it. What makes you think—'

'What is it, then?'

'Come on, Mum. I don't know what it is and neither do you. You're imagining things.'

'I'm not. The boys are in trouble. They must be looking for someone.'

'Stop!' Alex took Lily by the shoulders. 'What if you're right? All we have to do is try the numbers.'

Lily looked ready to cry, something Alex had rarely seen. 'And say what, Alex? Please think about it. Scoot and Kyle get more and more withdrawn. It's only been a couple of days but they look different.'

The door opened behind Alex and she barely had time to stuff the folded paper into her jeans pocket before she was knocked forward by the force of the handle jabbing into her back.

She let out a loud yelp and Lily pulled her to one side. 'Who is it?' she said.

The door swung all the way open to reveal Scoot. 'Sorry,' he said, his face scrunched. 'I didn't expect it to be open.'

'Then knock,' Lily said, 'or shout. Or come to the Dog for a key.'

Scoot sidled in, his face scarlet, his fair hair

147

plastered to his head. 'I left a couple of my books here this morning. I need them for tonight – on my break. I was going to run up and get them so I wouldn't be late for work. I'm sorry.'

Alex caught her mother's eyes and immediately looked away. 'No harm done.' She rubbed what would be a nasty bruise on her back.

'You'll need a key,' Lily said. She kept swallowing as if her mouth was dry. 'We'll get one made.'

'Thanks,' Scoot said and raced upstairs.

They heard him slam the door to the bedroom the boys had used. His footsteps moved back and forth – and things banged and rustled.

Now Lily really did look close to tears. 'He's looking for it,' she whispered. 'The list.'

'Stop worrying. I'll take it to the police and ask them to check. I'll just say I found it and wondered if there was any way to find out who it belonged to. Who might be missing it.'

Lily sniffed and passed Alex on the way toward the back of the cottage.

It didn't have to be anything to worry about, Alex thought, starting to follow. Her mum was finding skeletons everywhere.

The bedroom door opened with a bang as it hit the wall inside the room. Breathing hard, Scoot rocketed down the stairs. He shot outside, closing the front door behind him.

He wasn't carrying anything.

Eighteen

When they walked into the parish hall, they were greeted by a too hearty wave from Dan O'Reilly. 'Tony, Alex, great to see you. Come on over.'

Her eyes unusually wide, Alex looked up at Tony. 'No one's ever that glad to see me,' she murmured.

'I always am,' he replied without cracking a smile. 'Which reminds me of what I've had in mind for hours.'

She didn't look at him again but he'd known she wouldn't. That's what a man got for telling the truth – the cold shoulder. And all he wanted was to take her to bed.

'Hello,' Tony said, putting an arm around Alex's shoulders – safe enough since she wouldn't make a scene here. 'We know it's getting a bit late but if you could spare . . .' A trestle table and its occupants caught his eye.

'Harriet and Mary,' Tony said, raising his voice and smiling broadly when the ladies turned from what looked at a distance like strips of photographs. 'What are you doing here?'

The table had been moved a distance from any work station and a single female officer sat across from the Misses Burke.

'Mary thinks—' Harriet started.

'Miss Burke,' Dan interrupted firmly. 'You'll

149

understand if we keep this between us for now, won't you?'

'Alex and Tony already know I saw the dead woman,' Mary said, moving her head to accommodate focusing through her thick glasses between the photos and Alex. 'We did what you suggested, Alex, and spoke to Dan about it. It's very annoying though. These are such bad photographs.'

Not smiling, or worse, laughing, was difficult and essential. 'We'll talk later,' he said.

'Sit,' Dan told them and they dropped into two chairs on the opposite side of a desk where he sat. A battered, scratched metal desk but a bit more businesslike than the trestle table of previous occasions.

A multi-fold screen partitioning the hall almost in half was a new addition.

'Everything's awful,' Alex said, trying not to show surprise when Tony took her hand and gave a warning squeeze. 'Er . . . look at it. Rain, rain, rain. Do you think we could get a really big storm? I do and then it . . . well, it's not very nice out there.'

Dan grunted and Tony gave her a reassuring smile that made her want to kick him. He might as well have patted her head.

'When did Mary Burke tell you about seeing the deceased?'

'It was yesterday, right, Alex?' Tony said.

'But you two didn't think you should come to me with the information?'

'No,' Alex said promptly. 'I knew Mary would come herself when she was ready. It isn't my place to interfere. I suppose you do know she doesn't see very well.'

'I should think anyone who knows her does. But from the way she talked about the woman I saw, I don't think she was imagining things.'

'You're busy,' Tony said. 'We could get to what we have tomorrow.'

'Never too busy for you and Alex,' Dan said. 'Detective Constable Harding checked in a little while ago. I understand you two had a nice chat, Alex.'

Smooth innuendoes were one of Dan's specialties. Alex wished she hadn't come. 'Nice young man,' she said, making a rapid inventory of what she'd said to him at the Dog.

'Alex and I have something to share with you,' Tony said. 'We can't tell you much about it really, but we're hoping you'll know how to get it back to its owners. We've all gone through the misery of losing something important – or it looks potentially important.'

Doing her best to straighten the page again, Alex put it in front of Dan.

'Bugger it!' Bill Lamb said by way of announcing his arrival. He dripped across the floor, shaking his hat and himself. 'Cars all over the place. I had to park down by the road and, of course, the sodding sky chose that moment to compete with Niagara Falls.'

He wiped a wet hand across his eyes and saw Tony and Alex. 'Bloody wonderful,' he muttered, giving them one of his unblinking stares.

'Bill,' Dan said evenly, hooking a thumb in

151

the direction of the Burke sisters. If they'd heard Bill's cheery entrance, they showed no sign.

Bending over the numbers, Dan ran a forefinger down as if there were columns. 'Where did you get this?'

Framed by her short, dark curls, Alex's ears turned red. 'On the floor,' she said. 'It's phone numbers, isn't it? We wondered if there was a way to find whoever lost it. It drives you mad to make careful notes of something important then lose them.'

Making slopping sounds with his shoes, Bill approached, arms spread, and pushed his chin forward to see what Dan was looking at. A fat drop fell from his chin onto the paper.

A hard glance from Dan and his partner drew back an inch or two. 'Phone numbers,' Bill said. 'What are they?'

'That's what we hope to find out,' Tony said. He had long ago decided that being nice to Bill caused the man more annoyance than any negative approach.

'They're hoping we can find out who lost this list,' Dan said.

'Have you tried calling the numbers?' Bill said.

'We didn't like to,' Alex said. 'It could be awkward.'

'So you'd rather we did it? Makes sense. Harding's good at setting the right tone, guv,' Bill said. He didn't try to hide what he thought of anonymous lists of phone numbers.

'Give it to him and tell him to try them now,' Dan said. He waited for Bill to leave before giving Tony a penetrating look, but he called after Bill, 'Tell him to make a copy and give this back to me. OK, there's something going on that you two don't want to tell me about. Or you don't want to, but you think you ought to. Where did that list come from and why are you being cagey about it?'

Tony looked at Alex.

'I'm not the enemy,' Dan said.

'Did you find any sign of someone poking around the Gammage cottage?' Alex pressed her mouth into a firm line. She crossed her legs and jiggled a foot.

'My head is spinning,' Dan said and Tony was grateful the man kept his voice down. 'We're talking about telephone numbers. If you picked that piece of paper up in the street you wouldn't be here with it. But you are and now you're back talking about the murder scene again.'

'No,' Alex said hotly. 'All I asked was . . . OK. Tony?'

He felt cornered but also relieved she'd given up her tight hold on what was said. 'We've got a messy problem. We're trying to do what's best for everyone but we could be making a bad situation worse.'

Dan got up and retrieved his trench coat and hat. 'Just a minute. Harding!'

Detective Constable Harding yelled, 'Yessir,' from the back of the hall. He jumped up and strode over to his boss. 'Guv?' he said.

'When Harriet and Mary Burke are finished, please drive them home. You've got one of the pool cars?'

'Yessir.'

'Right.' He gave Bill a faint salute indicating, Tony thought, that he'd done the man a favor by not asking him to do the driving duty.

'These numbers, guv,' Harding said. 'Maybe I'm mad but I think it's a string of burners. I haven't called them all yet but I thought I'd just mention that. No reply, no answering message for any of 'em so far.'

'Try them all,' Dan said, turning to Tony and Alex with raised eyebrows. 'I suppose you heard that. Of course you did. Let's go to my interview room – otherwise known as my car.'

Inside the Lexus, Tony and Alex sat in the back seat while Dan sat sideways in the driving seat with his back resting against the door. 'Sorry about this,' he said. 'But there's no privacy in there. What's on your mind?'

'Kyle Gammage found the body in Underhill.'

Dan's brows rose slowly. He took off his hat and threw it onto the passenger seat. 'Tell me something I don't know.'

Rain beat a tattoo on the car roof and the windows were already steaming up inside.

'He and Scoot are anxious about drawing any attention to their family.'

'Why?'

Tony kept looking directly at Dan. 'Sid Gammage drives a truck. Long haul and at night because it pays well. I don't know all the details but they need the money to pay off debts, and because Sid hopes to give the boys a decent higher education.'

Dan rubbed absently at the long scar on his jaw. 'That's no different from a lot of families.'

'There's no mother in the picture.'

'It happens.' The detective leaned his head back against the window and Tony noticed how tired the man seemed.

He frowned, and glanced at Alex who was drawing in the condensation on her window with a forefinger.

She had stepped out of this. However much or little Dan learned from them was up to him. 'Sid isn't at home most of the time. The boys are afraid social services will get wind of it and interfere.'

It was Dan's turn to frown. 'There's no one looking after them?'

'We all are.'

'I got that but I thought you meant for a night or two. You're talking about more than that?'

In a small voice, Alex said, 'Yes. I've never met Sid Gammage.'

Dan's attention shifted to Tony and he shook his head, no. 'But they're staying at Lily's now and we're keeping a good eye on them. They're not going short of anything and they're good boys.'

'Damn, wouldn't you know there'd be unintended consequences to this enquiry. There almost always is.'

'We don't have to do anything in a hurry,' Alex said. She shifted to the edge of her seat and put her hands on Dan's forearm where it rested along the back of the seat. 'I honestly think they'll run if there's any mention of taking Kyle into care. Scoot's old enough to be on his own.'

'Is he?' Disgust hardened Dan's expression. 'People shouldn't have kids if they can't take care of them. No way is a seventeen-year-old up to taking care of himself and his brother, and a home' and everything that goes with it. What's their father thinking of?'

'I'm sorry but we'll have to contact Sid Gammage.'

'I expected you to say that,' Tony said. 'We don't have a number for you but the boys must have it.'

'Tony wanted to tell you about it at the start,' Alex said in a rush. 'As usual I thought I knew better and we could take care of Scoot and Kyle. It's so unfair. The murder is nothing to do with them. Dan, seriously, Tony didn't like keeping this from you.'

For a moment Dan looked ready to speak, but he closed his mouth and looked away. 'Thank you both for coming to us now. It was the right thing to do but I might have chosen to hold off just the way you did. Is Scoot working tonight?'

'He's already there,' Alex said.

'We think the list of numbers is his and he came back to Lily's cottage to look for it only Lily already had it.'

'I'll be by to talk to Scoot after a while,' Dan said. 'I was going to see if I could have my old room back at the Dog. If so, I'll talk to the boy there.'

Nineteen

Radhika was nice. She let him do things that she wouldn't have if she didn't trust him.

'I need to put more hot water in Naruto's bottles and make sure she pees and poops.' Kyle grinned at Radhika. They talked about things he'd never say in front of other ladies like her but she was different, a real belter. 'I never knew baby cats couldn't do those things on their own.'

She looked away from the computer screen. 'I expect Tony told you the mother normally takes care of those things. The kittens must be stimulated, then the mother makes sure they are comfortable afterwards. Such good mothers they are. Almost as good as you.' Radhika laughed.

Kyle felt a blush creep up his cheeks. She was beautiful. Such black, shining hair and big eyes. Under her white jacket she wore a brilliant sari in blues and greens with bits of gold. Radhika was the most beautiful person in Folly-on-Weir . . . perhaps in the whole of the country.

He turned on a tap in the deep sink and waited for the water to get warm enough – but not too warm. After filling two large spare plastic pop bottles, he exchanged them for the cooled ones presently wrapped in a piece of fleece he used to make a warm pen inside a crate. Naruto snuggled against one big bottle, her ears still folded over and her eyes light blue. She was always hungry and her demands turned raucous if she wasn't fed quickly enough to suit her.

'She might walk pretty well by next week,' Kyle said. 'I like the way her fur feels.'

'Everything will happen quickly if she is really well cared for,' Radhika said. 'And she will be. She is calico and I think she will be very beautiful. I like her orange nose and the black fur around her eyes.'

Kyle had the syringe ready to feed her and lifted the kitten carefully from the crate. 'I know,' he said before Radhika could speak. 'Really small bits so I don't choke her.' The kitten latched on and her wrinkled little ears twitched against her head.

'I don't have to worry about you,' Radhika said. 'You are very careful. It's getting late, Kyle. See, the light is gone. You should be on your way. I thought Tony would be back by now.'

He didn't want to leave Naruto but he knew she was right.

The phone rang and Radhika answered in her lilting voice. A moment passed and she said, 'Oh, dear. I am so sorry. She must have been lost on her way here. I will get her at once.' She hung up. 'Katie is in another cottage down the street. I shall go for her. Answer the phone, please.'

It rarely happened that Katie went off course going between her favorite places but everyone in the village knew her.

Kyle settled in a chair with Naruto. She fitted in the palm of his hand and looked so helpless, but she greedily took food from the syringe. He had to keep pulling it away. Thank goodness they would have proper little bottles for the milk replacement by tomorrow.

Tony had bought an Amazon Echo and they moved the machine from room to room in the clinic to listen to news, or weather, or more often, music. Kyle didn't think much of the music choices but Tony liked jazz so there was a lot of that. It played now and Naruto almost felt as if she was purring.

He turned his back to the door. What would any of the boys at school say if they could see him now?

An arm shot around his head, covered his eyes, so quickly he sucked in a big breath and coughed. A yell stuck in his throat.

He threw out his right arm and felt the syringe fly from his fingers.

A piece of tape was slapped over his eyes and a second across his mouth, so quickly he writhed and slipped to thud on the floor.

Like a sleeve made to fit his body, a sheath that felt like canvass was tugged over him, plastering his arms to his sides.

Naruto! He yelled inside his head but she shrieked and was gone, knocked away from him, and his attacker lifted and slung him over a shoulder.

A sharp jab in his leg made him momentarily stronger. He kicked, punched and twisted.

Quickly, his muscles turned hard and useless. He couldn't move.

He let his face fall forward, fall and fall.

Twenty

Dan sat on his bed in what he'd come to think of as his 'old room' at the Black Dog. The overnight bag he carried in his car was already unpacked. With pillows stacked behind his back and his legs stretched out, he felt comfortable to the point of being sleepy.

His mobile was beside him on the mattress while he waited for Calum's Skype call. He hoped the call would come in before Scoot showed up.

Getting out of his jacket and tie, kicking off his shoes and settling to let his mind wander was wonderful. Which showed what a narrow existence he lived outside his work. He couldn't even imagine going down to get a pint, or getting in his car to drive elsewhere and find tipsy laughter, reddened faces and phony friendship.

Chintz curtains at the very slightly open window lifted to bring the sound and the smell of rain into the room. He began to drift a little and had the thought that one day he ought to come here just to spend a couple of days for a break.

The ridiculousness of the idea jolted him wide-awake, and so did the Skype signal.

'Hello, my boy,' he said, knowing his grin was wide enough to be silly. 'I've been looking forward to hearing from you all day.'

'You have?' Calum's pleasure showed, too. 'I thought it was never going to be time to get up here to my room. They're all busy down there talking about a holiday in Spain, so I did a runner.'

'Spain, huh?' Dan said with a slightly unpleasant curl in his belly. 'Where in Spain?' Not that he'd ever been there.

'I'm not sure. Barcelona, Madrid, Cordova – is that what it's called? They want to go for Christmas.'

Christmas in Spain? Why not Austria or Bavaria or somewhere with a bit of snow and ice haloes falling around the street lights?

'Dad? That doesn't sound like fun, does it?'

'I don't know, son. I've never been.' He looked at his boy's face, so much a young copy of his own and the tousled black curls probably much like his hair right now. He had a sudden thought and sat up straighter. 'Hey, it's my turn this year.'

'Whew,' Calum let out a long breath. 'I thought you'd forgotten and I promised myself I'd wait till you said it. I'm to come to you this Christmas.'

Dan narrowed his eyes. This wasn't going to wash, no matter how Corinne put it to him. He swallowed. 'Would you rather go to Spain than come to the chilly old Cotswolds?'

'Are you kidding? I love it there and I'm coming even if you won't have me. I know my rights and this Christmas I'm to be with you.'

Dan chuckled. 'Oh, well, in that case I suppose I'll have to take you even if I don't want you.'

'Da-ad,' Calum said.

161

He would not think about potential difficulties. 'You're coming and we're going to have a great time. Should we go out for dinner?'

'No way. We'll cook it. We always eat at home at Christmas.'

They had always eaten at home but Corinne had done the cooking while Dan and Calum 'helped.' 'At home it is. I'll order a fresh turkey and we'll cook all the trimmings.'

'And have a tree?'

'What do you think?'

They stared at one another in silence with tight smiles on their faces. Calum was too old not to think about how different it would be, no matter how hard they tried to capture good memories. But he would make it fun for his boy and watching him would be his own fun.

'You didn't throw out the decorations, did you?' Calum asked.

Dan swallowed around a lump in his throat. 'They're exactly where they're always stored, in the attic. Would I miss taking them out one-by-one and remembering where we bought them? We should add a couple of new ones.'

'Can we go to the Christmas shop at that garden center?'

Dan felt his breathing get shakier. 'You bet. Perhaps this is a good year to buy the tree there. They have beautiful ones.' All the things they'd done as a family still had the power to hurt. Not because he wanted everything back as it had been, but traditions were hard to ignore.

'Dad, have you thought anymore? About the thing we talked about?'

Only every time he had a free moment and at night when he tried to sleep. 'Yes, I have.'

'So have I. I know me mam won't want me to go for good but there's got to be a way around it. I'll miss her but we can work that out. It's my life, too. Not just yours or hers. I never got to decide what was going to happen to my family. Now I still don't have any rights. Supposedly. Only I do and my right is to spend more time with you.'

Oh, lovely, now his eyes stung. 'Hold on a sec while I get some water. It's dry in this room.' It wasn't but it was a reasonable excuse.

With a glass in hand, he sat in the room's only chair this time. 'Back again.'

'What room?' Calum asked, frowning.

'It's at a pub and guest house called the Black Dog in the village of Folly-on-Weir. I can't remember if I ever brought you here.'

In a sharp voice Calum asked, 'Are you on holiday, then? On your own?'

Dan knew better than to laugh. 'I've got a case down here. It's easier to stay than drive back and forth each day.' And there was nothing at home to draw him there. 'With any luck it'll be cleared up soon.' But there was something off kilter about the case so far.

If Mary Burke had indeed seen the victim three weeks before she died, what had she been doing in Folly? Where was she from? Why wasn't anyone looking for her?

Those answers would solve the case but no answers were coming.

'I'm going to talk to Mam,' Calum said, jolting

163

Dan. 'I'm going to tell her I want to go back there and back to my old school and friends. She wants me to be happy, I know she does. I'm not happy. I keep wondering what each day is for. Sometimes I take long walks to stay out of everyone's way and try to figure it out. There's nothing here for me.'

'Your mam's there.' His son's words, his tone, gave Dan a nasty feeling. 'I thought you were OK with the way we've worked everything out.'

Calum sighed. 'You never asked, Dad. Neither did Mam. You told me, is all. I don't think I can keep on hoping something will change when it never does.'

The not very veiled messages weren't lost on Dan but he didn't want to think that his young son found no satisfaction in his life. He did know that Calum wouldn't be the youngest kid to get down enough to throw everything in.

'What date do you come for Christmas?' Dan said.

'I don't know. Early December, I suppose.'

He needed to talk to Corinne quickly, preferably without things deteriorating into anger. 'When I get off the phone, I'll check the dates.' *Careful*, he told himself, *careful*. 'It's hard to get any extra time with school starting again after the holiday.'

'I've thought of that,' Calum said eagerly. 'How would it be if I could stay there for the winter term. It would give everyone a chance to settle down and decide how they were thinking. I—'

'Wait a minute.' Dan drank from the glass of water. 'You're rushing ahead too fast. I'll talk to your mam first.' *And hope she doesn't throw a fit and blame the whole idea on me.*

'But do you think it's a good idea? Would you like it if I stayed?'

Whatever happened he must not blame Corinne for Calum's unhappiness. 'I think it's a lovely idea . . . if your mam likes it. She loves you the way I do, son, and that's so much it can hurt when you're not with us.' Great, adult thought processes pressed on a young boy. 'As long as we know the times you're gone aren't forever, we can handle it.'

'So talk to her about it,' Calum said, his voice rising with excitement. 'It won't be forever, just for Christmas and winter term. Then I'd visit Ireland again. And Bram's boys will have much more room when they move in. Mam's house is bigger than theirs, but not so big two of us kids wouldn't have to share a room. This is perfect. Please say it's perfect.'

It wasn't. 'It's past your bedtime. Tuck in and remember I'll be on this case for all of us. I'll not put it aside, I promise. But don't keep watching your mam as if she's about to lay an egg. She'll smell trouble. I've got to work out the right time.'

Calum smiled. Dan wished he saw more confidence in the boy, and that he felt more himself.

'You'll do it, Dad,' Calum said. 'Night.'

Twenty-One

When Radhika arrived at Mrs Marroway's cottage there had been no answer to the knocker. It was too dark to see much but there seemed to be no sign of Katie in the yard and when Radhika plucked up the courage to raise her umbrella high so she could peek through the letterbox, a lamp was on but Katie didn't come barking to the door, which she would have if she were alone in there.

Mrs Marroway was a spry, but caustic, eighty-something and liked her walks. Perhaps she hadn't expected Radhika to come so quickly and decided to take Katie for a stroll down the lane. The rain wouldn't have deterred the woman.

Radhika knocked again. No result.

The street lights were on and there was no sign f the tall old lady or the big golden-white dog, 1 either direction. Ducks still bustled on the tiny raindrop spattered stream in front of the cottages. Water overflowed gutters. But the occasional quack, and the sound of heavy rainfall were all Radhika heard.

Mrs Marroway could have decided to take Katie to the clinic, but Radhika had left by the front door and if Mrs Marroway went the back way, they would miss each other.

Radhika took her mobile from the pocket of her raincoat and punched in the clinic number.

The first time it went to the answering machine, she thought Kyle must have hesitated before answering and then had to situate the kitten before he picked up.

She tried again, threading her way across a tiny bridge to an alley between two cottages. It was easier to go in through the back door, except for the plethora of puddles, which were treacherous once the light faded.

Kyle didn't answer.

Hitching up the skirts of her sari, Radhika ran, pulling to the side of the track as a vehicle passed and splashed her with muddy water. Her sandals made it difficult but she hurried on until she could go into the clinic. She flapped her umbrella to dislodge some of the water and put it in the kitchen.

'Kyle,' she called, 'I'm back. Did Mrs Marroway call again? Is Katie here?'

He didn't answer but she was already at the door to the little office that doubled as overflow for recovery animals. Kyle wasn't there.

The door to the crate where Naruto was kept remained open. She fled to the examining room, and the little surgical suite, dashed to the sitting room at the back of the cottage. Called up the stairs.

Nothing.

Back in the office, she stood just inside and tried to decide what to do first. She would not make anyone panic until she was sure it was necessary.

But she was panicking.

A loud squall – a sound of helpless disgust

confused her. Almost like a hungry newborn baby.

The sound came again and she saw tiny Naruto plop from her legs to her tummy and wobble back and forth, rooting around in the rug with her face, looking for comfort.

Radhika scooped her up. She took one of the still warm bottles from the cage, settled the kitten on top and held her close to her body. The thud, thud of her own heart sickened her.

Snatching up the phone, she tried Tony's number. No answer. What was going on? Alex didn't answer either. She dialed 999 and asked to be put through to Chief Inspector O'Reilly's people at the Folly parish hall.

The dispatcher started to ask questions. Radhika gave the clinic address, said a child was missing, then demanded the parish hall number again. 'They are close to us,' she insisted. 'They can come quickly.'

At the other end of the line someone new picked up, 'Lamb,' said a voice she had not forgotten.

'Kyle is missing,' she said in a babble. 'Kyle Gammage. This is Radhika at the veterinary clinic. He stayed here while I went to get Katie, only she was not there. I think something has happened to him. I need help. Now.'

'On my way,' Bill Lamb said. 'I'm only minutes away. Hang in there.'

While she waited, Radhika took some fleece and put it between Naruto and the bottle. She couldn't manage filling a new syringe and holding the kitten so she dipped her small finger in some milk and the little creature sucked hungrily. No teeth yet, and for that Radhika was grateful.

Clattering in the hallway warned of an approach and Bill Lamb, hatless, his crewcut hair flat to his head and dripping, met her as she left the office.

He put out a hand and she held it hard. 'He's gone.'

'You think he ran away?'

'No! The kitten was on the floor, on her own and the syringe for feeding is there, too. She is an angry little girl but well, I think. I do not know, I just do not know. Has he been abducted, Bill? Who would kidnap a boy? I don't think he has any money or anything like that. Nothing anyone would want.

'Tony and Alex do not answer their phones. I do not know where Katie is. I should not have left Kyle here on his own.'

He took her firmly by the shoulders and backed her into an armchair. 'Let me start making calls.'

While he listened for an answer, he paced, peering out of the windows when he reached them. He spun around and said, 'Guv. Good. We've got another problem. I'm at Tony Harrison's clinic . . . no, he's not here. Radhika called me. She was called away by a neighbor who supposedly had Katie. She couldn't find the woman or Katie and came back. The boy, Kyle, she thinks he's gone missing.'

'He has!' Radhika said loudly. 'He is gone, I tell you and he left the kitten—'

'Hush, Radhika, hush.' Bill sat on the arm of the chair and put an arm around her shoulders.

He had always been so nice to her, especially when she had been in her worst trouble.

'Guv, I haven't had a chance to look around. I only just got here but the boy isn't here and from what Radhika says, it's possible Kyle didn't leave of his own volition. Do you know if Tony and Alex are there? Radhika says their phones are off. I can call the bar and find out.'

'Oh, well I'll leave that to you then.' Bill frowned and rubbed her shoulder. 'Right, I'll round up people to come here and search.'

Bill got up and made calls in rapid succession.

With Naruto back in the cage, Radhika prepared warm food for the syringe.

When she held the kitten again, she felt tears and blinked them away. She must be strong.

'We'll find him,' Bill said and she looked at him through a watery veil. 'Don't cry. Please don't. It's shock you're feeling.'

Careful not to crush the kitten, he put his arms around her and eased her forehead into his chest. 'Help's on the way. Let us do the worrying.'

'But that lady was killed,' she said, sniffing. 'Near the Gammages' cottage. It is so fearfully strange, Bill. There is something that joins these things. There must be.'

He smoothed her hair at her temple. 'Perhaps.'

With less ease than he'd held her, Bill set her away from him. She looked into his face, at the way he frowned, the sharp downturn at the corners of his mouth. 'Sit down, please. Best to be as calm as you can. Someone will come and make you tea.' He kept looking at her with that puzzling expression.

'I am calm,' she said, swallowing. 'If I have done the wrong thing, I am sorry. I should not have insisted on bothering you at the parish hall. Wrong. It may make it difficult for you. I'm sorry.'

He took a step toward her but multiple footsteps approached from the back door.

She fed the kitten.

'You couldn't do anything wrong if you tried,' he said quietly.

'Warren, sir,' said the first constable through the door. 'Where would you like us to start?'

Twenty-Two

Scoot came through Dan's door as if he expected the worst, possibly execution. Until the boy knocked, he'd forgotten calling him to set up a meeting only minutes before Bill's little bombshell from Tony's clinic.

'Come in.' Should he send Scoot away? No, it was time to be blunt about anything that might help in this case. There had to be connections between events, and the Gammages were part of those connections.

First Dan needed information on Sid Gammage and how to get him here, then he'd have to tell Scoot that his brother was missing. The latter was a miserable prospect.

'Sit down,' he told Scoot, indicating the one chair. He had a thought. 'When's the last time you saw Katie? The dog?'

'She's downstairs. In front of the fire.' Scoot sounded a bit shaky. 'With Miss Mary and Miss Harriet, and Bogie. Your big detective brought the ladies back and saw them inside.'

'Good.' He couldn't think of a plausible explanation for asking about the dog without giving away the whole plot. He'd talked to Alex who had said she would get Tony and come up.

There was no point in not getting to the must-ask questions. 'Have you seen this before?' He showed him the piece of folded paper Lily had found and given to Alex.

'Yes,' Scoot said clearly, gripping the arms of his chair.

'It's yours, right? From one of your notebooks? Might as well ask rather than go through all your books and waste time.'

'It's from a composition book.'

'What are these numbers?'

'Just numbers.' Scoot sounded anxious.

'Let's not be stupid,' Dan said. He felt sorry for the boy. 'And please don't take up valuable time we don't have.'

Scoot frowned. 'I don't know what you mean. They're numbers.'

'They're phone numbers. Anyone can see that.'

Slowly, Scoot dropped his face into his hands, he nodded his head, yes.

'What are they? Whose are they? Don't mess around.'

'I'm not.' The young voice broke. 'I can't say.'

'You can and you will. I'd rather you tell me yourself but if I have to prompt you I will. Whose numbers are these?'

The kid curled over, his forehead all but on his knees.

'I've got to know. All of it. I have to get in touch with your dad. Would any of these numbers help me do that?'

'No.' Scoot shook his head.

Someone knocked on the door. Dan gritted his teeth and opened it, standing back as Alex and Tony walked in. 'Sorry we couldn't be reached on our phones before,' Tony said. 'We both turned them off when we were talking to you earlier.'

'Sorry we couldn't get here earlier,' Alex said.

Dan really felt like saying he wasn't sorry. 'Shortage of chairs, unfortunately,' he said. 'Feel free to sit on the bed.'

'Sit here,' Scoot said, standing up, his eyes suspiciously bright.

Could be that getting these three together was a good idea. 'Scoot was just going to tell me about this,' Dan said, holding up the notebook page.

'Perhaps we should come back later?' Tony said.

'No, no,' Dan said. 'I think we should all be here. Take the chair, Alex. We've got questions to be answered. At least Scoot told me where Katie is now. That's one puzzle off my mind.' There should be someone present for Scoot during questioning anyway.

Tony gave him a sanity-questioning look and sat on the bed.

'Why didn't you go down and check?' Alex

said. She looked pinched and irritable. 'Or just call the bar. You know she's often here.'

'I'd only just found out she was missing. Or Radhika thought she was missing.'

Alex frowned. 'Does that mean Kyle's back? We checked in with Radhika. She told us what happened earlier. Where was Kyle?'

'Hold on,' Dan said, pulling Scoot against him as he would have rushed from the room. 'We've got everything in hand, boy. Calm down.'

'Is something wrong with Kyle?' Scoot said, sounding out of breath. 'What is it? Where is he now?'

Tony reached for Scoot and caught his arm. 'Sit beside me, old son. Alex and I were only told there'd been trouble a little while ago. When we saw you here we thought you knew about it, didn't we, Alex?'

The only answer Tony got from Alex was silence. She pressed her fingers to her mouth.

'From the way Radhika spoke,' Tony said, 'it sounded as if you had things sorted out.'

'That's right,' Alex said with a withering look at Dan that would have daunted him if he hadn't been on the receiving end of many similar looks before. 'I certainly wouldn't have expected you to be pushing Scoot for information on a piece of paper when you hadn't told him Kyle's missing.'

'I must know where Sid Gammage is,' he told her, keeping his eyes on Scoot's. 'Your dad has to be told about Kyle. And he'd want to be here with you anyway.' Gammage should never have left his children alone.

Scoot looked frightened. 'Those are numbers my dad used to call me. I kept them because they made me feel I could reach him if I had to. Why would he keep using different numbers? I couldn't reach him at his regular mobile number, either. Where's Kyle? Tell me.'

'Hold on, please, Scoot.' Dan folded the paper again and put it in his pocket.

'Can't you find out anything from the list of numbers?' Tony asked.

'They've made advances on that but mostly no. These days you can get numbers that look as if they're in a different area. No problem at all. Either the sim cards are being changed out or he's got single-use burners and he's tossing them who knows where.'

'He's driving his own truck, though, right,' Tony said. 'There's got to be paperwork on it somewhere – probably in the cottage.'

'It's not his truck,' Scoot said, shivering. 'It belongs to the company.'

Dan sat on the other side of Scoot from Tony. He looked hard into the boy's face. 'What company? Hugh doesn't have the name of any company on your application for work.'

'I gave the home information. Dad doesn't like anyone contacting where he works. Where's Kyle?'

Dan got to his feet. 'What company?'

'Podmore Hauling and Storage,' Scoot said quietly. 'Near Northampton.'

Dan snatched up his mobile and called Bill Lamb. He gave him the information needed and told him to see if there was a night answering

175

service. Then he asked for a progress report without mentioning Kyle's name. In this case, no news wasn't good news. He had to get to the parish hall and oversee the search.

'We've got everything under control, Scoot,' he said, pulling on his jacket and an anorak. To Tony and Alex he added, 'I'll send someone to keep an eye on things. Please keep Scoot with you.'

'Where's my brother?' The boy's voice rose higher with each word and he stood up. 'Tell me.'

'We'll find him. Hang in there, for him and for all of us and don't try to take things into your own hands or we'll be looking for both of you.'

'Alex?' Scoot said.

'You'll be fine with us. We'll stay at Corner Cottage.'

'We don't know how,' Dan said. He couldn't keep the kid in the total dark. 'But Kyle left the clinic while Radhika was running an errand. He'll turn up. Either he'll go back to the clinic, or he'll come here to meet you. Isn't that what he usually does?'

Wild-eyed, Scoot nodded, yes, but Dan felt like crap when he left the room.

Twenty-Three

Before nine the next morning, Joan Gimblet strode heavily across the saloon bar.

Polishing a table, Alex watched as Joan brought

a hand down smartly on the counter bell. She brought it down several times.

'Good morning, Joan. At least it's dry. That's a treat.'

Joan swung around. 'There you are. Can't stop to chat. Very busy day today. But I promised Martin I'd come in and personally remind you that the youth center is opening at three and, of course, we want you there. And Tony. I know you've said you can't come but we know you will.'

'You must be so proud,' Alex said, polish in one hand, duster in the other. 'I'd love to come but a few things have us at sixes and sevens at the moment and, of course, we're usually pretty busy here then. If I'd had more notice . . .' *I still wouldn't have come if I could help it.* She did feel a sliver of shame.

Joan's face took on a puce hue. 'Well, I was going to mention that. Paul said he'd come down to remind you but he forgot. *Men.*' She rolled her eyes. 'Anyway, please close up at least between 2.30 and 4.30 so we can have a good crowd. We'll have drinks and snacks. There'll be a ribbon cutting and there are awards to be handed out.'

The best way to deal with Joan was to acquiesce – more or less. 'I'll see what we can do. I hope everything goes really well.' She would post a notice near the bar and make an announcement about the youth center. She would not be closing the pub.

Joan nodded but her expression turned sly. 'There was a policeman outside Lily's cottage

177

all night, isn't that right? Is everything all right there?'

'Absolutely blooming,' Alex said. She didn't offer a word of explanation and got some satisfaction out of the disappointment on Joan's face as she walked out.

Tony had spent the night scrunched on the small-scale couch at the cottage and she had shared her mother's bed. She had suggested to the policeman who had been put on duty outside that he make an occasional stroll to the back of the cottage so that Scoot might see him and lose any ideas of running off in search of his brother.

Now a full search was underway for Kyle and the school premises were being patrolled. Scoot had been horrified at the latter but they'd managed to persuade him that none of the kids would know why the school was being watched.

Hugh leaned cautiously around the wall of bottles between kitchen and bar. 'Is she gone?' he asked.

'You saw her and pretended you didn't?'

'I heard the bell, then I heard her talking to you. Doesn't take two to get the gist of Joan Gimblet's demands. Awful woman.'

Guilt crept up on Alex. 'She's a bit difficult but I don't think everything has been as easy for her as she'd like us to think. I'm not closing up for her, though. I'll announce it and make sure there's a sign up, but that's it. I'll have to find someone to go and represent us, maybe with some flowers for Joan.'

'Nice idea,' Hugh said. 'Someone's coming

178

walked toward him, holding her bottom lip in her teeth. 'Kyle could be dead. That woman was killed near their cottage and they haven't found a suspect or a motive, or anything – they still don't know who she is. I'm wondering if Kyle knew something and they decided to keep him quiet for good. Whoever "they" are.'

'We can't do anything but wait, Alex. I know that's the hardest part, but what choice do we have?'

Automatically she touched her trouser pocket. Fortunately the days had grown short. Darkness was the only thing she was waiting for now and then she would follow the choice she'd already made and use the key to the Gammage cottage that Scoot had given her.

Twenty-Four

All day they'd waited and all day they hadn't heard a word about Kyle. Alex hadn't seen Dan or Bill, or any other police officer she knew. Tony had come in on his way from the clinic to one of the outlying farms and he looked as worried as she felt. If he had known what she intended to do – what she was on her way to do now daylight was fading – he would have found some excuse to try stopping her. He would use logic to talk her out of it, but this was the one thing she could think of that would make her feel she was being potentially useful. She was taking action, dammit. How long could you carry on with your life, pretending your heart wasn't in your throat and you expected to choke soon? Any effort to find the boy was worth it.

Yes, she was impulsive, and yes, she took chances, but she would need a brain transplant to change her instinctive behavior. And it should be remembered that she had escaped any scrapes she'd got into – so far.

Radhika had gone over every moment of the previous evening with Alex, all the way to getting a phone call about Katie, then returning to the clinic to find Kyle wasn't there. Not a single clue either of them could pounce on.

The Range Rover was still parked at the Black Dog. Without any comment, Alex left the saloon bar and went into the kitchen. She slipped into the back parking lot, took her bike from the storage room where she sometimes kept it and yanked open the gate from the parking lot into the lane beyond. She didn't dare ride along the hard-pack with its thick, exposed roots, potholes and voraciously reaching bramble branches, bare except for the thorns, so she pushed her way to a side road past the dairy and cut back again, behind the village, until she reached roughly paved surfaces where she could ride.

On the other side of Folly, three small roads to the right would take her to another that led to farmland and scattered buildings beyond Underhill. Alex took the middle road, knowing it had the best surface. She was so grateful the rain continued to hold off, but her legs were cold as she pedaled.

A long arch of crooked branches, reaching for each other across the road, closed her in. The bicycle lamp bounced off one tree trunk after another in an eerie ballet that sucked her through a moving, low-light tube enclosed in darkness. She was reminded of a movie about some mini-aturized human traveling through a person's insides with all the rings and ridges on various canals. Yuck.

There was nothing to fear. A lone ride at night was exactly that – you did it on your own. No distraction, just mile after mile and plenty of time to think about what she was doing and why.

Sweat dried on her back and grew icy. Her Barbour jacket felt suddenly too heavy. She couldn't remember why she'd chosen to wear trainers, but she'd had a good reason at the time. Tonight they didn't stop the chill from cutting through her feet.

Then she was where she'd intended to be, at the first corner of the lot where the Gammages lived. Hiking her bike over the fence wasn't easy but she managed and took the extra precaution of chaining it to a pole.

Under the cover of gnarled and dormant fruit trees, she went cautiously forward, watching for any light or sign of life. The key to the cottage was in her pocket. Scoot had given it to her when she told him she wanted to look around in case Kyle had been there and because it was all she could think of to do.

He had whispered his thanks and the hopeless-ness in his eyes brought her close to crying. But it wasn't long before she struggled to hide fury building inside her. Innocent people set upon by maniacs. How long would it take the police to find the culprit? Her first instinct had been to send him over to Corner Cottage, but in retrospect, the less time he spent alone and worrying, the better.

Alex crept forward until she came to the edge of the trees. She scanned the entire area. No police vehicles or activity to be seen in the adjoining field. No lights in the cottage. The thought of the boys living out here alone made her sick, and sad. It couldn't be allowed to happen again.

If Kyle came back in one piece she would track Sid down herself and work something out with him. She wanted no part of separating a parent from his children.

She had decided to start with the outbuildings, getting to the one where the lone visitor seemed to have disappeared for last – except for the cottage itself.

The largest outbuilding, stone but with a rusted metal roof, didn't want to let her inside. The doors rattled but were stuck at the top as if the wood had swollen.

There was no padlock and she put her weight against one door while shaking the other by a hasp with no padlock. Rusty edges cut into her fingers but she kept banging with her back and yanking on the hasp, constantly aware of the noise she was making and fearing the arrival of her mystery man.

Without warning, the door behind her back gave way and she sat on a concrete slab with enough of a jolt to send a shock through her spine. The door kept swinging inward and Alex was confronted with a dark colored van in an otherwise empty space.

She got up, made sure the key to the cottage was still in her pocket, and went to try the driver's door. It opened and a dim inside light came on. Despite an indefinable sweet odor, the vehicle interior was clean. No wrappers from chocolate, or empty food bags. The carpets looked as if they'd been vacuumed and she could see through the windscreen that the body of the van, although old, was free of dirt.

With her heart hammering at her ribs, she peered into the back seats and floor, then went around to open the back. It wasn't locked. What was she afraid of finding? No one would be mad enough to leave a body here.

Nevertheless, she opened the doors slowly and let out a great grateful breath to find another empty space.

Two other outbuildings yielded nothing more sinister than a lawnmower, a leaf blower and garden tools hung from hooks all along the walls.

At the cottage, Alex stood at first the front, then the side door, listening. The wind didn't blow, branches didn't sway and from the building came silence so deep it ached in her head. No, she would follow her plan and save this for last.

She carried on to the building where the man had gone in, but she hadn't seen him come out. It was constructed of brick, with a flat roof covered with grass and moss. The faintest of moons washed from behind thick dark blue cloud but Alex was glad of it.

When she turned the handle, the door opened. Closed inside, she dared to turn on her torch, to the lowest setting. This was where the Gammages kept things they used most often. And she sniffed at the pungent scent coming from hanging strings of onions and a basket of fallen ripe apples loosely packed around with strips of newspaper.

The sight of Kyle's muddy bike saddened her. No prospect of his having used it to go somewhere, then. Methodically, she searched around every pile of boxes, between every box. She moved things out to see behind them and replaced everything as she went. A small, red pedal car was stored in a corner. It kept company with a miniature wheelbarrow and a plastic mower. A mesh sack filled with balls hung from the wall. Wickets and scarred cricket bats stuck out of a box. The Gammages must have lived here most, if not all, of the boys' lives.

Climbing onto a wooden crate to check along a shelf, she had to grab on to stop falling off when the crate wobbled.

With a crash, the door slammed open.

Alex screamed and dropped the torch. She tried to turn her head but she still had her hood up.

'Who are you?' A man's deep voice yelled, and before she could answer two large hands caught at the back of her jacket and swung her down. Unable to gain her balance, she landed on her face against the wooden floor.

He kept a fist between her shoulder blades, pressing her down. 'Who are you? Where are my boys?'

'Alex Duggins from the Black Dog,' she squeaked out. 'I was looking for Kyle.'

'Shit,' he said forcefully. 'What are you talking about? What do you want here? There's nothing worth stealing.'

She shivered uncontrollably and didn't say another word. Her constricted throat felt as if it were being squeezed.

'Get up!' He yanked her to her feet so roughly she almost landed on the floor again. 'What do you mean you're looking for Kyle? Where's Scoot?'

Her thoughts steadied and she belted him with one fist. A short person could harm a tall one in ways they didn't expect.

His yelp satisfied Alex . . . until her brain started to move, like mechanical parts in need of oil. 'I'm so sorry. I thought you were going to hurt me.'

He leaned against a wall, slightly hunched and making hissing sounds as he sucked in air.

'Who are you, please?' She could get away and run, but not if she had made a terrible mistake about this man. 'Tell me who you—'

'I'm Sid Gammage,' he said through his teeth. 'I live here. You'd better run and hope I don't get over this quick enough to run after you. *Women*, you're no good, not one of you.'

'But you came up behind me in the dark, Mr Gammage. You grabbed me and I had no way of knowing you were Scoot and Kyle's dad.

187

People are looking for you.' She retrieved her torch and switched it on.

He turned to look at her with eyes so much like Scoot's it was another shock. 'Whose looking for me? Why?'

What should she tell him? This was horrible. She was looking at a man she had thought might be a murderer.

Perhaps he was a murderer.

She reached for the door handle, but he grabbed it first. A very tall man. Sinewy and hard-bodied, by the look of it. His blond hair was receding but still, he was nice looking in a hawkish way.

'I'm Alex Duggins, Lily Duggins' daughter.'

'I met Lily a long time ago when her girl was young. She works for her daughter at the Black Dog now, doesn't she? In Folly.' He frowned. 'Flaming hell! You're the daughter who owns the pub.'

'I already told you that. And I know Scoot because he does a few hours work for me each day. A super boy. He works hard and looks after his brother, and . . .' Her voice trailed away. What did Sid already know? What was his story? She could easily say something that would make all this turn out very badly – for her. And she could tell him exactly what Dan wouldn't want him to know before he talked to him.

'And what?' he asked. 'Why are you here?'

'OK. I can understand the question. Kyle has been missing since last night. Early evening, really. The police are looking for him. No luck so far. I came out here to see if I could find any clues to where he'd gone. See, his bike's still here so he didn't ride off somewhere. I haven't been in the cottage yet.'

'My god,' Sid muttered. 'Since yesterday? Haven't the police looked out here?'

'They must have,' Alex said, feeling guilty for her lack of faith in them. 'I wanted to see for myself. Everyone's spinning their wheels. We haven't heard a thing today and we're worried to death.'

'I'm going into the cottage. If you decide to get out of here, just do it. I wouldn't blame you.' He pulled out his wallet and showed her his driver's license. 'That's me. Just in case you stay, you'll know I am who I say I am.'

'I think we should get back to the pub,' Alex said. 'Scoot will be there. Kyle usually comes to meet him when he's finishing up.'

'I want to see my boys,' Sid said. 'It's been too long. You must have driven here. Would you be all right with taking me back to Scoot?'

'I came on my bike but you've got your van.' She flinched, ready for more anger over her poking around.

'It won't start. Battery's dead.'

He opened the door and went outside. 'I'm going to check in the cottage. Where's your bike? You'd better get along back. I know some short ways to Folly. I'll walk.'

The night remained still but the moon was higher, throwing spiny shadows of brambles across the ground.

'How did you get here?' Alex knew she should just walk away but she couldn't do it. She wanted to find out if he'd been the man she'd seen a couple of days ago but didn't know how.

'I hitched a ride,' he said. He gave her an assessing look. 'Someone should have told you not to be riding around in the dark on your own. You're not much taller than my Kyle. You'll be scared all over again, but will you let me walk along beside you to the pub? I won't blame you if you tell me to push off.'

He was right, she was scared, but not only of him. As long as she hadn't thought about someone attacking her, she'd been fine. She giggled – an out-of-control reaction. She'd already been attacked. Why should she be afraid now that she knew how to take advantage of being height challenged?

'Glad you find it funny. Give me ten minutes. Ever ridden on the handlebars of a bike before?'

Twenty-Five

Kev Winslet was in the position he enjoyed most, the center of attention. Hugh got a kick out of the way the man rolled from heels to toes, did a little bounce, and repeated the process.

OK, Alex, where are you? If I didn't know you'd taken your bike I'd have the police here by now.

'You lot missed a good do,' Kev announced, red enough in the face to show he'd already had more than enough to drink. 'Champagne! How about that? And some good grub. Fiddly, but good. They're going to have an open house next week. More champers and grub. We were only in the one big room today. All the mod cons, I can tell you.'

Sam Hadley, Liz's husband, was giving a hand clearing tables so Juste could stay behind the bar to help and Scoot needn't fall behind on the washing up. It had been Alex's idea to keep the boy busy and she was right. Sam took a silk chrysanthemum from an arrangement and stuck it behind Kev's ear. 'Saw you going on your way, lad,' Sam said. 'Would have sworn you were going courtin' with that great big bunch of fancy flowers you had.'

Kev whipped away the flower. 'You're jealous because Alex didn't ask you to be her emi . . . emisry. Stand-in or whatever.'

That brought him gusts of raucous laughter.

'We were all invited, you know, Kev,' one man said. Others chorused an agreement. 'We'd rather drink here, isn't that right, lads.'

A roar of approval went up.

Lily came through the bar from the restaurant. 'Anything?' she whispered in Hugh's ear.

'No. Are you OK with me giving O'Reilly a jingle shortly?'

'Yes,' she told him solemnly. 'I ask you, who rides a bicycle, on their own, at night?'

'Evidently your daughter does. Deliberately. She wasn't snatched, I can tell you that. She sneaked out.'

Lily gave him a withering look that warned him to step carefully with criticisms of Alex.

'It's up to her when she comes and goes,' Lily said. 'I don't want to call Tony yet.'

'She could be with him. That's where she usually is.'

After a long sigh, Lily said, 'Let's give it fifteen minutes, then we'll call Tony first, then the police.'

Hugh gave her a mock salute and said, 'Yes, marm.'

'You been to see that youth center yet?' Kev said.

'Nope.'

'It's something. Most people don't live as jammy at home as that place.'

'I think we can take it Kev's impressed by the youth center, folks,' Hugh said, softening any sting with a smile, despite the snickers. 'Maybe you can get some sort of membership. Have they got pool tables? A swimming pool, maybe? Sky's the limit – lap dancing with appropriate ID?'

'Smart arse,' Kev said. 'It's about time the youngsters had a good, safe place to go around here. It's got that special heating and cooling. Geo-thermal, they said. Saves a lot of money. Joan Gimblet kept going on about it. Martin explained it. How the ground's a steady 55 to 57 degree Fahrenheit and this gizmo uses that no matter what temperature it is above the ground, but Paul shut him up in the end. He said Martin loves the sound of his own voice and he should save it for the stage. Said he was boring everyone asleep. We had a good laugh about that, I can tell you.'

'We're going to put *you* on the stage if you keep going on about it,' Sam Hadley said.

More laughter. Major Stroud roared, 'A good one to miss, I'd say, chaps. Unless you like curtseying when you give the mayor a bouquet.'

Scoot came into the bar and touched Hugh's arm. He hitched his head toward the kitchen and went back there.

'There's someone making a lot of noise out there,' Scoot said. 'A real racket.'

Hugh flipped on the outside light, threw open the door and looked out. He heard scrabbling and a man said, 'Hold on. We're doing more damage. Sit on the hood.'

'What is it?' Lily gave him a push from behind and they both tottered down the single step. 'For crying out loud.'

Holding onto Alex to stop her from falling, a tall man stood with one foot on the ground and the other on a bicycle pedal. The machine had run into the side of Alex's Range Rover.

She struggled, half of her on the bonnet of the vehicle, the other half tangled in the bike's handlebars.

Twenty-Six

'This is informal, sir,' Dan said. The flat look in his eyes said he expected this to be anything but informal. 'I understand we've got the dining room to ourselves. After you, Mr Gammage.' Pointing

193

a file folder in its direction, he indicated the passageway from the kitchens leading to the restaurant.

Tony had just arrived. He could feel Alex staring at him and looked at her. Somehow she must think he had called the police. He shook his head, no. 'May we catch our breath, Dan?' he said. 'I just found out about Alex's adventure. My father called me. What alerted you?'

The man he assumed to be Sid Gammage held Scoot to his side and looked, wild-eyed, around the kitchen.

'I called,' Hugh said. 'It was time the police were here.'

'And I agreed,' Lily added. 'I wish there had been more time for Sid and Scoot to talk, but we don't always get what we want.'

Sid gave her an almost fond look.

'Sid and I met a couple of times years ago,' Lily said. 'I used to live in Underhill, remember.'

Tony was relieved when Alex smiled at him. Her hands were held under her arms in an unnatural fashion. Probably sore from her handlebar ride, he thought. Her face was smudged with dirt and her clothing looked ready for a thrift store – if they'd take it. 'Thanks,' she mouthed at him.

'Are you OK?' he said.

'Apart from my shredded pride, I'm fine.'

'Have you caught your breath now?' Dan said. His face pulled tight in a mask to cover irritation. 'Are we allowed to get on with the very serious issues the police are dealing with here?'

'Whoa,' Tony said. 'Hugh gave me the short

194

version of what's going on. Looks to me as if you wouldn't be any further forward with your "serious issues" without a little help from some people here. What's the news on Kyle?'

Bill Lamb entered smoothly, as if on skates. 'I think you forget the way things go here. We ask the questions. You give the answers. If some of you take the law into your own hands, that doesn't change the balance, unless you get arrested for interfering with an investigation.'

'Bill . . .' Dan said, and paused with his lips parted as if about to launch into a tirade. 'Would you take Scoot and Lily into the snug.' He raised a brow at Lily. 'Is it empty? If not, would you kindly clear it?'

'Follow me, please.' Lily was expressionless.

'Bill,' Dan said again. 'Just a general chat about anything that comes to mind, right? Perhaps they'll remember something useful.'

Bill's smile didn't reassure Tony. He held an arm out to Alex and slid it around her when she came to him. 'Can't let you out of my sight,' he muttered. 'You're incorrigible.'

She leaned her head against him.

'Have Detective Harding join us in the dining room,' Dan said.

Tony could sense the other man sizing up his options. He couldn't be sure how Sid Gammage would behave when confronted. But he decided Harding would be there primarily as the second official pair of ears.

He felt Alex's hand flex at his waist and glanced down into her scratched face. Damn, more than once the thought had crossed his mind that perhaps he should try to get her far away from here and pray they didn't settle in another wasps' nest of intrigue . . . and death. 'You OK?' he said quietly.

Alex raised her chin. 'Not really. But I'm better now than I was.' Her smile was slightly reassuring.

With his two charges, Bill set off along the passage from the kitchens. They would cut around into the snug doing their best not to draw much attention. Scoot looked back at his dad who gave him a comforting smile before the boy was out of sight. Tony liked the way the man was with his son.

'I'm sure this isn't convenient,' Dan said to Hugh, 'but I hope you and Juste can hold down the fort.'

'Liz Hadley is here now. We've got her husband, Sam Hadley, helping out, too. We'll manage just fine, thanks.'

They went to the same table in the main dining room as they'd used before. The curtains were open and this time nobody attempted to close them. They sat and Tony saw how Alex gripped the edge of the table.

Sid frowned but held his silence.

'This is an informal chat,' Dan said, echoing his opening comment. 'I gather Alex was there at the cottage when you arrived, Mr Gammage, we—'

'Sid,' the man said.

Dan gave a brief nod. 'I'd like to hear you both talk about your encounter. That way I won't put Tony through having to wait for a repeat performance from Alex.' He gave Sid a long stare and Tony lost any softening of tension he'd started to feel.

Alex's hand crept along the table edge until their fingers touched.

'I've been away from home working,' Sid told Dan without hesitation. 'I wanted to get back and check on my boys. This job is lasting a lot longer than I expected. That's a nuisance but I need the money.'

'When was the last time you were here?' Dan asked.

Sid frowned. 'Don't remember the date. Several weeks now.'

Dan's surprised reaction was a good performance. 'Really? You weren't here in the last few days, then? Possibly more than once?'

'No.' It was Sid's turn to look puzzled and Tony could have sworn it wasn't put on.

Alex shifted in her chair. She hung on every word and he wondered what she made of Sid's denial. There was no solid reason not to believe him.

Harding came into the room and pulled a chair up at Dan's shoulder. 'Detective Constable LeJuan Harding,' he said. Tony sensed Alex smiling and raised a brow at her. She wiped the smile from her face at once.

'Mr Gammage,' Dan said, and Sid didn't offer familiarity this time. 'Our records show you own a Yamaha motorbike. 1998 m 500, dark blue and black. Is that how you got to Underhill this evening?'

'No, it's still at the yard I work out of.'

'How did you get here, then? We know your van is in a shed near your cottage.'

'Got a bus then hitched the last bit.'

'Why didn't you use your motorbike?' Dan rested his elbows on the table and used a conversational tone.

'I've got a heavy work schedule. I'm going to be in trouble for leaving in the first place, but if I'd got the bike out I'd have been overheard. I slipped away to the nearest bus station.'

Harding made a couple of notes in his book. Dan glanced at the constable and nodded approval. 'Why aren't you free to come and go, Mr Gammage?'

Sid stood up and took off his anorak. He draped it over the back of his chair and Tony could almost hear him using the diversion to think, and fast. 'I am free to come and go. But I've got a contract. A certain number of trips in a certain amount of time. I'm well paid and I want to keep the job; I won't if I mess about and get behind. I'm going to have to hope I can talk my way out of leaving for Harwich again tonight.'

'You intend to leave again – with Scoot on his own and Kyle missing?'

Sid surged to his feet. 'What the fuck are you doing about finding my boy? Why are you sitting here jawing at me when there's a thirteen-year-old out there somewhere on his own – or with some crazy?'

Dan leaned back in his chair and clasped his hands behind his head. 'Feel better? Let off a bit of steam, have you? Or was that a smokescreen you were blowing?'

'We're talking about my son,' Sid said, still on his feet. 'He's been gone since yesterday. I'm not letting off steam. I'm scared, you tosser.'

Alex took hold of Tony's hand and held on tightly. She turned to him and pain was written on her face, pain and fear. Kyle had already become special to her.

'Harding,' Dan said. 'How about some coffee. Sound good to anyone?'

Mumbled responses followed and Harding slipped along the back passage to the kitchens.

'Do you sleep in your cab when you're away, or have you got a place somewhere?'

Sid took moments to change gears. 'Sometimes in the cab. Not if I can help it. When things run late in Harwich there's no choice. I've got a room in Northampton – at the yard. It's not much but I don't need anything but a place to sleep and wash up. Sooner I'm finished with this stint, the better.'

Scuffing his heels, Harding returned. 'They'll bring it through,' he said, and sat down again.

'I've got something I'd like you to look at,' Dan said, flipping open the file he'd put on the table. 'Not the best thing to look at but take your time, please. It's important. Do you know this woman?'

Sliding into his chair again, Sid bent over what Tony could see was a woman's photo – a close-up of her face and shoulders. The dead woman, he thought.

'Gawd,' Sid murmured. He looked closer. 'She was strangled, poor bugger.' He looked up at Dan.

'I just want you to tell me if you've seen her before.'

'No.' Sid let out a long breath. 'Poor woman. She was strangled, wasn't she? And knocked about as well? No, I never saw her before.' He turned his face away.

'You're sure?'

Sid nodded, yes. He looked a bit sick. 'Who is she?'

'That's what I was asking you about. If you'd seen her or knew her. So far she hasn't been identified. I thought you might have come back because of her.'

Alex increased the pressure on Tony's hand.

'What do you mean?' Sid asked.

'There had been an idea she might be your wife.'

The totally blank stare Sid gave Dan couldn't be manufactured unless he was a RADA graduate. 'I haven't seen or heard from my wife for years,' he said. 'It can't be too long to suit me. And this isn't her. That one would be about 35 for starters. This woman's older. Nothing alike.'

'Where is your wife?' Dan asked. 'You're still married?'

Sid put his hands over his face and rubbed. His fingers trembled.

'I don't know where she is. Haven't seen her since she left us ten or so years ago. And yes, we're still married. Wouldn't know how to find her. Don't want to. I want to know what's being done to find Kyle.'

The unpleasant photo still lay on the table. Dan put the end of a long finger on the corner. 'Anything said here stays between us,' he said. 'Anytime you think you want a solicitor we'll call him or her for you or get you one.'

'Why the hell would I need a solicitor?'

'I'm giving you the option, is all. This woman's body was found in that copse in the field behind your cottage. Kyle found her.'

Laughter from the bar penetrated absolute silence in the dining room.

Liz Hadley came through with a tray and paused in the doorway, evidently sensing the strained atmosphere.

Quickly, Dan slid the photo into the envelope. 'Thank you, Liz,' he said. 'Leave the tray please. We'll deal with it.'

Tight-lipped, Liz walked away. Alex reached for mugs but Harding stood up and said, 'I'll do that. Four coffees?'

They each took a mug but ignored a plate of sandwiches.

'He's only a kid,' Sid said. 'No one would take seeing a dead body like that well, not easily, but at his age, it's going to mark him. Has he run away? Did he leave a note or tell Scoot?'

'We don't think so on either count,' Dan said. 'Scoot's shattered because Kyle's gone, and if there's a note we haven't found it.' He went on to explain what had happened at the clinic.

'So he was snatched. Who would . . . some sick bastard, that's who, that's what you think, don't you? You think he's been killed because whoever did the woman in thinks Kyle might be able to finger him. Did Kyle say he saw the killer?'

Everyone sat still and silent.

Surely, Tony thought, if the killer had been Sid and Kyle knew it, he would have been in a terrible state. The kid wouldn't have been able to hide it all completely. That was a rubbish idea.

'I'd prefer to think Kyle's alive and well, Mr Gammage,' Dan said finally. 'If Kyle knew who the killer was, I don't think he could have kept it to himself. Alex, did you agree to come here from the cottage with the boys' father?'

'Yes,' she said clearly, raising her chin and meeting Dan's eyes. She launched into a detailed description of what she had done to leave the Dog and ride to the fields behind Underhill and delivered a slightly more halting account of searching the out buildings where Sid found her.

Tony moved his chair closer to hers, thinking about what he already knew, that Alex would always be her own woman and she'd do what she thought she must.

'Thank you,' Dan was saying.

Harding continued to write in his notebook and a man with a Scandinavian appearance tapped on the doorframe.

'Barry,' Dan said. 'Any luck?'

'Yes. Some. If you can break away, sir.'

Dan got up. 'This is Detective Constable Harding's partner, Detective Constable Trafford,' he said. 'He's been working on some details for me. I'll be right back.'

Tony and Alex drank coffee. Sid sat and stared into space. He looked like hell. Too tired to sleep, too tired to stay awake. His eyes were red-rimmed, the whites bloodshot.

Harding looked over his notes and appeared to edit them.

'This is horrible,' Alex said. Tony might have guessed she'd never manage to remain silent, or to stop herself from trying to comfort Sid. 'Detective Chief Inspector O'Reilly is a good man, good at his job. He may not seem to have any leads but you can be sure he's making progress.'

'Can I?' Sid said, and sighed. 'How? He hasn't shown me any. Sorry. You mean well. I don't understand what's happened or why anyone would take Kyle unless he knows something that could be inconvenient. And why haven't they found someone who saw him taken?'

'There are a few cottages near the clinic,' Tony said. 'The people who live there are all old and some are bedridden. I see the visiting nurse stopping in and meals get delivered. I don't suppose the police would get much joy there.'

Sid had straightened his back. He held his mug between two fingers and pushed it back and forth. 'There's got to be someone.' he said. 'That dead woman. Did anyone see her around here before?'

'No,' Tony said automatically. 'Except one of the ladies who runs Leaves of Comfort. It's a tea shop.'

'Who is she?' Sid leaned forward. 'She runs a shop? She must know what's what around here,' he added.

Tony caught Alex's eye and gave a slight

shake of his head. Best not over-involve the sisters.

'If she . . . If that dead woman came through here, someone else must have seen her. The article in the paper . . .' He left his mouth open and his eyes looked down. 'It must have been in the news.' He looked up again. 'I don't get to see a paper with my schedule and there's no TV in my room. Has there been anything?'

Tony clenched the muscles in his jaw. He felt suddenly ill at ease, as if the atmosphere around him had changed. Or as if he was missing something important. 'We can get you the papers from the last few days. The little local one doesn't usually have anything interesting to write about so it's full of all this.'

Harding crossed his arms and kept his eyes lowered.

Dan appeared from the passageway. 'Don't get excited but there's progress at last,' he said, although he didn't look as if he'd won the lottery. He seemed to hesitate, looking from the group at the table to the papers in his hands. 'It might be better if we asked Tony and Alex to leave now,' he said.

Tony started to get up.

'Unless they aren't interested, I'm fine with them staying,' Sid said. 'They've cared about my kids – got a stake in them, I'd say.'

'If you're sure?'

Sid nodded, yes.

'Right.' Dan sat down again. 'We've reached Mr Gary Podmore. I believe he's your boss.'

For an instant, Sid looked startled, but then he

said, 'Yes,' and rubbed at his eyes. 'I'm just a driver. I do as I'm told. Ordinary bloke. This is a good job for me. All I want is to keep my family together. Nothing fancy. But I ran up a lot of debts over the years. It's hard to get ahead. I want my boys to have a decent chance in life.'

'Yes,' Dan said. 'I think that's what most of us want for our kids. Mr Podmore backs up the story that your job is routine. You say you make special trips and you're paid big money for them. We'll probably be speaking with Mr Podmore again just to clarify things. Are you sure there's nothing criminal—'

'No!' Sid slammed his hands down on the table. 'I drive all night and sometimes into the middle of the morning. It's not easy. Get loaded up one end – someone else does the loading – and then I don't even see the truck till the next job. Only thing is I don't get any downtime except for a few hours' kip if I'm lucky. That's why the pay is good. I wouldn't want to do it forever but you can do just about anything for long enough to build a nest egg.'

'You aren't on the Podmore books, is that correct?'

Sid frowned. 'I hadn't thought about it but I suppose that would be right. This is separate, something Gary does for other people's good more than himself. Gary gives me my pay check. Now I think about it, I did know it was separate. But when I want to, or the job's over, I can go back to my old job.'

'Sounds as if it's working out well all around,' Dan said.

205

'It would be if Kyle was here,' Sid said, and rocked from side-to-side in his chair. 'You must have some thoughts about what's happened to him.'

'We've got ideas,' Dan said. 'Do you think he could have gone looking for you?'

'He hasn't taken his bike.' Sid poured more coffee, which had to be cold, and gulped it down. 'I suppose he could be trying to catch up with me. He wouldn't go without Scoot though. And you all said he was at that vet place. He's not the sort of lad to walk away from responsibility. The woman there told him to wait for her. That's what they said.'

Dan ran a finger down the top sheet in his stack of papers.

'You said there was progress,' Sid said. 'What? You must have found out something about Kyle.'

'I was thinking about getting a clearer picture of some of the players in this case,' Dan said, not looking up.

'Tell me what you know! Don't fuck with me, O'Reilly or you'll be sorry.'

'Will I?' The detective achieved something close to a cherubic smile. 'I do hope not. That'll do it for now then. I'll ask you to stay at your cottage, Mr Gammage. We'll transport you there.'

'Bloody hell.' Gammage's face gleamed with sweat. 'I'm not playing games with you. There's no reason to stop me from going where I want to go. I've got to get to work and I want Kyle found.'

A brief glance passed between Dan and Harding. 'No,' Dan said, 'I can't make you stay but I thought you'd want to.'

'I do. But I can't.' Sid got to his feet and swung his anorak from the back of the chair. 'If someone could give me a lift to a bus, I'll check in with you every couple of hours. Unless I can help here. Can I?'

'No,' Dan told him. 'Do you have any objection to Scoot staying in Tony and Alex's care? And Kyle if necessary, when we get him back?'

Sid looked at the floor. 'No objection.' He took out his wallet and pulled out a wad of notes. 'If I see Scoot again now it'll only upset him more. Give him this. And in case anyone has any questions about Tony and Alex looking after the boys, you all heard me agree. And you know where to find me.'

Dan started for the front door of the restaurant. 'I'll take you out and get you a lift.'

Raising his brows at Alex, Tony got up and went to the windows at the far side of the room and she came to stand beside him. They watched Dan talking to an officer while Sid stood apart.

She dropped her voice, 'Did I hear what I thought I did?'

'I think so,' Tony said quietly. 'It could have been a genuine slip.'

'So what do we do?'

'Figure out why he would lie about seeing a paper – if he did, and it sounded like it. We don't want to make trouble for them if there's nothing there.'

Twenty-Seven

After another night at Corner Cottage, this one spent on the couch vacated by Tony who had brought in an air mattress, Alex was glad to move her stiff body around.

When she got back from dropping a dejected Scoot off at school, she dragged herself into the cottage with thoughts of the comfortable bed at her house swimming around her head. Come to that, she could use the room she kept at the Black Dog and pull rank while she slept.

Scoot worried her. He'd passed on her suggestion that he stay home from school. He said he was better there with his mind taken off Kyle a bit. But the light had left Scoot's eyes and he dragged along, looking at the ground. Like Alex – only with so much more understandable reason – he was desperate for news of his brother. He feared the worst, of that she was sure. But so did she. She kept going over events leading up to his disappearance, searching for a way it could have been avoided. Nothing, except a nagging idea that she should have been able to help somehow.

She had paused at the front door, looking out at a morning when mist tucked itself into the creases in rooftops, into the pointed rocks on top of dry stone walls, even hovered above the gardens and along the road. Cottages where lights were still on inside, and the Black Dog with smoke from the chimneys starting to rise in darker wisps, looking soft as if the misty air were a gauze filter drawn across them. It all seemed more enigmatic than inviting.

Alex shut the door firmly. Giving in to fear would only make her sad, more introspective – and useless.

Bacon. She smelled it the instant she reoriented to her surroundings. Tony cooked a mean egg and bacon breakfast but she hadn't expected him to do anything like that here. Still, she smiled a little at the thought of fresh food and a cup of strong coffee.

In the kitchen, she was startled to see Lily at the stove, an apron over her black work dress, spooning sizzling bacon fat over eggs in a frying pan. Bacon and fried bread, tomatoes and a pile of mushrooms were keeping warm on a platter atop an unlit burner.

Tony sat in the corner behind a tiny, scrubbed wood table that could be folded down against the wall when not in use. He looked disgustingly well-rested and pleased with himself. An overnight bag had come with his air mattress and he'd clearly showered and dressed in a clean sweater and trousers with the sparkling white collar of a shirt crisply visible at his neck.

She ran both hands through her hair and rubbed. 'Don't you look smug, Dr Harrison? You obviously slept well.' He was the solid presence she needed.

'I did offer you my air mattress,' he reminded her, and he had – with or without him in it.

209

She wrinkled her nose. 'You needed the extra length. Morning, Mum. You look spiffy, too. I'm letting the side down but I clean up nicely. Let me take over for you there.'

'You sit down,' Lily said. 'You both need time to think and get yourselves sorted out – personally, I mean. You're both worn out and you, Miss Alex, have got to stop running off into dangerous situations without as much as letting us know where you are.'

'If I'd told you what I was going to do yesterday, you'd have slowed me down. I might have missed Sid altogether and that would have been a pity. It didn't feel so great at the time, but in retrospect, it was the best thing that could have happened.'

'I didn't expect him to take off for Northampton or wherever last night,' Tony said. 'How could he go before knowing Kyle's safe?'

Lily looked over her shoulder. 'I've got a theory on that. I think he knows where Kyle is and isn't worried about the boy.'

'Oh, I hope you're right, Mum,' Alex said, although she doubted the theory. 'We're getting on toward forty-eight hours. That's way too long. Scoot's brave face is slipping and the self-sufficient act isn't fooling anyone. Sid popping in like he did and then leaving again hasn't helped.'

'I thought I might go and take a look at this Podmore operation Sid works for,' Tony said nonchalantly, not even flinching when Lily all but dropped his plate on the table in front of him. 'I want to see exactly what the place looks like and the activity going on. What Sid's quick

210

departure did for me was raise a whole lot of suspicions.

'Dad would lend me his car, not that I think Sid would recognize my Range Rover if I was unlucky enough to have him see me. But it might be a good idea to make sure.'

'You will not, Tony,' Alex said. Her mum had put a mug of coffee on the table for her and she swallowed a mouthful too fast. It was hot and she coughed.

'I'll pretend you didn't say that,' Tony said, digging into his food with relish. 'Lily, you can cook my breakfast anytime,' he said.

Alex's throat burned and her eyes teared up. 'You can't go on your own,' she sputtered.

That got her a pitying look and no answer.

'I wish neither of you would keep taking things into your own hands,' Lily said. 'Dan is working hard. I see his people all over the village, and we know they're doing a lot we don't see. Why not let them do their work?'

'Do you think Sid would have showed up at the Dog last night if I hadn't gone to their cottage? He wouldn't have had any idea of a connection to the pub so why would he?'

Lily kept cooking. She said, 'He might have gone there anyway. Don't you think Scoot had told him where he's working?'

'No,' Alex said. 'I don't know why, but I'm sure he didn't. When I mentioned it, Sid didn't show he knew what I was talking about. From what I can gather, Scoot started with us after the boys were left alone and if I had to guess I'd say he's making extra money in case they need it to

211

live on. And that's probably part of why he didn't tell his father. He was afraid Sid wouldn't like it. Also, it's obvious they're supposed to keep to themselves and now that's been splintered.'

'I agree,' Tony said.

'It's an awful thing for a boy of that age to have so much responsibility. When I asked, he said they have money and everything's paid for. The rent and so forth. But I do think he's very worried and now, with Kyle gone, I don't know how long he'll hold it all together.' Lily put a plate in front of Alex, brought two full toast racks to the table, and joined them.

'Scoot's stronger than you think,' Alex said. 'He's introverted, yes, and naturally quiet, yes, but I also think he's probably got a steel spine.'

'He may need it,' Tony said. 'We know there's a lot wrong going on, but I won't be surprised if it turns out trouble is closer to home for Scoot and Kyle.'

'If Kyle ever shows up,' Lily said quietly.

Surprised at her mother's comment, Alex took hold of one of her hands. 'Mum, he's coming back, I know he is. He's got to.' Her lips trembled as she brought them together.

'There's an angle I've thought of,' Tony said. 'I wonder how the rent on the cottage gets paid – other than when Sid shows up like he did last night and left money for Scoot. That's all part of the Gimblet holdings. We can't ask Joan about it but agents who would handle the property would know if the rent was paid up and how.'

'And they won't tell you,' Lily said, sounding exasperated. 'Tell Dan your idea.'

'So that he can tell me to bugger off?' Tony cleared his throat. 'Sorry, but I'm browned off with the way the coppers keep things close to their chests. If I speak to them, can we be sure they'll follow up?'

'If they listen – which they should – they'll look harder at Sid than they may be looking already,' Alex said. 'Not that I'm so bothered about that anymore. I just don't want to say anything that sounds like an accusation if all it does is bring more trouble on the Gammages – if Sid hasn't done anything, that is.'

Tony narrowed his eyes in thought.

'I'm going to get cleaned up,' Alex told them.

When she got back downstairs she expected Tony to be gone and planned to make sure she either caught up with him if he went after Sid, or that she followed him.

He was sitting where she'd left him. 'Lily's gone to work. Mary called. I always expect to hear Harriet, not Mary on the phone. She says she would appreciate discussing the woman whose picture was in the paper.'

Alex stiffened. She gripped the back of the nearest chair. 'She already spoke to the police about that. What else could she possibly have to say?'

'Sounded as if she'd like both of us to go to their cottage,' Tony said. 'It would be easy to brush them off but too often they've been right on with something.'

Twenty-Eight

'You can understand why I hesitate to go back to the police,' Mary said. 'I don't think they believed a word I said the first time.'

Harriet had already served tea and biscuits they were still too full from breakfast to eat.

'Is that what you think, Harriet?' Tony asked.

She sat in her chintz, overstuffed chair and crossed her wool-stockinged ankles neatly. For a moment she concentrated on her tea and the currant biscuit sitting in solitary splendor on a beautiful floral plate atop one arm of her chair.

'How should I know?' she said finally. Today she wore a plum tweed skirt and woolen cardigan, a plum silk blouse – and plum hose. The trouble in her eyes belied her indifferent tone. 'Mary hasn't said if I can be trusted with her bombshell information either.'

Oliver, the sisters' gray tabby, sauntered his sinuous body to sit at Tony's feet. The cat placed all four feet tidily together and passed a pink tongue around his lips.

'You wouldn't like my biscuit,' Tony told him.

'Yes, he would,' Harriet said. 'Shortbread is his favorite. It's the butter, I think. It's up to you, of course, but he would definitely appreciate a crumb.'

Tony offered the treat.

Oliver turned his head aside as if offended.

Tony placed the crumb on the carpet.

Oliver sniffed it, gave Tony a dramatically evil glance, and chewed the morsel, spreading small crumbs in his wake. But these he cleaned up before walking slowly over to stare at orange, one-eyed Max curled on Mary's lap.

'He doesn't really hate Max,' Mary said. 'He just has to keep up his reputation.'

'Hates him,' Harriet contradicted. 'Wishes he'd drop dead instantly.'

Since Alex had seen the two cats getting cozy when it was really cold, she grinned. 'Oliver just has to keep the newcomer on his toes. What did you want to see us about?' Drinking tea and chatting was all very nice, but she and Tony needed to get to work.

'What's happened to Kyle's kitten?' Harriet asked. 'That baby creature means a lot to him.'

The question startled Alex but it was Tony who answered. 'Naruto, as Kyle named her, is at the clinic. Radhika is looking after her. She's not big enough to be adopted out yet.'

Mary gave a little titter at that. 'If that lovely boy comes back, I'd like to see how you intend to give his cat to someone else. She may be one of the main things that keeps him strong – needing to get back to her. Scoot told us all about it.'

'We just need to get Kyle back,' Alex said. 'I'm not thinking about anything else.' She would be now. Who knew what Kyle's living arrangements would be, if and when he got home. She breathed through her mouth and felt sick with worry.

'Of course,' Harriet said, but she didn't look either Alex or Tony in the eye.

Mary took off her thick-lensed glasses and polished them on a lace handkerchief. 'My eyes are rather bad,' she said.

A huge understatement. 'Yes,' Alex said. 'But you do so well. You've learned to make a lot of accommodations, haven't you?'

'Exactly.' Sitting straighter in her velvet wing-back chair, Mary's face lost any sign of the sweet old lady. 'I have and I'm very good at them. I may have to start reminding certain people that I'm still the most reliable dart player at the Black Dog.'

'As if you'd ever let any of us forget,' Harriet said with a half-smile, but she didn't remind her sister that she played more from long practice and instinct for the board than her ability to see.

'The first time she came she didn't stay,' Mary said vaguely, picking fluff from Max's back and rolling it into a ball.

Alex looked at Tony who had not reacted.

Mary shifted in her chair, accommodating her arthritic hip. 'Didn't even order anything. I'm not usually behind the counter, you know. Not often, anyway.'

'What are you talking about?' Harriet wasn't usually snappish but she spat out the question. 'We can't waste these people's time with rambling.'

'Explaining is not rambling.' Mary put her glasses on again. 'I'm setting up what happened. If you're bored, why not go for a walk, or read a book?'

They all waited for her to continue.

She looked at each of them. 'She didn't stay the first time. Hardly got through the door. And the man didn't come all the way in at all. Just held her arm and from the expression on her face, it was painful.'

'Just a moment, please,' Tony said, shifting forward. 'Is this the woman you think looked like the one in the paper of the one of the dead woman?'

'An E-fit photo,' Alex added. 'They say they can be really good.'

'It was her,' Mary said shortly. 'Whatever the man said to her, I couldn't hear him. He pulled her out.'

'This man, what did he look like?' Tony asked.

'I don't know. He was behind her, but he was rough and nasty. I would have called the police after I'd thought about it. I don't do these things without thinking carefully first. But she came back about five minutes later and seemed all right so there was nothing for me to report.'

'That's not true,' Harriet said, an unaccustomed flush on her neck. 'You never mentioned this man to me or to the police. You say you didn't because it didn't matter but now you change your mind. Why?'

Mary shook her head. She pressed her hands to her cheeks. 'I did think about it. I really did. But I already worried they wouldn't believe I'd seen the woman at all. If I told them about the man, too, they could have been convinced I was on a flight of fancy. Everyone thinks I'm as blind as a bat. I didn't say because I didn't want to be

217

embarrassed if it was nothing to do with anything. Now I'm so angry with myself. Silly pride and from a woman of my age. Dan will be furious with me . . . unless he doesn't believe me.'

'Mary,' Tony said, getting up, 'are you sure you saw a man come in behind this person?' He took the old lady's cup and saucer and went to pour her more tea.

He made Alex smile, despite how serious everything was. A man who was a natural care-taker wasn't always easy to find, or not among younger men.

'I'm absolutely sure,' Mary said. 'Why didn't I follow them and look outside? I would have been able to describe him then.'

'We all think of what might have been the best thing to do after the fact.' Tony gave her the cup and saucer again. 'Drink that and don't worry. We're with you and we'll help with this. What do you think you want to do?'

'You know what I have to do.' Mary gave him a watery smile. 'I have to go and see Dan O'Reilly. I'll call the parish hall and find out where he is.'

'Drink your tea,' Tony said. 'We'll go with you. Solidarity helps. Perhaps you didn't take any notice of this fellow.'

Mary choked on her tea. She found her hand-kerchief and touched it to her lips. 'Oh, no, not that. That way lies the doddery old lady reputation. Don't take any notice of her, they'd say. She imagines things and embellishes them. Absolutely not. Complete details this time.'

Harriet cleared her throat and set her own cup

and saucer aside. She still hadn't touched her biscuit. 'Something does worry me about this,' she said, keeping her eyes lowered.

'Tell us,' Alex said. 'We need to get all of our concerns out in the open.'

'Oh, look!' Harriet said. 'Those are flakes of snow, aren't they?'

Now Alex looked at Tony and they both raised their eyebrows. He went to the window and checked outside. 'Tiny flakes,' he said. 'They won't come to anything. It's much too early for that.'

'Stop shilly shallying about,' Mary said, with evident relish at turning the critical light on Harriet. 'Tell us what's on your mind.'

'It's nothing really. I'm probably worrying about nothing. But I just wondered if there was any possibility . . .' Harriet wound her handkerchief through her fingers.

'Yes,' Mary prompted. 'Get to the point.'

'Could this put you in danger, Mary? That's what I'm getting around to. Could someone decide they should put a stop to your giving evidence against them, especially since they've killed once?'

Twenty-Nine

Bill Lamb turned up the collar on his trench coat and tried to keep his attention on what Dan was saying, to him and to Harding and Trafford.

Radhika, standing on the other side of the High Street from the Black Dog, splintered his concentration. Either she was waiting for someone or wanted to give that impression – when she didn't look his way.

Since the other night when he'd got carried away at the veterinary surgery, no matter how innocent it might have seemed, he'd lectured himself to keep his distance. They came from two different worlds and although he thought, in weak moments, that he wanted to try making a real connection with her, he knew how impossible even trying for a future with him could make her life.

'Anything on tire tracks outside the clinic,' O'Reilly was saying. 'And don't bother telling me it was raining and muddy and a lot of people had been there that day. Tell me they got something from under a bush where the vehicle had parked to one side. Anything, but don't say there's still nothing.'

Bill felt Radhika staring at him. When he looked back she bowed her head and turned toward the green.

'There's still nothing, guv,' Harding said but he didn't risk one of his careless grins. 'Forensics did what you asked and went over everything a second time. Like before, there's fingerprints galore – and animal prints – but nothing we've been able to get a match from.'

'Right.' Dan crossed his arms tightly across his chest. 'Then I want the fingerprints of everyone who lives here. Not the bedridden ones, or the kids, but everyone over the age of twelve.

Even that could have holes in it if there were several of 'em.'

'It would have to be someone old enough to drive,' Trafford said. 'They couldn't have carried him away without someone seeing something.'

'Old enough to drive means able to drive for our purposes. And where there's farms, there's youngsters of ten who could get a vehicle to move. We just aren't going that far until we've eliminated the rest. Beat coppers canvassed the houses and businesses around . . .?'

'Nothing,' Harding announced. 'They didn't get replies at some of the cottages. Most likely because the people aren't ambulatory.'

'Do it again. You two this time. Split it up – it only takes one to knock an old-person's door. Who spoke to this Mrs Marroway, the one who was supposed to have called Radhika about the dog?'

'I'd have to check the log,' Trafford said. 'But I'll go back anyway.'

'I think I'll do it this time,' Bill said. 'Another call came in from forensics. They reckon they've got a minor detail on the murdered woman they'll be getting in touch about,' Bill said.

Radhika was walking very slowly toward the pond at the village green.

'Why don't you pop over there and ask Radhika to go through that conversation with Mrs Marroway again?' Dan said, indicating the lone figure on the green. 'Now might be a good time.'

Fortunately, Bill thought, he wasn't the blushing kind. He didn't bother with subterfuge and pretend he'd only just noticed Radhika. 'Will do. I'll catch up with you, guv.'

It was spitting with rain. He jogged across the road and walked rapidly after her. She wore a dark raincoat over a gold-edged sari in orange and yellow, but she had only the thin silk scarf over her hair.

When he drew near he called, 'Radhika, it's Bill.' He hated the thought of her being frightened by his approach.

She turned to face him, worry in everything about her, from her eyes to the guarded way she held her body. 'I'm sorry,' she said. 'I knew you'd see me and come over when you could. I shouldn't have done that.'

'Why not? Next time call out so I'm sure it's me you want.' As if he hadn't known very well. He tipped his hat farther over his eyes and offered her his arm. 'Let's find shelter. You're getting wet.'

She hesitated a moment before putting a hand beneath his elbow and holding the material of his trench coat. 'Under that tree?' She indicated a massive beech that was holding on to its leaves still.

Without comment, she walked in that direction, knowing that if his colleagues were watching they'd see him walk Radhika out of sight and have plenty of snide remarks when they saw him again.

Far enough beneath the tree's canopy, they could watch rain water dripping heavily from leaves at the outer ends of the branches but it was dry closer to the trunk. There was no meeting of sky and land to be seen. Everything melded into one fuzzy grey wall. The pond had a roiling mist across much of its surface and ducks hugged the bank, their heads tucked beneath wings.

If he hadn't clamped her hand to his side, she would have moved away. 'Doesn't the weather here bother you?' he asked. *What did they say about the British? Without the weather, they'd have nothing to talk about?*

'I love it here. Everything about it. Sunny days, grey days, stormy days – and when it snows I am happiest of all.'

Her voice, soft but clear, had too much of an effect on him. 'Well this may be a happy year for you. It's supposed to be a very snowy winter.' *More weather.*

She took a long, deep breath and let it out slowly. 'Do you think Kyle will come back?' she said.

'Yes,' he said with conviction, knowing he should be less definite. 'We're doing everything we can to find him. I think there's someone who knows a lot about what happened. Well, that's an obvious statement, but I mean someone besides whoever took him – if that's what happened.'

She put the back of a hand to her mouth. Her very dark eyes were huge. 'I think so, too. I think they could come and tell you if they had the courage.'

'You think more than one person did this? That doesn't have to mean one of them did it against their will and the other is causing them to keep quiet.'

'No.' She shook her head. 'I don't know anything except this is my fault. If I could turn back the time, I would.'

He studied her. 'What do you mean, your fault? How could it be?'

'Because I left Kyle alone in the cottage. If I'd said I would come for Katie once Tony got back, or just said I couldn't leave because I was on duty, it wouldn't have happened. I didn't think. I often don't think.'

'You mean you should have told an elderly woman she had to look after a big dog until someone felt like getting her? And if you'd stayed, who's to say you wouldn't have been taken, too?' He was supposed to have her go through that evening again, from the beginning, but she seemed emotionally fragile.

'At least we would have been together,' Radhika said. 'He wouldn't have been so afraid. Bill, he must be very afraid.'

If he's still alive.

She watched him as if she trusted him to make it all right. 'I'm glad I'm not looking for you, too,' he said.

When she leaned against him his muscles tensed. He put a hand on the back of her head and held her there.

'You are not responsible. This Mrs Marroway. We've been told she's spry and gets about a lot. But she's uncooperative. Our Officer Trafford talked to her and said she was annoyed at his interruption. She more or less ignored him and said she was talking to her sister on the phone. He tried again, twice, but either she was out or

224

didn't answer the door both times. I'm going back this afternoon. We'll make getting to her a priority.'

'Have you checked to find out which number the call came from? The one I answered?'

'I'm sure that's been done,' he said, but he wasn't. 'There's only one Mrs Marroway and she lives in that cottage.'

Radhika looked up into his face. 'Will you ask her if she went somewhere that night?'

'Yes.'

'Ask if she saw anything when she was walking, if she was walking. They say she walks at all hours. I wonder if she saw a vehicle going toward or away from the clinic.'

'I see where you're going with this but you would be more likely to see something than her. You said you left immediately for her cottage. You'd have passed any vehicle.'

She spread her hand on his chest. 'No, Bill. Not necessarily. I went between two of the cottages near the clinic and walked down the front side. I wouldn't have seen someone back there.'

'Stop blaming yourself. She called you, you said. Then I think she must have let Katie out and the dog ran to the Black Dog.'

'Bill, I think I made a really big mistake. Her voice . . . the voice sounded unusual, very high. I need to hear her speak again. I thought and thought and I've decided it was a man pretending to be a woman.'

Thirty

The sisters walked into the parish hall with their shoulders brushing. Taking strength from one another, Tony supposed. He had tried, as had Alex, to reassure both of them but Mary in particular was visibly shaken.

She had climbed the steps outside the hall extremely slowly, having refused to use her walker. She didn't want to look like 'a doddery old fool,' she insisted.

Harriet took her hand and they went together toward Dan O'Reilly's disaster of a desk.

'Can I help you, ladies?' Tall, blond and self-assured Officer Miller came from behind the screen, her arch smile as tight as Tony remembered. Then she saw Tony and Alex and the smile was an instant memory. 'DCI O'Reilly isn't back yet,' she said.

Harriet glanced behind her and caught Tony's eye. 'We'll wait,' she told him. 'No need to keep you and Alex, though.'

'No,' Miller said. 'I'm sure these two can manage on their own. Why don't you tell me what's on your mind and I'll pass it along, if necessary?'

'Officious prat,' Alex muttered.

Tony chuckled. She could be relied on to interject the unexpected.

He got folding chairs for Harriet and Mary and

set them up in front of Dan's desk where precarious piles of papers hung on despite all odds and every inch of surface he could actually see bore deep scratches.

'We'll stay with you, unless you want to get rid of us,' he told the sisters jocularly, and grabbed two more chairs. 'No point in rushing back out into the rain.'

Officer Miller ignored him. She sat in Dan's chair and pulled a memo pad toward her. 'So what is it?'

'I'd like to wait for DCI O'Reilly, please,' Mary said. 'He would only want to hear what I say for himself, anyway.'

'You can trust me to be a good judge of that,' Miller said. She glanced at Alex for the first time and Tony wondered what could have led to such deep dislike. Officer Miller released the malign expression from her face only to replace it with a basilisk stare that was even more alarming and pointless.

'Any chance of some tea?' Alex asked sweetly. 'I think you should have some bags and boiling water. They were sent over from the Dog much earlier, weren't they?'

Without another word, Miller headed back behind the screen.

'I'd like to see what's going on back there, wouldn't you?' Alex said.

'If you work out how, I'm with you.' Tony pushed his coat back and stuck his hands in his pockets.

Harriet looked back at them. 'Tea bags?' Her lip curled.

As Alex and Tony dropped onto the hard, metal chairs, the rumble of voices approached the front doors and Dan came in with Bill and Harding. The detective constable nodded at them, gathered what looked like a large-scale map, and left again.

Dan and Bill spoke in low voices by the door. Bill took off his hat and ran his fingers through his hair. He looked troubled.

'Afternoon,' Dan said, striding toward his desk. 'A reception committee. Now what?' He tossed his coat over the back of a spare chair and his hat on the seat before sitting down.

Bill had gone behind the screen.

'I was just telling Tony how much I'd like to see what you're hiding behind the screens,' Alex said. 'Academic curiosity only, of course.'

Tony looked sideways at her wishing she were more circumspect, just occasionally.

'That's why the screens are there. To shield all our fascinating secrets from nosy parkers' prying eyes.' Dan laughed, softening what he probably sincerely meant.

'I'm the one who wants to talk to you,' Mary said. 'I should have made myself clearer when we came in before. A black woolen hat and sunglasses, I think, but I was in a bit of . . . I was caught off guard by what happened and then I didn't reconstruct it all as I should have. He was a lot bigger than her.'

Tony winced. He kept his eyes on Dan.

The man was good with people, Tony would give him that, even when they didn't make any sense. He leaned forward over his desk and said,

'Let's take this slowly, Mary. Back up and start again. Who was bigger? Who wore a woolen hat and sunglasses?'

Mary's profile showed blotches of color in her powdered face. 'Stupid of me. I'm very nervous, Dan, that's why I'm . . . yes, I'll start again. That's the sensible thing to do.'

She reached for Harriet who held her hand once more.

'I didn't tell you everything. About the woman who came into Leaves of Comfort to buy Bath buns and Vimto.'

'The woman you think matches the description of the dead woman?'

'Yes. Yes, of course. She came in twice. Or she came in, went out, and came in again. It was all one event really, d'you see?'

'I'm sure you'll make certain I do.'

'Take a breath, Mary,' Alex said and patted her shoulder.

'She came in for those things but before she could get them a man put his head around the shop door and made a clicking sound with his tongue.'

Clicking sound? And now there was a hat and sunglasses but before the man had been behind the woman so he couldn't be seen? Could be, Tony thought, that coming here had been a horrible idea, at least until Mary settled down. He caught Alex's eye. She was as off-balance as he was.

'You said you couldn't see the man,' Harriet said.

Tony barely stopped himself from groaning.

229

'You meant fully see him, didn't you,' he said. 'Because she hid most of him.'

Dan shook his head as if in disbelief at the prompt.

'It's not entirely that,' Mary said. 'When he clicked his tongue, she went toward him, completely cutting him off from me. It wasn't a sunny day. That should have seemed odd with his sunglasses. But he did have the hat on so one could say he was prepared for all eventualities.'

Mary frowned, concentrating, while they all waited. Tony held his breath.

'I'd forgotten the hat and glasses until just now,' Mary said. 'Oh, I do hope my memory isn't failing. I couldn't bear that.'

'I'm sure it's not,' Dan said, matter-of-factly. 'Police questioning can be a bit daunting. Tell me everything in your own time.'

Miller approached with four mugs of tea on a tin tray. She left the tray on a corner of Dan's desk and didn't ask if she should bring a fifth mug.

'You can have mine,' Harriet said, to no one in particular.

'And mine,' Mary added. '*Tea bags.*' On her lips the words sounded like quiet outrage.

All the mugs stayed where they were.

'She went to him and I saw his hand around her arm. He pulled her outside. There was no conversation at all. Out she went and the door closed.'

Dan appeared to be counting off points on his fingers. 'So, woman in. Man in. Woman and man out. Now we get to the woman coming in again.'

'Absolutely,' Mary said. 'Then it was exactly

the way I explained it before. She bought Bath buns and Vimto and left.'

'I do see,' Dan said. 'You can't be more specific about the man?'

'I'm sorry, I was a bit upset by his rudeness and the way he made that awful noise as if he were calling ducks. Frightful. Her shoes were wet and you know what that does to color. But they were blue.'

Thirty-One

Dan rested his elbows on the desk, put his hands over his ears and shook his head slowly from side to side. No, no, no. This damnable village was enough to drive the sanest of men mad, not that he thought he qualified for the sane moniker anymore, if he ever had.

He hadn't attempted to speak to anyone since the entourage had left the building. At least Tony and Alex both had the grace to shrug and turn up their palms.

'You OK, boss?'

He raised his face to see Bill and gave another negative shake of the head. 'Tell me I didn't imagine that our victim was shoeless when we got to her.'

'She was barefoot,' Bill said. 'The boy, Kyle, reckoned she was wearing trainers but we think he was too scared and confused to know much about anything.'

'It seems he was probably right,' Dan told him. 'Why would he come up with blue otherwise. She had on fancy trainers when he found the body. Which means someone swiped 'em before . . . who was the copper who got to Kyle first and saw the body?'

'Constable Burrows. He's the one who responded to Kyle's call first. Miller was right behind him.'

'Right. Get me Burrows – on the phone will do.'

His mobile already in his hand, Bill took off to find the constable's number.

'What the hell happened to them?' Dan asked himself aloud. He shoved himself back in the chair and clasped his hands behind his neck. 'That can't be. I'm desperate enough to make things up.' Some ideas were better left alone.

'Burrows, guv,' Bill said, jogging up and handing Dan the mobile.

'Burrows,' he said. 'DCI O'Reilly here. You were the one who went with Kyle Gammage after he called in the body, right?'

'Right, sir.'

'What did she have on her feet?'

Silence had Dan chewing the inside of his mouth. 'And I expect you were there when the police surgeon came.'

'No, she didn't get there for some time. SOCO was coming in, though. I passed them on my way out, sir. I wanted to get the boy away and there were plenty of uniforms without me.' The man took an audible breath. 'I don't remember what she had on her feet. I'll have to think about it.'

'Burrows, did you see the victim's feet?' Dan could imagine not noticing – or, unfortunately, he could imagine some people not noticing.

'No, sir,' Burrows said so quickly it sounded as if he were grabbing a lifeline. 'I didn't. The boy was in a terrible state. I gave a quick check for a pulse and obviously she was dead. She'd been dead a while.'

'Thanks,' Dan said. 'I may get back to you later.'

'What's going on?' Bill asked. He picked up a mug of cold tea and drank it down as if he didn't notice its condition.

'Pull up a chair,' Dan said. He filled his partner in on what Mary Burke had said.

Bill crossed his arms over his chest. He still wore his trench coat although it was soaked at the shoulders. So far he hadn't talked about his encounter with Radhika. 'So, one more character on the stage but the plot is just as much of a mystery. Or is it?' He looked up at Dan. 'It's not a leap to think that was the killer.'

'But what does it give us on him. Forget the hat and glasses or whatever. He was a lot heftier than the victim. That would cover a lot of men.'

'Or women,' Bill said. 'Not likely but some women are built like that. We can't rule it out.'

Dan didn't say just how unlikely he thought that was. 'Kyle saw a man from a bedroom window at the cottage. He said he was big but again, no useful details. We need to speak to the boy again.'

'We need to find him,' Dan muttered. 'Would your best guess be that he's done a runner or that he was snatched?'

233

'I don't know,' Bill said.

Dan shook his head slowly. 'Did Radhika have anything useful to add?'

'Yes.' Turning sideways on his chair and crossing his legs, Bill studied his own fist. 'First, she insists it's all her fault he's gone because she should have stayed with him. I hope I put the lid on that.'

His sergeant was more than enamored with Radhika, Dan thought. 'She'd better get over it.' If these two decided they wanted a future together, it could be a difficult match. Or maybe not. What the hell did he know?

'I'm going to this Mrs Marroway's myself,' Bill continued. 'On the phone she was very short and when Trafford went there – three times – he was either as good as turned away or he couldn't get any answer at the door. Radhika said something interesting though. She thinks the call she got at the clinic wasn't from a woman. The voice was artificially high-pitched and now she thinks the caller was a man pretending to be a woman. When she got to Marroway's cottage, the woman was out. And now we know Katie was at the Black Dog. Radhika wanted to know how long Katie had been at the pub which is a reasonable question.'

'It's a question that should have been asked before now,' Dan said. 'Why don't you try to speak to this woman Mrs Marroway now?'

Dan's mobile rang. He tucked it between ear and shoulder while he made some notes. 'O'Reilly,' he said, distracted. He covered the mouthpiece and said to Bill, 'The dog was at

234

the pub by the time Scoot came up to see me but I didn't ask him when she arrived there. Our Mrs Marroway has questions to answer . . .' He took his hand from the mouthpiece. 'Repeat, please. I didn't get all of that.'

He stared at Bill and felt muscles working in his own jaw. 'We're on our way,' he said.

'This is news we didn't want,' he told Bill. 'We've got another body. Adolescent male.'

Thirty-Two

The crime scene was behind the new youth center. Men in muddy overalls stamped with a firm's initials that meant nothing to Dan, stood aside from a SOCO tent he was surprised to see already erected.

A uniform sergeant unwound blue and white crime scene tape while a second officer hammered in stakes they were using to help secure the perimeter.

The sergeant saw Bill and Dan and came toward them. 'Bendix, sir,' he said. 'We're waiting for the police surgeon.'

Dan quelled the desire to say they were usually waiting for Dr Molly Lewis. 'Right. Who's in charge?'

'You sir,' Bendix said and reddened. 'I mean, apart from you there's a Detective Inspector Cooper who happened to see the vehicles going by.' He indicated an ambulance, a SOCO van

235

and three police cars. 'He's staying until you take over, he says.'

And the man was in with the victim, not Dan's favorite thing to find at his crime scenes. 'That's the youth center?'

Bendix put his hands on his hips and nodded, yes. 'Fanciest one I've ever seen. Not that I've seen many.'

The building covered a large area surrounded with what looked like fresh sod and planted with new trees here and there. Mostly one story, a much smaller, separate structure had two stories. The place looked as new as it was. Dan hadn't realized it was completely finished, but then, he hadn't seen it before. Over his left shoulder, in the distance, a rambling, yellow stone house stood on a flat-topped hill above terraced land. Numerous outbuildings were far enough from the house not to obstruct the view – or detract from its solitary charm.

'That's Woodway?' Dan asked. 'Mrs Gimblet's home?'

'Yes, sir. Woodway Farm, it's called. I believe the mayor's brother shares it with her and her son. There's a lot more of it you can't see from here.'

'Impressive.' He gave the sergeant a nod and carried on toward the tent. A man with sparse gray hair, a deeply-lined face and a notable belly hanging over his belt, came out to meet him. He had stripped off his SOCO suit and dropped it as he approached.

'Andy Cooper,' the man said. He didn't smile and from the purplish bags under his eyes and his shambling walk, Dan decided he might

236

actually be too worn out to care what impression he made. 'I was driving by so I thought I'd come and see if I could help.'

'Good of you, inspector,' Dan said and introduced himself and Bill. They all shook hands. 'Where are you headed? Or perhaps I should ask where you're from?'

'Harwich is my patch. I'm checking out some of the isolated outfits that might throw light on a case we're working on. Heading over to one or two small towns. Bradford on Avon for one. Nasty business you've got here.' He jabbed a thumb toward the tent behind him. 'Looks like a lot of anger went into that. Whoever put him in the ground didn't think it through properly. You know what that is over there, I take it.'

Dan cast about for what the man was talking about and realized there were signs of digging behind the tent – and that several of the workmen were leaning on shovels.

'The pile of dirt should have given me a hint,' Dan said, giving the grave a passing glance. 'Brain block. We've had a long few days.'

'Tell me about it,' Andy Cooper said. 'We need more hands but do we get 'em? No way. Just the usual bollockings about how long we're taking.'

'Anything in particular you noticed here?' Dan asked. 'We shouldn't keep you from what you want to be doing.'

'Apart from being able to smell anger around that kid, no. Your forensics people are coming in in dribs and drabs. Must have woken 'em up from sound sleeps.'

'Bit late for that,' Dan said. 'That's the thing with these country cases. Our people have to come quite a way and some of them don't get the concept of getting on it right now.'

Cooper must have felt Dan's impatience to get on. 'I'll cut out then,' he said. 'Let me know if you need to ask me anything.' He handed over a card, took one from Dan, and ambled toward a green Fiesta parked on a nearby lane.

'I wanted to ask what case he's on,' Bill said. 'But I figured he'd have said if he wanted us to know.'

Dan filled his lungs to capacity and let the air out slowly. 'Let's take a look, shall we?' It wasn't really a question.

Bendix had stood at a respectful distance but now he fell in behind the detectives.

Dan snapped his fingers and turned to the man. 'I remember you, don't I?'

'Previous case, sir. In Folly-on-Weir again. Strange one.'

Rolling his eyes, Dan said, 'It's always something strange in Folly, sergeant.'

At the closed flap to the tent he paused. He would never admit it but his heart rested in his throat and there was sweat on his back. He picked up two SOCO kits and pulled on his own, including the mask he hated. Bill did the same but didn't immediately move on. He scuffed at the ground and met Dan's eyes. 'I'm not looking forward to this, either. Alex and Tony—'

'Yeah,' Bill said. 'To say nothing of Scoot and his father. Bloody awful.'

He lifted the flap, ducked and walked in.

There should have been more activity but the crew who had got there were efficiently busy and one man pulled down his mask when he saw Dan. 'And you are?' he said, politely enough.

'DCI O'Reilly. This is my partner, DS Lamb.' He worked out his warrant card and held it out for the man to see. 'We're on a case in the area.' He balked at saying he thought this incident was related.

'We've been taking pictures and doing what we can without the pathologist's direction,' the man said, not bothering to identify himself. Most SOCOs were not police officers but purely forensics types. They marched to a very different drummer. 'No ID found yet. Want to take a look.'

'Thanks.' Unfortunately 'no' wasn't an acceptable answer.

He saw what he hadn't realized outside. Next to the victim a hole opened into the ground and from the way it looked, this had been where burial had taken place, not out there. 'A trench,' Dan said. 'They were digging a trench. Why?'

'Some sort of trouble with the new geo-thermal system. Take a look.' He waited until Dan peered down to see a tidy line of pipes that curved up and down and followed the trench to where it continued outside the tent. 'New fangled heating and cooling set-up. It's getting common enough, I've been told. They had trouble with it, sent for help from the outfit that put it in and they started digging, looking for the problem. They couldn't find anything above ground. Then they ran into their problem – the body buried in the trench and covered over. Apparently everything was put back fairly perfectly.'

The body lay under a sheet of heavy plastic used to protect it from the introduction of new residues. Dan pulled it back and stared. He felt an exclamation climbing to his lips but made sure he shut up.

'Is it him?' Bill said behind him.

Still holding up the plastic, Dan stepped back to let Bill see.

Bill dropped to his knees and looked closely at the head. 'Why would anyone do this?' he said. 'What could make them mad enough – or crazy enough to do it?'

The body was dressed in a torn, striped T-shirt and jeans with one leg ripped open from knee to hem. There was so much blood that the arms and exposed leg were caked. Bones protruded from the left lower leg where the jeans were torn. The feet and hands had been pummeled with something heavy and sharp enough to crush and mangle.

Blood made it impossible to know the victim's coloring.

Even worse, even more sickening, the face had been beaten until it resembled a bloody hamburger – flat, inhuman.

Dan had put gum in his mouth when he entered the tent. It didn't do much but at least it kept his stomach from emptying at the stench. There was earth liberally distributed all over the body, crammed into the holes that were all that was left of the nose and filling the gaping mouth.

'Holy Jesus,' Bill murmured and crossed

himself. His lips moved as if he were praying.

'What have we got?' Small, blond Dr Molly Lewis entered the tent with more technicians.

'A nightmare,' said Dan.

'Should I get hold of Sid Gammage to see what he thinks?' Bill asked. As experienced as he was, his complexion was gray. 'I could go and transport him.'

'No,' Dan said. 'I'd have to be sure myself before I'd do that.'

He glanced at Molly who looked back at him. She squared her shoulders. 'Right. I don't know how many photos have been taken but I'll want more. Turn on the recorder. Get the video going.'

Getting up slowly, Bill said, 'Look for whatever was used to strangle him.'

'Yes.' Dan didn't recall feeling much worse than this. 'And they should keep their eyes open for his shoes.'

Thirty-Three

Scoot leaned his bike against a wall at the back of Tony's clinic. He'd stuffed a comb into his backpack that morning and now he raked it through his hair, flattening it down as much as he could. Grateful it hadn't actually rained yet, he wiped the inside of his jacket over his damp-feeling face and used the same spot on his hands. His nails were clean enough, his jeans, too, his trainers were dusty, but he couldn't help that.

His stomach rumbled. He was using his lunch time to come here and he hardly remembered breakfast.

Shrugging back into his jacket, he checked to be sure his wallet was still in his jeans pocket and went to the door at the back of the cottage. A sign in front of the building said to come around here. Another sign on this door announced he should walk in and go through to the office – wherever that was.

He climbed the two outside steps and pushed the door open. The little hops and spins in his stomach didn't help a thing. A nasty thought stopped him for a moment. Kyle had been taken from here. He had probably been bundled out through this hallway. Scoot swallowed, closed his eyes for a moment, then worked to relax his jaw. His eyes prickled but Dad always said men didn't cry. He would laugh after he said it, but Scoot knew they were a family who only managed to stay together because they kept on being strong and loyal.

He couldn't relax.

It was a small place and he heard both barking and the sound of a voice from a room ahead and to the left. Another sign here let him know he'd come to the right place and he tapped the door tentatively.

Radhika – and Scoot knew her, had seen her before – swung open the door, a phone still at her ear. Scoot could tell she was surprised to see him but she waved him into a crowded room where animals rested in crates. Supplies and folders crowded a desk and the top of a filing cabinet and there were bottles of pills in a plastic tray.

'I'll call you back later,' Radhika said and put the phone aside. 'Scoot? It is Scoot, isn't it?'

'Yes,' he said in a wobbly voice that embarrassed him.

She frowned, and he was afraid she would cry. He wouldn't know what to do, if she did. Next he didn't know what to do when she put her arms around him and hugged.

Those tears he'd fought got dangerously close again.

She released him. 'I'm . . . I can tell you I'm worried because you must be also. Have you heard anything about Kyle?'

He shook his head. 'No. Nothing, and no one comes to say what's going on. I'm sure they think getting the information by listening to the adults is enough, but it isn't. When someone is missing as long as this, they're usually dead, aren't they?'

He hadn't intended to say that but he wanted her to tell him he was wrong.

'I don't know. I tell myself that lovely boy will come back to us soon. He is so special, so kind. Scoot, I didn't see anything useful. He left while I was gone and out of sight of this clinic. I am so sorry I couldn't stop what happened.'

Scoot nodded, not knowing what to say. He looked at the crates. A large gray dog watched him from one, eyes very sad and droopy.

'Is he going to be all right?' Scoot said, pointing. 'He doesn't look good.'

Radhika laughed and despite himself, Scoot smiled at the sound.

'He is a big, strong, healthy boy,' she told him. 'Of mysterious origins as Tony insists on calling dogs who aren't recognizable breeds. This spoiled one is called Baby by his owners who adore him. He needed a pad sutured, nothing more. If you walk on glass, silly Baby, you will cut your feet.'

A small sound came from the crate beside the desk.

'Is that Naruto?' Scoot asked, going closer and dropping to his knees. 'Yes, I think it is. Kyle described him so many times I'd know him anywhere.' He pushed a fingertip through the mesh and made noises although the kitten had his head pressed into a fleece blanket and didn't look up.

'Her,' Radhika corrected him. 'She is tiny. Would you like to hold her?'

Scoot opened the crate himself and gently lifted out the kitten. When he put her against his neck, she tucked her face into the hollow there and almost sighed with satisfaction.

Another laugh from Radhika. 'She must know you and Kyle are brothers. See how contented she is.' She stroked the kitten with the back of a forefinger.

Scoot held the cat with one hand and worked his wallet free with the other. 'We're going to adopt her. I expect Kyle told you that.'

Radhika stopped smiling. 'We hadn't talked about it.'

He felt a ripple of anxiety. 'Has someone else adopted her?'

'No. Where would you keep her?'

'We'll work it out,' he told her. Like so many things in his life, this was one more to be worked out. 'There is always an adoption fee. I remember that from when we've looked at posters for cats and dogs in shelters. I'll pay that now, and pay for the surgery to . . . what do you call it?'

'Spay,' Radhika said and she still wasn't smiling.

'Yes. Well, when it's time, that will be paid for.'

He took out some bills, trying not to think about when they would get more money from their dad. He still ached from having seen him only to watch him leave again. Scoot couldn't believe his father would have gone away if he had a choice. 'What does it all cost?'

'I'll have to find that out,' Radhika said but he heard how her voice strained.

'There are forms,' he told her. 'I saw someone fill them out in a pet shop once. When Kyle gets back I'm going to give Naruto to him as a coming home present.'

He couldn't look at Radhika's big, sad, dark eyes. She made him afraid that she didn't think Kyle would come home, or that they would have no way to keep the kitten.

Scoot straightened his back. 'I'd like to get the forms signed now and put Kyle down as the person adopting Naruto.'

'But—'

He held the kitten close to his neck and avoided looking at Radhika. 'Please,' he said quietly. 'Kyle will come home and want his kitten.'

Thirty-Four

Northampton was foreign territory to Tony but his sense of direction didn't desert him. Once past the outskirts he had found a car rental agency and left in a small, nondescript gray Ford Fiesta with enough miles to account for the dings in its clean but dull gray exterior. Remembering his story for wanting the 'cheapest car on the lot' made him smile: He was low on funds and his own car had broken down.

His dad's Lexus was in a paid car park several streets from the rental agency.

Thanks to Scoot and with a little unconscious help from Sid, he knew the man supposedly worked for Podmore's Hauling and Storage. A call to the plant had brought little joy; he was told Sid no longer worked there. He hadn't tried to find out about the secondary Podmore business Sid said he was with now, not during the first call. After a wait he'd phoned again, got someone different on the phone and asked about the other plant. He was told he'd have to contact Mr Podmore directly about that since they had nothing to do with it at the main plant.

That seemed too easy, even if he didn't have the vaguest idea where to go next – until he used the laptop he'd brought to find out what he could about Gary Podmore and his company. It was disturbingly simple to get details on someone, particularly someone who was fairly well-known in the area, including gems like how many speeding tickets he had been given. He had never been arrested. The only business address was for the main plant.

Tony had seen a good photo of the man, found his address and telephone number. He used the latter to call and ask if he could speak to Mr Gary Podmore about a shipment. He was told to wait. The phone number was right! In the following silence he hung up and set out to find his way to Podmore's address.

What next? Tony parked in a small track above several empty lots that sloped down to the Podmores' road. He had a clear view of the impressive three-storied, multi-pillared, white house. The hauling and storage business must be booming. He settled in to wait.

Nagging at his brain was the certainty that Alex would be looking for him by the end of the evening. She would expect him to show up at the Dog so they could drive home together, as he'd said he wanted to. From the way time was passing, that wouldn't happen. He checked his mobile and saw she had already tried to reach him. If he called back . . . he couldn't call her yet, not without telling her where he was and dealing with her demands that he let her come and be with him.

With a map spread wide over the steering wheel as if he were lost and trying to find his way, he was soon wishing he'd thought to bring at least a bottle of water.

His own vehicle was parked at his dad's house,

at the far side of the drive where it wasn't visible unless the gates were opened. They were closed. But that didn't mean Alex wouldn't call his dad and Tony hadn't been able to make himself ask him to lie.

An hour passed, and he moved closer to the house, parking on the same side where any leaving car would pass nearby. Darkness had settled on the quiet area and streetlights had come on. Tony put away the map and hunched down. Rain began to fall, growing quickly heavy. Tony shook his head. How long should he wait on the hope that his quarry would leave the house and lead him to Sid Gammage?

He got his answer sooner than expected, at least to his first question. A very dark-colored car drove out and passed him. All Tony could tell was that the driver was probably male.

In movies they made following moving vehicles look relatively simple, or at least possible. Tony began to doubt he'd pull it off at all and soon wished he'd kept the Lexus with its more powerful engine for overtaking. The car he was after moved onto better lighted streets and he saw it was a black Mercedes. The presence of other cars reduced the risk of being seen but made it more difficult to make sure he didn't lose Podmore.

He trailed him to the outskirts of Northampton and prayed he wasn't heading for the plant he already knew about.

Much sooner than Tony expected, they headed into an area of warehouses and rundown houses, most of them apparently abandoned.

The Mercedes drew up near tall, double gates constructed of new-looking layers of tight metal mesh. From what Tony could see of the tops of what lay behind, there had to be something that wasn't obvious to keep safe.

The gates slid open, gradually disappearing into pockets on either side. Tony saw no choice but to drive by. If he stopped on this now empty road, he'd be too obvious.

Podmore was turning into the open gates as Tony passed and he saw a mostly empty yard surrounded with utility buildings. Two lorries were parked at the far end with people walking back and forth, loading the back ends with anonymous-looking boxes.

Tony didn't see anyone who resembled Sid Gammage.

A right turn took him along another dingy, deserted road with no lights showing anywhere. When he reached the end and would have to turn right or left, he gave a soft exclamation. For all the secure gates at the front of the place, Podmore's had a second entrance at the back and as he passed, one of the lorries pulled out and turned left to go back the way Tony had come.

He angled right to drive around the compound, but not before he saw the second lorry leave and follow the first. It was the sight of Podmore's car following behind them that confounded Tony.

These back gates didn't close again. There must be more departures planned. That or there was nothing of value left to protect.

Sid mentioned he 'lived on the premises.' He

had to have meant the premises where he worked and that meant here. Right now he could be having his evening meal or talking to another worker.

Going in without leaving a clue to where he was would be asking for more trouble than anyone needed. He drove around the corner and out of sight of the gates and mounted the Ford's two right wheels onto the pavement.

He hadn't known he would send a text to Dan O'Reilly until he'd pulled up the contact information. Now caution was everything: 'In Northampton. Hoping to find Sid Gammage. Something not right with him, but I only care about getting him back to Scoot, and if we're lucky, Kyle. Will keep you informed.' How cryptic could he be and still hope they would track him if they had to? 'Driving local rental car. Not 24 hour agency. Closed nights. Used real name.'

It wouldn't be a piece of cake but if he hadn't showed by morning, they could follow the breadcrumbs he'd given them. His dad's car would be safe and eventually found.

He sent the text and turned off his mobile.

In almost complete darkness, Tony left the little car. He doubled back to where the back gates of the plant still stood open. That still bothered him but there were possible excuses and he was committed now.

His head and face streamed with rainwater. Slicking a hand across his eyes, he slipped through the gates and to the corner of the first building. A weak beam of light from beside garage doors didn't give him any comfort but at least he got some idea what was ahead of him.

Not much.

No vehicle, only two more inadequate lights beside other doors. Puddles filled potholes in the asphalt and the camber of the surface had been humped so much on one side of the yard that water rushed downhill toward the warehouses. Tony heard the gurgle of drains and wondered how often they overflowed to flood the buildings.

He walked upright, deliberately confident. He couldn't fight several men if they set on him and dealing with one depended on a lot of elements.

If he appeared to pose no threat he could hope for a more-or-less peaceful reception.

Halfway along the facades a glow shone through filthy glass. Tony moved away from the wall and kept walking, looking sideways. No one moved beyond the window, or not that he could see.

The confidence was feeling shallower. If he wanted to find Sid, he had to knock on a door, or several of them until he came face to face with a human. A nasty thought turned his stomach but he quickly told himself that if there were man-eating dogs around they would be barking by now.

He rapped on a door with his fist. At that moment, he heard what had to be the back gates grinding shut. The temptation to run for escape came and went quickly. He probably wouldn't make it and if he was caught running away, what then when he tried to tell his reasonable story?

No one answered the door.

The bald, brash approach was one way. Why the hell not. Tony went to the lighted window, stood close and peered in. The sill was high enough for him to have to arch his neck for a better view.

A door to his right crashed open and a man built like a tank came at Tony. He stood his ground. 'Good evening,' he said. 'I'm—'

One heavy hand spun him around and the other slammed him against the wall hard enough to whip his head back into concrete. 'Hold it,' he shouted. 'Just hold your horses.'

The response was a fist to Tony's solar plexus that doubled him over. Another blow met his forehead and he jerked down. He couldn't catch a breath and his legs wanted to collapse. Fighting the pain in his gut, he stayed where he was, bent, his arms wrapped around his belly.

Dimly, he heard the front gates opening and the low purr of an engine. Blows, raining down on his shoulders and back stopped him wondering who was coming, and infuriated him.

He threw a punch of his own. If he could handle flailing horses while they delivered their foals, he could do damage to this creep. He met solid muscle and punched again with his other fist. A hiss of indrawn breath gave him a moment's pleasure before the next shower of punches.

'Yeah, boss,' the man shouted. 'Broke in. Don't know where or how. No vehicle.' This man had a thick, eastern European accent.

'OK, OK,' another voice, this one definitely

English, said loudly and very close to Tony although he didn't dare uncover to see who it was.

'What was he doing?' the same voice asked. 'Who are you, man?'

That had to mean him, Tony decided. 'I'm Tony Harrison from Folly-on-Weir.'

'Never heard of it,' the man said. 'You heard of it, Ellis?'

'Never, Gary. He's a thief trying to talk his way out.'

'Gary – whoever you are – would you call off your thug and give me a chance to speak?' Blood trickled into the corner of his left eye.

'Let him go,' Gary said. 'I'm Gary Podmore. I own this facility. Get him inside, Ellis. I'm getting soaked out here.'

He was bundled through the door Ellis had used and shoved forward repeatedly until they reached a room where he was pushed inside as the lights were switched on.

Internal, the room had no windows and odd pieces of sagging furniture around the walls. There was a TV. A battered refrigerator also stood against a wall with a metal table holding mugs, instant coffee and an electric kettle.

'Sit,' Gary Podmore said.

'I'd rather stand.' The idea of sitting while this pair stood over him didn't appeal. He swiped blood out of his eye, then wished he hadn't touched his swelling brow.

'Have it your own way. This is a business where there's little to steal unless you're planning to drive a lorry away. You wouldn't get far.

253

Give me one reason why I shouldn't call the police.'

Do call the police . . . Tony doubted he'd be fortunate enough to see the law rushing to his aid.

'Speak up,' Podmore snapped. 'You don't look like a burglar.'

He frowned deeply as if he were puzzled. His blondish hair and mustache made him look younger than Tony thought he could be. Jeans and jean jacket helped that.

'I'm not a burglar.' Tony's guts still ached. 'I'm looking for Sid Gammage. He works for you as a lorry driver. He said he's with a different part of your business from what happens farther south of Northampton. I think he meant he's based here.'

Podmore kept frowning. 'The plant in the Hardingstone area is the main one. In an industrial park there. This is just overflow.'

Instinct stopped Tony from mentioning what Sid had said about this being a completely separate operation. 'Yes. Where will I find Sid Gammage?'

Gary Podmore stared at Ellis who stood with beefy legs planted wide apart and a thunderous expression on his shiny, pockmarked face. He wore black hair slicked back with something greasy.

'There is no Sid,' Ellis said. He narrowed his eyes. 'But I was in the other plant when the police made enquiries. Do you remember that, Gary? When they phoned just a couple of days ago. The receptionist said they were looking for

254

someone and I think that was the name.'

Tony got an evil premonition of disaster for Sid . . . unless he'd been lying about working for these people.

Podmore snapped his fingers. 'It was. Sheila mentioned . . . Wait a minute. There was a driver called Sid. I remember first names and he was the one we let go some weeks back.'

Ellis shook his head. 'I don't think so, boss.'

'I can't check the records until morning,' Podmore said, 'but I'm sure that was him. Tall fellow. Quiet but a bit of a troublemaker. He got into it with some of the other lads and—'

'You're right,' Ellis said and in a toneless voice. 'Didn't he just walk off the job when he was disciplined? I think he did. We've been so busy, I haven't thought about him. Who talked to the police?'

'Don't know. Whoever took the call, I suppose.'

'Well, we'd better make sure what they were told. I'll do that tomorrow. Why are you looking for him?'

The rat Tony smelled was growing huge. 'I help keep an eye on his kids when he's away on jobs,' he said, feeling ridiculous and completely inadequate for the job he'd taken on here. 'They haven't heard from him recently and they could use some reassurance. I decided to come and see him.'

He waited for one of them to ask why he hadn't phoned. The question didn't come and he wondered why.

Tony tried to decide what to do next, other than get out of here. He couldn't demand to search the place.

'Doesn't seem he was a very reliable type,' Podmore said. 'It's a good job those two boys have you to lean on. Not that I suppose you want to be stuck with that for too long,'

'Sorry to bother you like I have,' Tony said. 'I never expected to find out Sid wasn't here. And I do think he's a nice enough chap, by the way.' He wanted to hit the right note, a non-threatening note. 'If you should hear anything from him, would you tell him Tony came by? I'll do my best to keep his boys from panicking about him.'

'Good for you,' Podmore said.

Ellis stood by the door. 'You'd better be on your way,' he said. 'It's late. Some of us have work in the morning.'

Gingerly pressing his midriff and wondering about broken ribs, Tony followed Ellis to the outside door and into the yard. The man made no attempt at an apology and Podmore didn't follow them.

'I'll open that gate,' Ellis said, nodding toward the end of the buildings. Those gates couldn't be seen from here. 'Where you came in.'

'Right.' As he walked away, Tony considered what he'd found out, or thought he had. At first he'd decided the trip a complete waste of time.

It wasn't.

Ellis shouldn't have known Tony used the back, or to be more exact, the side gates, even if they had closed after he entered the yard. It was open before so it didn't work automatically. They had been waiting until he came through.

Podmore returned to the plant as if he'd known Tony was inside and timed the arrival for after Ellis confronted him.

Now Tony thought about it, Podmore had driven quite slowly while he was following, as if he intended to make sure he found his way. Why, unless he wanted a chance to deny any knowledge of Sid's whereabouts?

The gate had slid open again and Tony went through and on toward the car.

Did he look stupid or could those two really think he wouldn't notice how at first they absolutely didn't know Sid, but then absolutely did remember him and what he'd supposedly done to get fired. And why would Ellis talk about the police contact – obviously intended to put Tony off continuing to search – about how it had been some time ago when he knew it could only have been in the past few days. It wouldn't be quickly forgotten, or mistaken for old news.

But the biggie to Tony was Gary Podmore's major slip. If he hardly remembered Sid or anything about him, how had he known the man had two boys? Not just kids even, but *boys*?

Was Sid alive?

Tony's mouth was dry. He couldn't stand thinking about what would happen if the man had died, or been made to disappear.

If Scoot was really unlucky he'd have lost both his father and his brother.

Thirty-Five

Earlier, from a bar window at the Black Dog, Alex had seen Dan driving by at speed with someone she assumed to be Bill Lamb. That had not been long after she and Tony had left the parish hall and taken the Burke sisters home. Tony had returned to the clinic. Hours had passed since then and not a word from anyone that would give a hint about the rush departure of the two detectives, or about Kyle.

The pub was closed and Lily had gone home to Corner Cottage with a very subdued Scoot. The boy had answered no questions about what was on his mind. He had asked her if Dan had mentioned any police progress in finding Kyle but then he fell silent for the rest of the evening, speaking only when spoken to and seeming completely removed from his surroundings and activities.

Hugh hung around, watching her while pretending he was giving extra attention to details already dealt with, but finally checked everything was locked up and went upstairs to his rooms for the night.

Alex was left in the bar with Bogie and Katie. She went into the snug and sat on a banquette with the dogs on either side of her.

Not one word from Tony since he said he was returning to the clinic. She had tried to reach him three times but only got his answering service. There was no answer on the phone at his house and she had yet to get up the courage to try Doc's home. So far she hadn't mentioned her fears to anyone.

Could Tony have done as he threatened and gone in search of Sid Gammage?

Radhika's number was on Alex's mobile. Much as she didn't want to concern Tony's assistant, she could answer at least one question.

'Hello,' she said when Radhika answered, tentatively. She didn't sound as if Alex had woken her up.

'Forgive me for phoning so late. Would you tell me what time Tony got back to the clinic this afternoon, I'm trying to reach him.'

Seconds stretched away before Radhika said, 'I am afraid for Kyle, and now for Tony, too. He didn't come back today although he said he would.'

Alex gritted her teeth. Wherever Tony had gone, it was under his own steam, she was sure of that – and irritated beyond being rational. 'It's all right, Radhika. We've both been really busy. I'll let you know as soon as I find him.'

Radhika didn't sound convinced but she accepted Alex's platitudes and they hung up.

He hadn't even gone back to the clinic!

She heard a key in the lock on the door to the inn but didn't move. There were several guests and she didn't feel like greeting them – unless it was Dan and he could give her good news.

The front door closed with a careful, click, and footsteps moved across the restaurant.

259

Alex listened, but then recognized the voices of a couple from Stoke who represented a china company. She had the brief thought that she didn't know how well the china industry did these days.

Where was Tony? Even if he had gone to find Sid there should have been time to make contact by now.

Calling Doc about his son's whereabouts was out of the question. But Tony could be at Doc's house.

He wasn't. Alex just knew it and she was scared. She didn't feel brave. Panicky was much closer.

And she was getting mad, dammit. What did he think he was doing, going off somewhere that kept him away all these hours and not getting a message to her?

Dead people didn't send messages . . .

For crying out loud, this wasn't like her. She knew better than to rush to conclusions.

He was too principled to play a silly game of getting back at her for the times she had taken things into her own hands. Wasn't he?

Unfortunately, the answer to that was, yes, which didn't make her feel any better.

Staying here and driving herself to crazy thoughts couldn't go on. She got up and the dogs followed her through the bar and behind the counters to the kitchen. She put leashes on them, grabbed an old duffel coat from the back of the door and her car keys before walking out into the night and letting the lock close behind her.

With Bogie and Katie swaying from side to

side in the passenger seat of her Range Rover, she drove to the clinic. Tony didn't answer her knock and his vehicle wasn't there. In the early hours of the morning she'd have been amazed if it were.

Back in the Range Rover, Alex rested her brow on the steering wheel. There was only one thing to do next but she hated it.

Lights shone bright through the windows of the parish hall. She parked, made the dogs lie down, and walked slowly to the front of the building. Several cars were there, but not Tony's. She hadn't expected it to be but she had hoped.

Dan's Lexus was pulled up in front of the hall.

Bill Lamb would have every reason to point the finger at people who meddled with police investigations.

She took a deep breath, went up the steps and pushed open the door. Her eyes took a second to adjust from the darkness outside to the light and activity in front of her. Detectives and uniform officers moved back and forth from behind the screens, conferring with personnel at the line of desks in front, looking at computer screens, and occasionally approaching Dan O'Reilly to talk in low voices.

Tony stood with his back to her beside Dan's desk, his hands clasped behind his back while Bill bent over the desk making marks on a chart.

'Tony,' Alex whispered. Weakness swept over her, a mixture of being so tired and so frantic. He didn't hear her but looking at his solid back, his hair curling and unruly from being wet, and realizing how she had dreaded anything happening

261

to him, she knew there was a message for which she didn't have time this morning. He mattered so much to her, so very much.

She almost stumbled forward but steadied herself and walked firmly to stand at his shoulder. 'You, Tony Harrison, are a selfish bastard,' she said.

Thirty-Six

'Gov,' she heard a man say. 'This is important.'

Tony turned and shrugged. He raised his palms and let his hands drop again. 'I'll tell you all about it, Alex. I wanted to call, I kept wanting to call you but I couldn't.'

He could have said, 'Now you know how it feels when you fly solo,' but, of course, he didn't. He might even have said, 'I'm a bastard?'. No, he wouldn't, and she was turning herself into something she disliked because she couldn't cope with needing someone, anyone, intensely enough to wonder if the world's lights would go out for her if he wasn't around.

'You're exhausted,' she told him, swallowing hard and taking in a swelling over his left eye and a cut from which blood had run as far as his chin and dried. She'd seen him looking tired many times, but not like this. 'He needs that wound dressed,' she said, to no one in particular. 'You're going to have a black eye with all the drainage there must be inside. Do you feel light-headed, or tired? You mustn't go to sleep, Tony.'

He smiled half-heartedly and she grabbed him by the shoulders. 'It's not funny. Have you been fighting? Have you been in an accident?'

The hiss of his escaping breath shocked her. He spread his hands across his mid-section and his eyelids drooped, or the one that could droop, drooped.

She grabbed a chair and said, 'Sit. Now. I'm sorry I'm being an idiot. I'm really sorry, Tony. You frightened me. Did you get beaten up?'

'Don't worry,' he said, sitting with a thump. 'I'll be fine in a year or so.'

Alex bit her lip but it didn't stop her from smiling. 'Brave men can be such a pain.'

With a hand on Tony's shoulder, she looked up into Bill Lamb's grin. He straightened that out quickly. 'He was beaten up,' he said. 'He's got a damn great lump on his head and he says none of his ribs are broken but we don't believe him. He won't get checked out at a hospital.'

Dan had left his chair and was talking to the officer who had come to him. When the man walked away, Dan looked up into the rafters as if looking either for inspiration or because he was out of patience.

He beckoned Bill over and they conferred very quietly.

'I wish I knew what they were saying,' Alex said to Tony without thinking. 'I mean—'

'You mean you wish you could hear them,' Tony said, propping an elbow on his knee and supporting his head on his fist. 'I know what you're thinking before you say it. But I want to know, too. Looks intense.'

Alex looked at the back of his head where more blood had seeped into his hair. 'Who did this to you?' she asked quietly.

'You don't know him but as soon as we get away from here I'll explain it all. I did try to find Sid and I think I got close. Too close for some people.'

Dan and Bill came toward them, picking up folding chairs on the way. 'Over here,' Dan said, heading for a far corner well away from anyone else.

Bill picked up Tony's chair. 'Lean on me if you need to,' he said.

It was fortunate Bill couldn't see Alex's face. She doubted she was hiding her surprise at this solicitation.

They sat where Dan had indicated. They were close together but facing the room.

'We haven't been back long,' Dan said. 'Tony had the sense to stop trying to drive back and call us. You're sure you didn't actually see Sid Gammage, Tony?'

More shocks. There was no attempt to cut her out.

'No. But I kept thinking he was either some-where there, or he had been. Maybe he was driving. Sending him out on a job would have been a natural. But they wanted me to go away thinking Sid didn't work for them anymore. That he hadn't for weeks.'

'This was Podmore's?' Alex asked, and closed her mouth firmly.

'Yes.'

Dan and Bill looked at each other. They nodded, presumably in agreement.

'This is privileged information. If I hear it from anyone else, I'll know where it came from.' Dan fixed them with dark, hard eyes. 'We know Sid has a motorbike.'

'He told me he did,' Alex said. 'He couldn't use it to get back and check on the boys because he said the sound of the engine starting up would have alerted other people and he wasn't supposed to leave where he works.'

Another long glance between Dan and Bill.

Dan lowered his gaze to the floor. He still wore his raincoat and shoved his hands in the pockets. Alex could almost hear him struggling to make a decision.

'We're searching for Sid,' he said at last. 'Seriously but carefully. We can't charge in where you were tonight, Tony. It might not be good for Sid. We can't be sure yet, but it's possible we're looking at a much bigger picture here.'

'The motorbike?' Tony said. 'Why is that important?'

'Look try to forget we mentioned it for now. I think you may be able to help us. How, I'm not completely sure but Tony has already opened up new avenues. You shouldn't have, but you did, Tony. We'd appreciate it if you'd at least get your dad to check you. We have someone returning his car.'

'Doc will check him over,' Alex said. 'What else has come up?' There had to be more.

'Be patient, Alex,' Dan said.

Bill cleared his throat and caught Dan's eye. The senior detective whistled out a breath. From his expression he was fighting with something he wished would just go away.

'Yes, of course,' Dan said. 'OK, Bill. You can leave me to it. I'll get back with you shortly but we should probably tell each other to get some rest. Did you ever get to talk to Mrs Marroway. The woman who was supposed to have called—'

'I couldn't even lay eyes on her unless I staked out her cottage and waited for her to come out. I contacted home health, which I should have done right off. Short of the long, she didn't make any telephone calls, not to Radhika or anyone she doesn't have a special connection with. She's completely deaf, poor woman, and apparently angry about it. Not that I blame her. Whoever made the call had one aim, to get Radhika out of the clinic. She had never spoken to Marroway and had no idea she's deaf. Radhika still thinks it was a man talking in a high voice.'

'Might have expected something like that. Get out of here and sleep.'

He didn't speak again as soon as Bill left.

Alex rubbed Tony's arm and they waited.

'We have another body,' Dan said quietly. 'Since yesterday.'

She felt Tony stiffen. 'Why—'

'Why hasn't it got out?' Dan said. 'Why haven't you heard about it before this? For once we kept things tight enough. The murder site didn't hurt. There was a small work crew involved but they were ready enough to swear themselves to silence. I doubt if that will hold.'

'You won't tell us where you found . . . it,' Tony finished awkwardly. 'Dan, is it . . .?' He knew he didn't have to finish.

'We're not sure.'

Alex couldn't swallow. She pressed finger and thumb into the corners of her eyes. 'Dan, do you think it is our boy?'

'I can't answer that. But we need someone who can try to identify him. Sid's AWOL. Scoot is a seventeen-year-old kid and he isn't in the best shape. I don't even know if I could use him if I wanted to.'

'But you must think this could be Kyle.' She knew she was right. 'Which probably means it is. What happened to him?' she finished in a tiny voice.

Dan bowed his head. 'I can't be sure about an identity, any identity, at this point.'

'Something awful's been done to him, hasn't it?' Alex said. Her hands and feet felt numb, as if she'd gone into shock. Of course, she hadn't gone into shock.

'There has to be more family somewhere.' Tony sat up straight now. 'Their mother, someone.'

'Their mother hasn't been heard from for years. We don't know what name she uses or even if she's alive. Apparently there's an aunt. Sid's sister. We tracked her last known address and she's not there. Her landlord says she hitchhikes in Europe every year and doesn't make contact. He doesn't know when she might come back or where she is.'

'Would it work for me to at least try?' Alex

said. She heard her own voice in her head as if it was far away.

'No,' Tony said. 'I will.'

'Get some sleep,' Dan told them. 'I'm grateful to you. If you could stand by in the morning, I'll let you know what I decide is best. I have to discuss this with my boss.'

Thirty-Seven

The sun hadn't come up. It couldn't have. After Alex left to take Scoot to school, Tony had stood at the front door of Corner Cottage, taking in the scene. The sky resembled a blast of industrial smoke driven before a tornado. Only the tornado was missing.

School buses had swallowed their loads of children and born them out of Folly-on-Weir. The first shops to open still hadn't put their wares on display outside and anyone abroad was muffled up against the chill day even though it looked colder than it really was.

Tony had closed out the gray morning and returned to sit in Lily's kitchen, drinking coffee. He and Alex continued to keep a close eye on Scoot and she was insisting on driving him to and from school. If he felt self-conscious about that, he didn't complain.

Lily had already gone to the Black Dog and Tony was grateful for a little peace.

Someone knocked the front door, but he stayed

where he was. Perhaps they would go away again. He hoped.

Rather than go away, his father's voice echoed through the letterbox. 'Tony, it's your dad. I have a key.' And he let himself in. 'Lily gave it to me. Where are you?'

With a sigh he got up and greeted his dad. The rapid once-over assessment was all too familiar.

'I thought I taught you not to pick on people bigger than you are.'

'Very funny. Good of you to come, but I'm just fine. Bit of a headache, some scratches and bruises, but nothing major.' If he mentioned the ribs his dad would want X-rays.

'What about the ribs?'

Sheesh, was nothing sacred around here? 'Great now,' he lied. 'The man shoved me but I went backwards and he didn't get in a solid blow. But the bruising is pretty uncomfortable.'

'That's good news,' his father said, passing him and going into the kitchen where he put his bag on the table. 'Let me just take a look at you.'

'You already have. Here I am.'

'Your head first.' His dad tilted up Tony's chin and studied his face. 'Nasty. I'm going to dress that wound in your eyebrow. I'll use a couple of butterflies. You should have had sutures last night. How do you feel – really feel?'

'Sore. No good lying. The man who decided I was the enemy is a big, brawny one.'

His dad guided him into a chair and looked at the back of his scalp. 'Good job you've got a thick head. But if you start feeling any of the symptoms you already know you should watch for, get to emergency.'

'Thanks. I think I'm doing better already.'

'Did you find out anything about Sid?'

Tony sighed. 'Only that I think he's in trouble. I knew his behavior didn't make a lot of sense when he was here that night and now I know why. Or I believe I do. He had to separate himself from what he really wanted – to be with his kids– and instead try to get back before the people who say he doesn't work for them found out he was gone. He could really have feared for the boys' safety. Dan O'Reilly knows all this. But I don't necessarily think he and the police are much farther forward than I am. You know about the second body?'

Doc James nodded his head slowly. 'Do they know who it is yet?'

'They say they don't but Alex and I are pretty convinced it's Kyle. I don't know the details of the death, but Dan would only say he couldn't be sure who it is yet.'

'They should be able to check dental records,' Doc said. 'He wasn't a patient of mine but if he ever saw a doctor there are records of that somewhere, too.'

'When she gets back, Alex and I are going to see if we can identify the body. The police can't make that call even if they think they know. I tried to get Alex not to go but she insists she's better at people details and she's probably right.'

His dad pulled out a chair for himself and sat down.

'Coffee?' Tony said.

His dad shook his head, no. 'Tell me you're not going to lose your wool over what I'm going to tell you.'

'That doesn't sound good, Dad. What's happened now?'

Doc picked up an empty coffee mug and filled it from the pot on the stove. He looked into the biscuit tin as if it might contain some magic elixir, and took out a sugar biscuit. He repositioned himself at the table in thoughtful mode.

'OK, I'm off to make my own enquiries,' Tony said. 'I never liked truth or consequences.'

'Pointless to try,' his dad said. 'No one knows what Dan and Bill know and if you found someone who did, they probably wouldn't tell you without clearing it with one of the detectives first.'

The coffee was thick enough to be one step from cooling caramel. It needed chewing. The twisted expression on Doc's face suggested his teeth needed sharpening.

Doc made to get up. It was chilly still and he wound a muffler more tightly around his neck.

'I'm going to tell you something, ever so nicely and ask you not to get angry and try to interfere with what's been decided. Just remind yourself that it would be wrong to interfere with the slow progress being made.' His father looked at the backs of his hands. 'Slow progress but progress. That should make you feel good. But if you plough in with a megaphone, shouting orders, not only giving away how little you really know but telling the enemy just how ignorant we are, it's over. They win. Either they're well enough

271

organized to do what they have to do and get away, or they just get away. Can you see how it might be of benefit to keep our powder dry a bit longer?'

Tony pushed his mug of cold coffee back and forth. 'This doesn't make me feel trusted, Dad. Let's get to it, the reason you came. What don't I kick up a fuss about?'

'Radhika remembered something. A small thing, she said, until she realized how big a thing it was. She did see a vehicle the night Kyle disappeared. She was hurrying and worried and it was over in a moment. She's having another fight with guilt. Everything is her fault for being stupid and careless.'

'Rubbish,' Tony said. 'Silly woman.'

'It might be better if you didn't use that term around her. Big, dark vehicle. Not new, she thinks. That was it. Passed her as she ran back to the clinic and she didn't give it another thought. I can see that happening.'

'So can I.'

'Another thing. She talked Dan, or I suppose I should say, Bill did, since he did all the talking for her, into letting her see the boy's body. She wasn't going to rest if they didn't let her.'

Images swam across Tony's mind. The horror of what Radhika might see, and eventually, if she identified Kyle, her collapse into self-recrimination.

'Will Bill be with her?' he asked softly.

'He'll be outside. It may even be over by now. Alex will go in with her.'

Thirty-Eight

'Radhika,' Alex went toward the woman with outstretched hands. 'Are you still sure you want to do this?'

Bill had driven Radhika while Alex drove herself. She had come to see the special connection between these two and to realize it would get stronger if the parts of their lives fell into place.

'I have to do this thing,' Radhika said to Alex. 'I will be fine with Alex, Bill – and you need to do other things,' she told Bill who looked thoughtfully over her head but turned and walked away.

'Perhaps he should have stayed,' Alex said. 'He knows the procedure better than I do. A technician will come out to get us.'

'I do not like to be needy,' Radhika said. 'In time a strong man will tire of a weak woman. This was something my mother told me. She was a strong woman. You have been to this place before?' She tilted her head at Alex.

'Once,' she said. 'They're kind here.'

Radhika wound an old, embroidered linen handkerchief through her fingers and noticed Alex watching. 'I found this in a small old chest of my mother's. It is the one thing I have carried with me through my travels. The chest has six tiny drawers and is no bigger than a box. It is a yellowing thing, very worn, but you can see it is

273

Indian and old. No one but me would want it but I'm glad my mother gave it to me. It would have no value to anyone else. I carry the little cloth with me to give me comfort when I need it.'

Alex had no response.

'My mother kept little treasures in her funny chest. To me it is the embodiment of her memories. Perhaps her hopes. I don't know. She was a lovely, kind lady. She died eight years ago.'

Alex held a hand toward the woman but at that moment, a door opened and a scrub-suited woman smiled at them. 'Are you here for the police identification?'

They were taken into a corridor where Alex was surprised to see Dan O'Reilly. He nodded briefly at both of them. She heard the woman in scrubs say, 'Viewing window?' but Dan shook his head, no, and ushered them into the big, scrubbed room where everything shone chrome or white, except for the green drape over a body shape.

'Take your time deciding when you're ready to do this,' he told them. 'If you are ready at all. Doesn't matter who you are or how experienced you may be, it's difficult in the extreme. If you feel you want to leave, just indicate. There's nothing to prove here except this boy's identity, if you know it.'

Alex looked at Radhika, who nodded, yes. 'All right,' Alex told Dan.

The boy beneath the sheet had that stillness only seen in death. The parts of his skin that weren't injured in some way had a bluish tinge to utter whiteness. His hair, curly and longish, was a dull brown. Alex concentrated on the right hand. She studied the curl of the fingers, the ragged nails, the skin so obviously young and not so long lived in. These were hands new to rough use. And she knew she was preparing herself for the face she had allowed her eyes to slip over.

Someone coughed.

Not Radhika or Dan, or Alex. Who watched them?

People spent entire lifetimes studying crime and criminals, and some became doctors of the dead, detectives who specialized in taking what the mad ones left behind and seeing the clues those people didn't believe they produced. Some would argue that it was wrong to brand all killers as mad, that it impeded justice in some cases, but even when the perpetrator was found 'sane' was there real conviction in the finding?

Alex's brain screamed the questions she had tried but failed to banish forever. Looking down on this child, for that's what he was or very little more, she wailed silently for the mother and father who had begun his life, for the atrocity of any life twisted and torn with such foul and inhumane abandon. *Even for an instant of bizarre bliss that quieted an unspeakable need, or to be rid of eyes that saw too much, threatened too much, to silence a voice that could ruin you, how could you inflict this?*

'Someone's child.'

She didn't know she had spoken aloud until she heard Radhika's whispered, 'Yes. And he was our child, too, all of us. We are all grieving for this lost son.'

Alex didn't know if it was right or wrong, but she lightly left a kiss on a broken cheek.

As she straightened, Radhika did the same and when she stood up, their eyes met and held.

'This boy isn't Kyle,' Alex said to Dan. 'I never knew it was possible to be so relieved and so completely devastated in the same instant. Please find whoever did this.'

Thirty-Nine

'Tony, it's Alex.'

She heard him mutter something.

'It wasn't fair to send your dad to explain, but—'

'I'm fine, darling. So's Dad. Just worried about you. Where are you?'

'Sitting on a wall at a car park in Gloucester. Tony, it isn't Kyle's body.'

'Thank God,' he said quietly. 'Is it wrong to say that?'

'No. I was relieved. I wanted to sit on the floor and cry for joy. And I was so sad and angry, too. The boy was about the same age, but a more muscular person. The hair was different, and the shape of the face. You already know the features were . . . I don't want to think about that. I don't want to remember. I want to know who he was and what he looked like. But what I want most is to know his killer's been found.'

They hung on in silence.

Alex kept her eyes at the level of passing feet, every size and shape. Conversation flowed by in a steady stream, and laughter and music from somewhere. 'Tony?'

'I'm coming to get you.'

'Thank you, but I'd still have my car here. I'll come home now. Have you heard anything else?'

'Message from O'Reilly's office to say he wants to talk to me later this afternoon. Not a word of explanation. Alex, will you hang up on me if I say I hate the feeling I can't reach out and touch or, or get to you when I want to?'

She looked at her phone. The passersby had become a ribbon of colors as her focus blurred. 'Of course. That was me hanging up. Or this is me hanging up. Darn it, Tony Harrison, if I didn't like you so much I'd probably love you.' She didn't wait for a response.

The sign for Folly-on-Weir gave Alex a little comfort. Home, her home and the place where all the people she loved the most lived, too.

Ahead, too distant to made out individuals, a small crowd milled back and forth across the High Street between The Black Dog and Corner Cottage.

Familiar prickling started at the base of her neck and spread, upward and outward. She drove faster, then slowed again, worried about the people in the road.

The first person she recognized was Lily, then Tony and Doc who were on their knees by the cottage gate. Alex's hands slipped on the steering wheel and she wiped first one, then the other, on her trouser legs. She braked and steered sharply onto the pavement in front of the pub.

When she opened her door and jumped out, it was into the stream of early afternoon regulars following Lily.

'Stay back,' Tony shouted. 'Go inside for now. Alex, please could someone help with that?'

'I will,' Major Stroud announced. 'Come along. Nothing to see here. We'll be in the warm, kiddies.'

Alex heard muttering about 'bleedin' kindergarten teachers,' but dashed to the opposite pavement. Kev Winslet got there at the same time. 'I saw it happen,' he said, puffing. 'I saw him get here.'

'Oh!' Her hands flew to her face. She started to shake and swipe at her eyes. 'Kyle!' she heard her own shriek and barreled into Tony's waiting arm.

Kyle sat on the path, just inside the gate, leaning against the nearest post, with Tony steadying him while Doc took his pulse and shone a light into each of his eyes. Gaffer tape held Kyle motionless, like a silver-gray mummy.

Forty

'What do you think, guv?' Bill asked, slamming the passenger door on the Lexus and stuffing two cups of what would be bad coffee into the holders. Looking back at the swinging glass doors at the front of the police station, he added,

'What are we supposed to think about this Ellis bloke? Do you think Gary Podmore knew his man was coming here with his so-called bleeding conscience?'

Bill's mobile rang before Dan had a chance to answer the question. The grin that gradually spread on his partner's face agitated Dan. He drummed his fingers, waiting.

'We're on our way there,' Bill said. 'Yes, yes, I'll get back to you.' He rested the mobile on his thigh.

'Come on,' Dan said. 'What's going on?'

'Kyle Gammage just got dumped outside Lily Duggins's cottage. That was Trafford at the parish hall. Whoever's with the kid wants to know if they can move him inside or do they have to wait for the police to arrive? Do they have to take photos for the case? They called the parish hall—'

'Is he conscious? Photos? Holy hell – he is alive, right? Say it!'

'Yes, he's alive. He's in good shape. Something about a lot of gaffer tape.'

Dan had already pulled into traffic. 'Why aren't we talking to someone there at the cottage? Call 'em, man.'

'That's what I'm about to do,' Bill said, thumbs flying. 'I've got Harrison's number. Get the boy inside, right?'

'Yes, dammit. And they're not to question him. Balls is – Harding's good with kids. They look at those muscles and think he's frickin' Superman or something. We'll have him go over and assess how ready Kyle is for questions. God knows what he's been through.'

'Harrison,' Bill said in the snarky manner he saved for Tony most of the time. Good job Tony found it funny. 'No questions for Kyle before our people talk to him. DC Harding will be there shortly. Get Kyle inside . . . Oh, did you? Anything else you've already done? Scratch that. How is Kyle do you think? How does he look?'

He nodded and made approving sounds. 'He didn't happen to say where he's been and who with, did he? . . . No. You're right, best to let him talk about it in his own time.'

Dan didn't interrupt Bill's end of the back and forth. It could wait until Kyle was ready for questions.

'Do we start carrying a chart around?' Dan said when Bill finally reached for his coffee. 'A list of characters and motivation, what we think the connections are so far? Ellis is a shocker. He hardly said a word when we were at Podmore's yard. I could never have even dreamed up the notion of seeing him walk into the station like that. I want to show Harrison the pictures from Interpol and get his reaction. Those people are fast and slick. But they haven't given us every-thing we need – so far. Good idea for Alex to come with Harrison.'

'You think Ellis is trying to stitch Sid up?' Bill said.

'You have a nasty, suspicious mind. Yeah, I think that should be a definite possible. But it's a whole lot bigger than that. I'd like to see the boy now but first stop has to be the parish hall and Harding will do a good job of getting things going with Kyle. We need a gander at this new evidence.'

They stopped talking but Dan would bet they were both moving the same things around in their heads, trying to make the pieces fit. The case was a nightmare – except for the return of Kyle Gammage. Dan had dared to doubt the body was Kyle's. The build didn't completely fit his memory of him. He was grateful not to have to tell Sid, and especially, Scoot, they'd lost Kyle. This was a bright spot. And he really liked the kid, too. He wanted to shut out the picture of the dead boy, and thoughts of tracking down his family.

Tonight he would be talking with Corinne. Her request – by email – not his. Hell of a day. He shook his head.

'Alex took off fast this morning,' Bill said. 'I didn't know she'd left the building until later.'

Bill had been engrossed in comforting an unnaturally still and silent Radhika at the time but Dan didn't mention that. 'I spoke with Alex after the viewing. Interesting woman. She really feels for that dead boy and his family. She's angry at the world about it.'

'Radhika, too. She stood like a block of ice. At least they may know who he is soon enough – although it won't take away the violence done to him.'

'You didn't let anything slip about—'

'Thanks for the nice vote of confidence,' Bill cut him off. 'What do you think?'

'Sorry. I'm getting paranoid. Nothing about this case stays still long enough to get nailed down.'

He drove faster than usual through Folly-on-Weir to get to the parish hall. 'I must be sick,' he said. 'I'm glad to see this place.'

Bill gave a short bark of laughter. 'Me, too. Deliriously.'

Forty-One

With Alex clinging to his arm, Tony muttered all the way into the parish hall. Once inside, she held him back while she shut the door. 'Calm down,' she hissed. 'I've got to be here, too, and I'm not flipping out. Dan and Bill don't know how ticked off we are and apparently, they wouldn't understand why. I want to be with Kyle, too. He's safe with your dad and Lily and Scoot, for crying out loud. And Officer Harding's there. This meeting with us had to be important to Dan and we'll get back as soon as we can.'

He wanted the whirlwind to stop, dammit. Just leave him alone to enjoy Kyle and all his moving, living parts, even if the boy was loaded with gum residue from the gaffer tape that idiot had used to restrain him. Lily was still working on some of the tape. 'What are these people, these cops, what are they made of? Don't they have any normal feelings? Why wouldn't Dan – and Bill – want to see Kyle before doing anything else?'

Alex's expression became threatening. He

could take a hint – eventually. 'OK. I'm OK now. Why did you bring Bogie with you?'

'Because he's my kid and he's getting separation anxiety. His mother can't be trusted to be there for him. Now shut up and let's do this.' Bogie's despondent droop, including flattened ears and baleful eyes, was laughable.

A little sheepishly, Tony glanced at Dan's desk. Evidently the detective was too busy to notice any little dramas going on around him.

Bill came from behind the secret screens and saw them. He actually gave a grin, a real, genuine delighted smile, and beckoned them over.

Dan looked up at Bill, then at Alex and Tony. His huge smile matched Bill's and he stood as they reached him. 'We needed good news and we finally got the best,' he said. 'He's a great kid. I'll be over to talk to him once I have everything down to a simmer here. We've been gone all day. Harding is really good with kids. Kyle will like being with him.'

'We would like to get back to Kyle, Dan.' Tony didn't feel like chatting with detectives.

'Dan,' Alex said quickly, 'we know you need to talk to us now but you'll understand our hurry.' She gave that lovely smile of hers, the one that reduced him to putty and he didn't like her wasting it on Dan O'Reilly.

The man kept on smiling. 'Of course. Our custom sitting room is where we left it. Shall we?' He led the way to the group of gray metal chairs they'd used before. 'Bring what we need, please, Bill.'

Dan sat and took a notebook out of his inside

breast pocket. Settling in didn't interest Tony; he sat without leaning back and Alex perched on the edge of her seat. Bill came with a folder and an envelope in his hands, and a brown paper sack, folded over and stapled shut, in one hand.

'Alex,' Dan said, 'we need to revisit your conversation with Sid the night you went to the cottage and encountered him in a shed. He said he came by public transport then hitched a ride. You told us his excuse for not using the motorbike.'

'And we already know it was probably a lie because you said the bike was found somewhere you haven't been ready to tell us about.'

Dan didn't rise to her evenly delivered barb. 'Here in . . . it was around here. It was buried in piles of leaves and brush. Sloppy job. It was bound to be found. I'd like you to really think about that night. Try to remember if there was anything that stuck out to you. You told me Sid said the battery in his vehicle was dead.'

'His van. Yes.' She frowned. Tony wanted to ask more about the hidden bike. She felt him shifting in his chair, and fidgeting. 'Like what else would I remember about it all, maybe?'

'When you went into the building Sid uses as a garage – anything in particular there?'

'The garage, or whatever, was empty except for the van. The van seemed pretty clean. It didn't smell great – in the vehicle or the shed. I noticed that. But I didn't find anything inside, including in the back of the van. Nothing . . . Oh, cripes, I should have noticed the light came on. Is that what you're waiting for me to remember? I saw the light but it seemed normal. I just didn't think about the battery.'

'So you don't think the battery was dead at that point after all?' Bill said.

'Obviously not,' Alex said, sounding irritated. 'Why would Sid pretend like that?'

'People lie,' Dan said. 'I'm more puzzled why Sid would snatch his own boy, then dump him – if that's what he did.'

'He – we don't know that happened,' Alex said. 'We need to talk to Kyle. Or you do,' she finished hurriedly. 'Better than Kyle, Sid has to explain. Kyle hasn't said a word about who took him.'

'Sid still hasn't surfaced,' Dan said. 'We're hoping we have a lead on when and where he'll show up. Your solo adventure to Northampton could be what shook that information loose for us, Tony.'

Was that some sort of approval? He gave a brief nod. There was something important he wasn't being told but he knew better than to ask.

'You wanted these,' Bill said, giving the papers to Dan.

'Thanks,' Dan said. 'Keep the evidence bag for Mary Burke.'

'Will do.' Bill joined them on the folding chairs.

Tony could hardly stop himself from asking what was in the bag. He and Alex stared at each other in mute agitation.

'We'll ask you to join us when we see the sisters,' Dan said. 'They trust you and it makes it easier for them to relax. We're more likely to get something useful from them.'

'Is that it, then?' Tony said, knowing Dan hadn't finished with them and wishing he'd get on with it.

Dan slipped a slim sheaf of papers from the folder and photographs from the envelope. 'Not much longer, I hope,' he said, tapping the papers. 'This is all compliments of Interpol. Pathology and forensics came up with some interesting conclusions on the woman who died in Underhill. At first they talked generally about her coming from Eastern Europe. Now they have a definite hit on Poland. Dental work was helpful and a plate and pins in her left forearm gave the details we needed.

'It didn't hurt that coincidence played its part. An NCA agent – National Crime Agency – crossed our path at the start of another case. He's been more than helpful with putting some of the biggest pieces together. Of course, we could still be way off base but we don't think so. We need another dose of luck to help us out.'

Alex fidgeted. She crossed her legs and folded her hands around her knee while she jiggled the foot as if it were on a tight spring.

'Look at these,' Dan said, taking out the photos and giving one of them to Tony and Alex. 'Anything you notice?'

A young woman looked back at them, unsmiling, thin-faced, nice-looking in a nondescript way but not happy to be having her photo taken. She had dark hair that curled to her shoulders and wore a turtle-necked jumper.

Dark marks looked like the remnants of a black eye.

Tony frowned but not for long. 'The woman who was murdered in Underhill.' He turned to Alex. 'Do you think so? From her E-fit picture this would be a few years ago but the features seem similar.'

Dan produced the E-fit for them.

'Yes!' Alex leaned over and compared the two. 'But we still don't know who she is? She's got a black eye in this one.'

'I think we may know who she is,' Dan said. 'But we have a way to go yet. Apparently she'd been badly beaten not long before this. The report said a forearm break was consistent with twisting action. I think we can work that out.'

The lovely Constable Miller came over at a smart clip. She ignored everyone but Dan. 'Guv, a Mrs Gimblet from Woodway Farm – the Lady Mayor of Folly, she says – she's on her way over and wants to be sure you'll be here. She sounds angry and as if we'd better all understand how important she is.'

Bill and Dan raised eyebrows. 'We're here,' Bill said, superfluously. 'Where has she supposedly been?' The latter was addressed to Dan.

'With her brother,' Dan said. 'Driving to see properties in the Lake District, the foreman at the youth center said. Not due back for another couple of days. Incommunicado supposedly.'

'Mm,' Bill said significantly. 'I imagine someone got to them with the news. It's still not in the media. I don't know how we've got so lucky. But it's a good thing they're back.'

'Is this code?' Tony asked, past caution. 'What the hell's going on?'

Miller had left and Bill looked pointedly at Dan who gave a slight nod. 'The boy's body was found buried in the heating and cooling system at the new youth center. Something blew a gasket so a caretaker called the people who put it in and they had to dig it up again. We were called and there he was, poor kid.'

Tony glanced at Alex who propped her forehead on one hand. 'How long was the boy dead when he was found. An estimate, anyway,' she said.

'Couple of days, our people think.' This was Dan. 'Which ties in with the timeline of Kyle's disappearance.'

'Bit of a coincidence,' Tony said. 'Kyle has to have some information that's useful. He may be the only one who does.'

'We have to be sure we don't make any false moves talking to him,' Dan said. 'Sid Gammage gave a sort of permission for you to stand in for him with his boys, but that could blow up in our faces. I'm making contact with the appropriate services now. Then I hope he's up to talking to us.'

'You want the other photo, boss,' Bill said to Dan. 'If that woman, Gimblet's on her way we may not have long.'

'Yeah.'

Looking at the picture Dan produced, upside down, Tony saw a man who didn't look familiar.

'Do you think it would work to take Mayor

Gimblet up to the gallery to talk?' Dan asked Bill.

The gallery was reached by stairs to the left of the front door. A dusty place with seats set out in theatre rows, it was only used for an all-parish meeting when there was an overflow of people – which almost never happened.

'Why not?' Bill shrugged. 'You might need a mask for the dust, guv.'

The photo Dan put in front of Tony and Alex showed a bullet-headed male with short, spiked and bleached hair. He glared out of the photo, clearly not a happy man.

Alex took the photo in her hands and studied it closely. 'No, never saw him before. Should I have?'

'I'm damned,' Tony muttered under his breath. He inclined his head to look at the face. 'I know him. Not looking like that. With dark, greased-back hair. The skin's the same, the features are the same. That's friend Ellis of the nasty fists. I'm not likely to forget him.'

He felt as much as saw Dan and Bill look at one another.

'OK,' Tony said, 'is there any connection between these two?'

'Interpol thinks so,' Dan said. 'Interpol doesn't mess around. Meet Dorek and Mina Sawicki, or Sawicka as she would probably have been in Poland. Husband and wife. Smuggling. Liquor, cigarettes, drugs – and the biggie, human trafficking. Dorek has a long rap sheet there. GBH – grievous bodily harm – on several occasions. He was accused of the beating his wife got but she wouldn't say it was him. Probably afraid he'd do something worse. They got to the UK and became Peter Ellis – known as Ellis, and Nicola Fuller – known as Nicky. And they supposedly didn't know each other anymore. They'd never met until they went to work for Gary Podmore. After that they were close.

'They were off the radar until Ellis saw a sucker in Gary Podmore. A sucker with the right set-up to send lorries back and forth to the continent, and a bottomless need for big money to support his expensive tastes. The quantities of goods that got moved were massive, worth a fortune.'

'How did you know to follow this up? I mean, what made you go to Interpol?' Alex had hiked Bogey over her shoulder like a cat.

'Like I said, an NCA agent was already putting things together. Not anything to do with Sid Gammage or Kyle's abduction, but he showed up when the dead boy was found. Just driving by. Sounds unlikely but he knew some loads of Podmore's alcohol and tobacco were finding their way into out of the way places, including parts of the Cotswolds. He was checking some leads, saw the activity at Woodway and stopped. Got there before we did.' Dan took back the pictures. 'I'm damned glad he did. Good bloke to know and there's nothing wrong with a little clean quid pro quo.'

Alex leaned forward. 'Completely off topic, but why is your Miller put off by me? I never met her before all this.'

Bill gave a bark of laughter and Dan glared at him.

'Just one of those things,' Bill said, clearing his throat. 'We all think Miller has a thing for Dan, here, and there might be those who have suggested—'

'That's enough, sergeant,' Dan said, but Tony noticed he'd turned pink.

'Yeah, well,' Bill said. 'It's dopey to think Dan would have a soft spot for a pain in the ass who keeps showing up in the middle of our investigations, anyway. But that's the word around the station. Some woman in Folly-on-Weir could be competition for Miller.'

'Any coffee over there?' Dan asked tightly. 'Take a look would you?'

Bill sidled off looking more pleased with himself than he should. Tony figured he'd pay for that later. 'So you have two cases here,' he said. 'At least two. The murder of the boy, then the original murder of the woman and how that ties in with Sid and Kyle – or does it?'

Dan drummed his fingers. 'Can I tempt you into a drink in that very fine snug at the Black Dog later? After everyone's settled down for the night that is?'

'Yes,' Alex said promptly while Tony thought about how he wanted to spend time with her beside him while they found out more about what had happened to Kyle, followed by some time with her beside him with no one else around.

'Tony?' she prompted.

'Sounds like a great idea.'

Bogey chose that moment to scramble down and make his way to Dan's knees where he looked adoringly into the detective's face.

'Traitor,' Tony murmured to himself.

Dan picked the dog up and he leaned against his champion. 'You understand we need to talk to the sisters?' Dan said. 'It's going to be much later than I'd like by the time I've had a quiet talk with Kyle. We have to have someone from child services there but we're working on coming to an agreement about who has custodial care of him. That would be you, Tony, and Lily, and Alex. Thank God you're all upstanding citizens, according to those who don't know you.'

Tony grinned at Alex.

'I think I know what Joan Gimblet wants but with luck, I can fob her off for a bit and get to Corner Cottage.'

Right on cue, Joan burst through the doors and stormed up to Dan. She didn't even glance at Tony and Alex. Her face was painted in not too attractive shades of puce with purple veins standing out across her nose and cheeks. 'Do you know who I am?' she bellowed. 'I'm the Mayor of Folly-on-Weir, that's who I am. What right do you have to disrupt and destroy my property without a by-your-leave?'

'Are you referring to workmen responding to a service call and finding a body in the geothermal workings of your heating and cooling system, Mrs Gimblet?'

'I should have been informed, not left to find out when I drove back onto my property.'

'Unfortunate, that,' Dan agreed. 'But out of any of our hands. This was murder, madam. We are in the process of finding out the deceased's identity. Do you have any ideas about that?'

'Me?' Her voice rose several octaves. 'What would I know about such things. What I want to know is who took advantage of a hole on my property to bury a body. Completely thoughtless and uncalled for.'

'Quite,' Dan said.

Alex's lips were parted in fascinated horror.

'Who else was at the farm, madam? We couldn't find anyone to talk to.'

'Martin should have been there. My brother was with me in the Lake District. He'll be back soon but I dropped him off to take a train. He has some business to attend to first.'

'Then I'll ask you to have Mr Sutcliffe check in with us when he does return.'

'Why?' She bristled.

'We will be questioning a great many people. I'm sure you're as eager as we are to get to the bottom of this vicious crime.'

Joan's brows drew together. She seemed to focus on Tony and Alex for the first time. 'What does that mean, vicious crime?'

'I'm afraid we can't disclose the details,' Dan said. 'Not at this point.'

'But I'm the mayor. And I own a great deal of land around here. I have a right to answers.'

'Not to questions about official police business, Mrs Gimblet. I've decided I'd like to have Mr Sutcliffe and Martin come to see me as soon as they show up. If I'm not here, I'll be called in. Now, if you'll excuse me . . .'

First Joan appeared shocked, then amazed. She drew herself up and flounced from the hall muttering threats about going to the chief constable.

293

'And much good may that do her,' Dan said with a chuckle. 'I want to go to Kyle now. Bill will come and you're welcome. But keep an eye out for signs he's getting overwhelmed.

'We'll see you at Corner Cottage. But don't forget that meeting later. I have a feeling you hold a more important key than you realize, Alex.'

Forty-Two

Showered and mostly devoid of the gum from the gaffer tape that had been applied across his eyes (Doc said whoever did that was a thought-less fool) and his mouth, around his body to hold his arms at his sides to just past his elbows, and around his ankles, Kyle sat on the couch in Lily's crowded little sitting room. He looked quite happy to be tucked in with a puffy blue quilt.

Bill took Officer Harding outside, to find out if Kyle had said anything important, Alex thought. The rest, including Scoot, who sat on the floor at his brother's side, stayed where they were.

She waited for Dan to say who should stay and who should go but he didn't, just chatted to Kyle in a friendly voice about everyone being glad he was back.

Kyle stayed quiet and watched first one, then another of them. The tape had left angry red marks on his face and what she could see of his arms. His wet hair was uncombed and stuck up at angles.

'Radhika had to go back to the clinic,' he announced suddenly. 'She has to look after Naruto.'

Alex swallowed. She hadn't expected the kitten to come up so soon.

'That's good,' Tony said easily. 'Radhika says she's doing well.' He sat on the arm of Alex's chair and held her hand.

'I don't know who took me,' Kyle went on, equally abrupt. 'I didn't see anything. He didn't speak. Once we got there, he just took me to where things were for when I needed them, like the bucket.' His nose wrinkled and Alex winced.

'Are you sure it was a he?' Dan asked.

Kyle shrugged. 'I think so. He took the tape off my mouth for me to have water and crackers, then put it back quickly. Almost choked me once.'

Alex made fists and dug her fingernails into Tony's hand. He kept holding on.

'Rotten,' Dan said. 'Any idea where you were? After you were taken from the vehicle, that is?'

Kyle shook his head, no. 'I was on the floor. On a sleeping bag, I think. I could move my hands a bit. I would have tried scooting to look for a way out but I couldn't see so I didn't do it.'

'How far did he drive you?'

Another shrug. 'Felt like I was going in circles. There was a smell in the boot. I think I was in the boot. I smelled it before, I think, but I was all muddled up.' He looked around and frowned. 'And I was too scared to concentrate.'

'We can go over that later,' Dan said. 'Any of us would have been scared. Are you hungry?'

Kyle shook his head. 'Lily gave me some fancy little sandwiches, like they have for tea. And I had orange juice.' He looked at Lily and the trusting smile he gave her squeezed Alex's heart.

Dan bowed his head, thinking. When he looked up his face was harder. 'Were you hurt? I mean, was anything done to hurt you? Anything you may not want to talk about.'

'No,' Kyle said promptly. 'Mostly I was alone. I didn't know when it was night or day. I just kept hoping he would say something to me – just to hear a voice. I hadn't done anything. Why would someone do that to me?'

Dan leaned back in his chair. He was so serious, there was no doubt he wanted to consider the questions before answering. 'You didn't do anything and taking you was a terrible thing to do. We have to work it through, Kyle. While you were gone, I think you were fulfilling someone else's need. I don't know what they needed. Then they didn't need you anymore, but you weren't hurt. That means something – I'm not sure what, but we will find out.'

'He took the tape off my ankles so I could walk, then held my shoulders and guided me along. There were steps and I felt as if it got colder where we went. I thought it was under the ground. He wasn't rough with me. His hands were big. I'm sure it was a man.'

'What did the trunk of the car smell like?'

Scoot said, stepping on Dan's questioning with no sign of realizing it might not be a good idea. 'Was it like oil or something?'

'No. A bit sweet, I think, but I couldn't concentrate.'

Alex studied the boy. He needed quiet and calm, and he didn't need to be peppered with questions for very long, but she wondered if what he'd smelled in that vehicle had been the same as the odor she found in the back of Sid's van.

'Mum,' she said. 'I need to get to the Black Dog for the evening. There will be a nosey crowd and it's not fair to leave Hugh alone. If you can stay here, I'll get back later. OK?'

Lily smiled. 'Of course.'

'I'll stay with them,' Doc said. 'This young man needs some peace. More questions in the morning, Dan? If you have them.'

'Yes,' Dan said. 'Good idea.' He glanced at Bill who leaned in the doorway and they sent one of their unspoken messages. 'We'll get out of your hair. I'll be at the Black Dog getting sorted out for a bit.'

He was almost to the door when Kyle said, 'Can Naruto come here? I won't be able to go back to our cottage to stay yet, will I?'

Dan turned and said, 'Not yet, Kyle. I'd like both of you boys to avoid the cottage for now – if Lily can put up with you for longer.' He grinned. Dan grinning was a younger, gentler version of the way they knew him, Alex decided.

The detectives left and Tony stood up with Alex.

'Will I be able to have Naruto?' Kyle asked.

297

'It's not like blackmail or something. It's not that I expect to have her because of anything else that's happened to me. It's just . . . well, what do you think?'

'She's yours,' Scoot said, looking only at his brother. 'I paid the money for everything she needs and signed the paper. It's an adoption paper. You adopted her.'

Lily raised her eyes to Alex's and smiled a mischievous smile.

'That's that then,' Alex said. 'The papers are signed – as long as your dad approves.'

Forty-Three

The saloon bar buzzed excitedly. Every few minutes, the volume of voices dropped as customers glanced around to see if they were either missing something, or being inappropriate. Pinging from the side room where the fruit machines held court didn't diminish. The excuse Alex heard for the exuberance was that they were celebrating Kyle's homecoming. She doubted more than a handful of them even knew what he looked like.

Alex had insisted Scoot remain at Corner Cottage with Kyle despite making her own work-load heavier. Tony wielded a mean dish cloth over the tables he efficiently cleared. He crumpled empty crisp bags and serviettes onto his tray among stacks of dirty dishes and glasses and tossed back laughing quips at those who gave him digs for taking himself down a few notches in the professional work chain.

'Did you give the sisters Dan's message?' he asked Alex in passing. 'If they're too tired, he'll have to wait.'

'You're joking,' she said. 'Being asked to stay has made their day. They're glowing with anticipation.'

'Right,' Tony said and slalomed his way through tables toward the kitchens.

Alex glanced behind her. No, she hadn't imagined that Mary's cat, Max, had not only been elevated from lying in his carrier to curling up on Mary's lap, but now one-eyed Max had graduated to sitting on the table, blinking that one eye contentedly at the fire. He settled into a more comfortable position and delved his nose into his front paws.

Well, if someone complained she'd have to have a gentle word with Mary and Harriet. But with his bright orange fur, Max looked very nice on the dark, polished table.

Kev Winslet, gamekeeper on the Derwinter estate, touched her arm and motioned he'd like to speak to her – privately. She checked that Hugh, with the welcome addition of Juste Vidal, was managing well and followed Kev into the vestibule.

'I saw DCI O'Reilly go upstairs earlier,' he said in a low voice. Alex noted that the man was fairly sober – unusual when she knew he'd been at the pub most of the day.

'Yes?' she encouraged him.

'He went out again but he was in a hurry so I didn't like to stop him. Not when I don't know if he's already been told what I was going to tell him.'

Much as she'd like to know what Kev had to tell Dan, prudence took over. 'You might try the parish hall. If he's not there, they'll take a message for him.'

Kev scuffed his boots and frowned. 'I trust you to help me out, Alex,' he said. 'You probably know anyway. I saw when Kyle Gammage was dropped off – dumped more likely – outside your mum's cottage. It was a couple of minutes before anyone else noticed. Lily was here and she saw him right after the vehicle drove away. And it was spitting gravel, I can tell you.'

Alex stared at him. She crossed her arms tightly. 'Kev, did you see who brought him?'

'No, dammit. It took a bit to twig what had happened. Whoever it was got in and out on the pavement side and fast. Then he was gone and that poor kid was leaning against the gatepost trussed up like the Christmas goose.'

'You have to speak to the police,' Alex said. 'Did you get a number plate?'

Kev turned red, more from frustration than embarrassment, Alex thought. 'I wish. I just stood at the window, gawping at the boy like he was an apparition while the van left like a bat out of hell up the High toward Underhill. But he didn't have to be going there, did he?'

'Van?' Alex screwed up her eyes. 'We thought it was a car.'

'No,' Kev said. 'No, it was a van. Darkish, I think, but I honestly didn't notice anything else but Kyle. Not even the make of the bloody thing. Fool that I am.'

'Lighten up on yourself,' Alex said. 'Anyone

could have done exactly what you did. I would have. I'd only have been thinking about Kyle. Would you mind running down to the hall? I'll give Dan a call or get him traced. He'll want to talk to you right away.'

She hadn't forgotten Dan would be meeting with some of them in the snug a bit later but she wasn't comfortable with the idea of inviting Kev to join them.

'I'll be off,' Kev said, straightening his shoulders. He pushed through the door to the outside and Alex was left mulling what he'd said.

Tony joined her and put an arm around her shoulders. 'I want to get my bid in now before you're distracted by the difficult stuff,' he said. 'Would you consider sleeping with me tonight? My place or yours, or even here at the inn? I'd probably rather stay close to Kyle and whatever's likely to develop there.'

She frowned. 'Here,' she said. 'With an offer like that, how can I refuse?'

Forty-Four

Dan had driven out and parked his car on the far side of Underhill, on a hillside overlooking a valley too dark to make out details at that time of evening.

Exactly on time, her time, Corinne had called from Ireland to talk to him. Sitting there in the space between evening and night, he played and replayed what she had said. He hadn't stood a chance of pressing for what he really wanted. She tried to be fair to all of them, but in the end, he doubted one of them would look forward to peace and acceptance ahead.

The first fat drops of rain hit his face through the car window. He'd rolled it down to let in the night air that always seemed full of promise to him. The end of what had gone before and the promise of what was to come. He'd been right enough on that one, only he was left looking at a hollow resolution to what he'd hoped would be so much kinder to him.

Perhaps he had concentrated too much on what he wanted. Yes, he knew he had, but there had been so little of what he wanted from the time of the divorce until now. And above all he truly wanted Calum to be happy. He wanted Corinne to be happy, too, but with the cold rain keeping his thoughts clear, he couldn't think that she was or would be. They hadn't made a success of their attempts at marriage and family. Why should he expect them to come to acceptable joint decisions now?

He held his mobile and waited for Calum's call. Corinne had promised she'd make sure their boy had privacy to speak to Dan. He would impress on him that there was a really positive angle to what his mother proposed.

No, he would let Calum talk as much as possible. Perhaps it was time to step back and be guided, not that he, Dan, had been able to take the lead in much about his family in recent years.

The mobile rang with the distinctive Skype, under-the-water resonance. Dan switched on and studied his son's face. Disappointment, hope, confusion – what was there, almost imploring him to point the way?

'Dad,' Calum said. 'I wanted Christmas with you.'

'And I wanted you with me.' That had been the deepest cut, the loss of a Christmas, an old-fashioned one, together, chasing the careless times they'd once known.

'So what do you think?' Calum said. 'It's so hard. We can't have everything we wanted and if we do what Mam says, I'll be in Spain for Christmas with Bram and his boys. And they'll be wishing I was somewhere else. And Mam will be trying to make all of us happy. And Bram just barges along with his grin and his thinking everything's just fine while some of us are fed up.'

Calum sounded too old and too sad. Dan could hardly bear listening to him. 'OK,' he said, putting a smile on his face. 'It's not what we want, or not all of what we want. But this is one of those times when we have to give a bit to get a lot. Look at it like that. You spend Christmas in Spain with your mam and then you come to me for school afterwards. We'll settle in and have a good time. You'll be with our old friends, and they'll be thrilled and so will you. And we'll have the evenings and weekends to do things. Your mam thinks we'll be happy with that and we will. It'll be hard over Christmas but hey, I've got an idea. I'd better grab it fast, I don't get many of those.'

Calum gave what almost sounded like a giggle. 'Go on, then.'

'We'll have a second Christmas. How about that? We'll do the whole thing just the way we said we would only after you get back from Spain.'

For a moment the boy went quiet and Dan's heart missed some beats, then Calum said, 'I'd like that. Can we have that tree, still?'

'Of course, the whole thing. We'll get a living tree and plant it in the garden afterwards. It'll be our tree, our memories. You'd better start writing your letter to Father Christmas.'

'Oh, Dad, I'm not a baby.'

'I am. I'm going to start mine.'

Calum laughed and at last he wasn't trying to sound happy. 'Just get me a convertible Jaguar – I mean, tell Father Christmas I want a convertible Jaguar, Dad. I'll let you drive it till I can take over. How's that?'

'A great plan,' Dan said. 'But I'm still going to work on my letter so start saving up your pocket money. Will you tell your mam we think her idea is just fine?' It had been presented as a take it or leave it proposition if Dan wanted Calum back in an English school for a while.

'I will,' Calum said. 'I expect she'll want you to tell her, too.'

'She will at that,' Dan said. 'And I'll do it. Now get you off to bed. Love you, son.'

'Me, too, Dad.'

The lights inside the Black Dog were dimmed by the time Dan drove into the front parking lot.

More time than he'd realized had passed while he was lost in the 'what ifs.'

He almost wished he didn't have to face a discussion about the case now. What he had lost seemed sharper than ever, even when he could look forward to some extra time with Calum. He didn't blame Corinne for wanting their son with her at Christmas, especially when she'd be surrounded by Bram and his boys. She'd need someone of her own. Funny how he still thought of himself and Calum as hers when he, at least, never would be again.

He turned the Lexus off. The wipers stopped shifting through rain on the windshield and the water closed him in. It was up to him to make Calum's life as good as it could be. He'd do that by getting along with Corinne and not rocking the boat. He did grit his teeth a bit at that.

The front door of the inn was unlocked and he walked in quietly, shedding his raincoat and shaking off as much water as he could before closing the door behind him. The place seemed very quiet at first, but then he heard murmurs of conversation. The reception committee waited for him in the snug.

Forty-Five

Always trying to get ahead of any really busy times, Lily already had a tastefully pretty string of fairy lights looped along at ceiling level above

305

the order window in the snug. There were a few weeks to go before Christmas but Alex was glad her mum initiated these things.

Tony sat close to her, his arms crossed, a serious expression on his face while Harriet and Mary smiled and laughed, clearly enjoying this break from their routine. Max was on a table again, hardly recognizable as the scrawny stray Alex had found in a rubbish bin, with a badly infected eye Tony had to remove.

Doc had stayed with Kyle and Scoot while Lily came to the meeting. He had also turned up with tempting newspaper-wrapped packages of fish and chips from the newly opened shop in formerly empty High Street quarters.

Alex smiled at the thought. 'We'll have competition from the new chippy,' she said. 'I don't want to see everyone making a steady diet of that stuff either.'

'Sounds good to me,' Tony said. He paused. 'I thought I heard someone come in. I expect it's Dan.'

The man himself threw a moving shadow on the glass panels of the door and came in. His smile didn't completely work, Alex thought. She hoped there wasn't more bad news coming.

'Good evening, all,' he said, taking off his suit jacket and jerking down his tie knot. He sat close to the Burke sisters and rolled up his sleeves. 'Whew, no peace for the wicked.'

'Did Kev Winslet find you?' Alex asked.

'Yes. Or I got his message passed on. Good for him to take a note of what he saw. It would have been nicer if he'd got the license plate but it's still going to help.' A slight smile, there and then gone, suggested the detective was pleased about something. 'Can I buy everyone a drink?'

Lily popped up and looked around expectantly. Tony had a half of Ambler, Alex a bitter lemon, the sisters – surprise – a Harvey's Bristol Cream each. Dan asked for a single brandy and Lily said she would join him.

When she returned and they were all settled, including Katie and Bogie under the sisters' table, Dan reached for the notebook from his inside jacket pocket. 'I jotted a few things down to keep us on track. Bill will stop in when he's finished at the parish hall. What do you think about what Kev saw? Alex, or anyone?'

'I'm not sure he spoke to anyone but me,' Alex said. 'And I sent him to you. Have you ever felt you missed something really momentous? That it was right there in front of you if you could only remember it, darn it.'

'Frequently,' Lily said amid an affirmative chorus. 'Should we try prompting you?'

'No, please!' Alex held up her hands. 'Either there was or wasn't something and either I'll remember or I won't.'

'About the van?' Dan said, ignoring her plea. 'Radhika saw a big, dark vehicle when she was going back through all that rain the night Kyle was taken from the clinic. Now we've got another one. Or the same one.'

Alex looked at his face; she felt a bit removed into her thoughts. 'It's probably too late,' she said, feeling a little sick. 'But could someone go check out, you know, the van?'

'I do know and it's already been done.'

'Is there a way to know if it's been moved?' She felt all eyes upon her.

'We made sure there was,' Dan said. 'And it has been.'

'What?' Tony raised his voice a little. 'Don't do this. Tell us.'

'I don't like keeping secrets,' Dan said, 'but sometimes it's necessary. As soon as I can give out the information, you'll all know. The thing is I think we're almost home but missing one or two very key points, or players, maybe I should say.'

Feeling self-conscious, Alex asked Dan if she could have a few words alone but when he agreed, she took Tony with her into the restaurant.

'This is the problem with group conferences,' Dan said. 'We have to think about each person present and what's suitable to share with them.'

'Yes,' Alex said. 'Dan, you don't think Sid did these things, do you?'

'We can't rule him out yet, but I think it's less and less likely. And Kyle would have known if it was his father. If we follow up the tip we've been given and he shows up where it's been suggested he will, then no, Sid could not have been anywhere near Kyle, certainly not today. We're hoping for final answers on that before morning.'

'I don't suppose it matters much now,' Alex said. 'But that smell in the back of Sid's van – I smelled it and so did Kyle, and that's what was used, isn't it?'

'Yeah,' Dan looked speculative. 'That's what we have every reason to believe.'

'I think it was onions and maybe apples,' Alex said. 'I smelled something sort of sweet in the back of the van but didn't think much about it. Then I saw boxes of fruit and strings of onions in the shed, the one Sid found me in. I didn't make a connection then, but now I wonder. If Sid didn't drive that van and take Kyle away, who did?'

'That's the major question,' Dan said. 'And so far there's a big gap where the answer should be. And another one around the identity of the boy who was killed, and whether there's any link.'

'Link?' Tony inclined his head. 'Why would there be?'

'I'm not sure enough to throw out guesses,' Dan said. 'But there is someone I need to talk to and if he doesn't show up quickly, we'll have to hunt him down.'

'Who is this?' Alex couldn't help asking. 'Someone we all know?'

'In a manner of speaking. We'll have to wait a while longer for that. Not too long and it's important he doesn't suspect we're waiting for him. Now I wish Bill would show up so we can finish with the sisters.'

Tony drew his brows together. 'I don't see what help they could be.'

'Just an attempt to get some confirmation on one point.' He looked as if there was something he wanted to say but didn't think he should. 'Let's get back in so I can deal with that now.'

Bill met them outside the snug door. He carried what looked like the same brown, stapled-shut bag he'd had at the parish hall. He took Dan aside and they spoke quietly together.

'We'd better go in,' Tony said, but Dan and Bill were right behind them when they rejoined the others.

'Hugh stuck his head out,' Lily said. 'He and Juste are still cleaning up but Hugh will come through whenever he's needed.'

'I think you can pass on what's been said,' Dan told her. 'I'm going to caution the rest of you not to mention what I'm about to show Mary to anyone outside this room. If you do, I'll know where it came from.'

Alex hated it when Dan gave one of his threats.

'Mary,' Dan said, 'take a look at these and tell me if they're familiar.'

Bill pulled on gloves and took a pair of blue trainers from the bag. 'What do you think?' he said.

Harriet started to speak but Dan stopped her with a hand to her shoulder.

'Oh, dear,' Mary said. 'Those are hers, aren't they? That woman who came into Leaves of Comfort? Blues are easiest for me to remember,' she told Harriet. 'It's greens I have problems with. Of course, they could be another pair of blue trainers but what would be the point in that?'

'Kyle thought they were on the dead woman's feet when he found her,' Alex said, and ignored Dan's displeased look – she supposed because she was talking freely in front of others. 'They weren't there when she was taken away, I understand. Where were they found?'

310

Bill and Dan's eyes met. 'Hidden in plain sight,' Dan said finally. 'Now I'm off to bed. I've got a feeling tomorrow will be a very long day. Let's hope it's also productive.'

Tony and Alex followed Dan and Bill into the restaurant and the bottom of the stairs leading to Dan's room. 'I've told the ladies I'll run them home,' Tony said. 'They aren't finished with their sherry yet.'

'What aren't you saying?' Alex asked. 'Can you tell us?'

Bill shrugged and Dan considered a moment or two before saying, 'Sid's motorbike was found a couple of miles from the murder scene, buried in a hole known to the perpetrator. They covered it up with brush and junk but they wanted it found – it was a bad job. And it wasn't there immediately after the crime or we'd have found it then. This was staged, we think. We hope. The trainers were in a saddlebag. Whoever went back for the shoes waited until after the search to put the bike in place.'

Forty-Six

It was well after midnight when Dan and Bill drove past Oxford on the A40 and headed for the M4 toward the east coast. They both had a lot of questions and hoped they were about to get answers.

'How do you feel about working with Andy

Cooper on this, boss?' Bill said. 'It's more or less his baby.'

'That's not the way I see it. He wouldn't have got this far without Ellis walking into the station in Gloucester and giving us his sob story about Gary Podmore and Sid. Just be glad he didn't decide to mention his wife. That would have thrown a spanner in. We'd have had to take him to see the body. And once he realized we knew the dead woman was his wife, he would likely have stopped talking and we might not have got this lead for tonight.'

'But you thought we had to bring in Cooper?' Bill's ambition showed more often these days. He wanted his bits of glory.

'Without him we'd have been much less likely to believe a word Ellis said. With Andy, it all fell into place – we hope. And we're relying on him to have a description of the lorry by now.'

Bill sniffed and from the corner of his eye Dan saw him nodding.

'Good time to make this drive,' he said. 'Traffic's light so we should make good time.' Rain was turning to sleet on the windscreen and he said, 'Bugger it,' with feeling.

'You spoke too soon about making good time,' Bill said. 'Not that a bit of bad weather has to slow us down much. I noticed you didn't mention this to Alex and Tony.'

Thinking about Alex was a no win for him at the moment. 'They don't need to know until we see how it ends up. Could be they'll find out soon enough.'

312

'So it's tobacco and booze Podmore's into?' Bill turned on the defroster, front and back. 'Big time, apparently. Any thoughts on drugs?'

'Ellis and Nicky have a history with drugs but what was found on her body was probably supposed to throw us off even more.'

'You don't think there could be some human trafficking now?'

'Damned if I know for sure,' Dan said. 'But I'm expecting it – Andy Cooper is pretty sure that's a major part of it. Hell, I just want to find out Ellis told us the truth about Sid and we can hook up with him. It's not lost on me that we could have been getting a line and Ellis had some other plan in mind for himself. Too bad we couldn't hold him.'

'Yeah,' Bill said. 'Too bad he wouldn't incriminate himself. By the time he'd finished he almost had me feeling sorry for the way Podmore tried to suck him in.' He laughed. 'Once we have enough, Podmore comes in, right?'

Dan smiled. 'Eager beaver. I should think that'll be the plan. I want to check in and make sure our guys have got him under surveillance still. They might try to cover up before they'd let me know they'd lost him. Nah, they wouldn't.'

'I thought we were being positive,' Bill said.

By the time they reached Chelmsford they'd been driving for three hours. 'Bit behind,' Dan said, gulping coffee they'd bought at a roadside services. 'This is cold, but at least it's wet.'

'Colchester soon,' Bill said, 'then it'll come up quickly.'

A soft-sided lorry blasted past them, throwing

up dirty water from the roadway. 'Sod it,' Bill said.

'You're jumpy, partner. Time to settle down. This will go well.'

'Positive again, are we? What, you've got a crystal ball now?' Bill sounded tetchy.

'I want to know why Ellis would snatch Kyle – if he did. To keep Sid in line is too simple, and it doesn't fit with this story about Sid being Podmore's lieutenant. But if Ellis didn't take our boy, who did? I don't like Sid for it.'

'Me either.' Bill leaned forward. 'Colchester coming up.'

'The terminal's in Parkeston. Never been there. Never had a reason. Cooper had better be where he said he would or we're out of luck.'

'From here we can see it unloading,' Cooper said. 'And we're close enough to nab him. There's no way for him to make a run for it in the vehicle and I doubt he'd try getting away on foot.'

Cooper had been lounging against a parking sign when Dan and Bill rolled in. They sat in his car of the day, a rusted gray Fiat, and watched through binoculars as the big red S of the Stena line ferry came into view from the Hook of Holland.

'Right on time,' Andy Cooper said. 'I suggest we approach at the same time as the customs officers.'

'Sounds good,' Dan said. He didn't like the uncertainty of the setup – too many chances for screw ups.

314

Forty-five minutes and the ferry nosed in to dock and soon enough the vessel started to disgorge its payload. All three of them watched, scanning every vehicle for an extended-sized yellow van with 'Northern Freight' in red on the sides.

Some vehicles got pulled aside for closer inspection, others moved on after a short exchange with customs.

'What if they changed the vehicle?' Bill said.

'We get home sooner,' Andy responded drily. 'But from what you told me and my own sources, we know what we're looking for. If he didn't miss the bloody ferry, he'll be there.'

'There!' Bill yelled.

'OK,' Andy said. 'Out, but not too close until he's stopped.'

A windowless yellow van emblazoned with 'Northern Freight' drove slowly down a ramp.

'He's stopped and talking to customs.' Dan kept the binoculars trained even though he was close enough to see fairly well. 'Holy shit,' he muttered. 'I don't believe it. Move. He waited for customs to move off and he's getting out and walking away. That's cool if you like it. Move, move. It's Sid Gammage I want. The van's all yours, Andy.'

The NCA officer fell in with them and ran flat out. Dan was almost glad of the cold rain that still fell. He and Bill ran, doubled over, dodging between cars, toward Sid Gammage's tall figure walking as if he didn't have a care.

'Wait,' Dan said, signaling Bill and Andy to duck lower. 'I think he's looking for his car, or some car. Son-of-a–. Ellis had to know this was the routine but he didn't mention it. Don't ask me why but I think this is probably as far as Gammage ever goes. He's going to slide off, or try to. There! Go, go, go.'

Cars coming and going got in their way and brakes screeched. Horns blared and angry faces stuck out of windows. Dan dashed on.

Sid reached a gold-colored Peugeot and fished in his pockets for keys.

Dan slammed into him as he started to open the driver's door and Bill hooked handcuffs on the man's free wrist. Sid tried to fling himself around.

'Best hold still,' Dan said. 'You've been telling too many porkies, Sid. We need you to explain that to us.'

'Got him,' Andy said. 'Nicely done.'

Sid looked at Dan and let out a long sigh. He closed his eyes momentarily and made no attempt to struggle when the second handcuff went on.

He might not be a shrink, but if Dan had to guess, he'd say Sid Gammage was relieved to be caught.

Catching his breath, Dan grabbed Sid by the coat collar and started to move him.

'Oh, fuck,' Andy said, in a low voice and with feeling. 'It's gone. I don't see it anywhere. Someone's driven the bloody yellow bird of a van away. Right under our noses.'

Forty-Seven

Tony landed on the bed beside her and held her so tightly she could hardly get any air.

'Can't breathe,' she sputtered.

'You didn't have any difficulty stealing my towel, madam. You were breathing then.'

'Why are you up so early? I want to fool around for hours.'

He rolled onto his back and spread his arms and legs as if exhausted. 'You've worn me out. It's eight already and I don't think I got four hours sleep. That's what sleeping with a sex fiend does to you.'

She punched his side lightly. 'You wanted to be here.'

'I did, didn't I? And I still want to be here. But I don't want some bright spark coming to knock at the door and ask if we want tea or something. It's more sedate to go down for breakfast.'

Alex giggled. 'Sedate? When were we ever sedate?' She tickled him until he convulsed over her and she got what she'd wanted.

Panting, tangled together, they waited until their breathing quieted.

'This could be a hell of a day,' Tony said, pulling Alex to lie on top of him. He stroked her in all the places guaranteed to drive her mad. 'I don't think Dan came back last night. Something tells me they were expecting things

317

to come to a head – or at least to move forward.'

'Let's have breakfast in bed,' Alex suggested.

'I don't think so. One of us would have to go down and get it and I don't want to put up with the comments. Not that I don't think they make them anyway.'

'Mmm.' Alex closed her eyes and turned her face into his neck. 'OK, we'll get up. Maybe I don't want this day to start. It's unlikely to be better than yesterday and apart from getting Kyle back, that wasn't great.'

Tony's phone rang. He picked up. 'Tony Harrison. Good morning . . . Do I? Well I *feel* chipper, too. Might as well start out on an optimistic note. What is it, Dan?'

He looked meaningfully at Alex and she shunted up to sit against the headboard.

'You do have Sid, though? Yes, sounds like a mess. Rather you than me. He's on his way to Gloucester? You're on your way. Gloucester, too?' His frown grew deeper. 'How did Ellis get away?' He screwed up his face in a giant wince. 'They set it up, then. Sid walked away and Ellis hopped in and took the truck while you were all busy. Still . . . well, perhaps you'll tell us more and perhaps you won't. Sure, we'll watch for Ellis but I doubt he'd come here.' He narrowed his eyes. 'I'm at the Black Dog now. Had to pick up Katie.' Lies weren't his style but Dan O'Reilly wasn't a man he wanted involved in thoughts about his own sex life with Alex. 'I'll take Alex aside and warn her, and we'll make sure Lily and Hugh know.'

318

Dan must have taken some time with his next explanation. 'I see,' Tony said. 'Why would he come back here? Wouldn't he keep on running once he got away? You think or you know he killed her?' Tony's face went blank. 'Oh, my god. Psychopath. He must be if he did that.'

Alex pulled at the sheets and coverlet and wrapped them tightly around her. She looked suddenly cold.

'Don't worry,' Tony said. 'I wouldn't dream of approaching him – not that I think we'll see him. You're right, though, better to be warned. Martin? He called the parish hall when? OK. I wonder where he is now.'

He scooted beside Alex with his knees drawn up and gathered her in beside him. 'But he didn't tell you this story he says you'll want to hear? We'll watch for him as well. Never a dull moment. See you when you can get here.'

He tossed the mobile on the bedside table and rested his chin on top of Alex's head.

'What?' she said breathlessly. 'What was all that?'

'Too much. That's what it was. They've got Sid in custody for some sort of smuggling. They caught him driving off a ferry in Harwich. I didn't get the impression he was under suspicion for anything worse.'

'Like kidnapping his own son?'

'Mm. Right. We're to watch out for any sign of the man they called Ellis, the one Mary thinks she saw. And we don't approach him if we see him, we don't do anything.'

'I don't need any encouragement to stay away. But I don't understand what's going on.'

319

'Neither do I except the net is closing on the people involved in all this. We go on as normal and keep a close eye on both boys. I am going to the parish hall to talk to LeJuan who can apparently explain it all better. Dan said when he and Bill get here things will be clearer, whatever that means.

'I couldn't figure out who worried Dan the most but if Martin Gimblet shows up he'd like us to string him along and get a message to Gloucester if they aren't here by then. He said something about Martin being potentially unstable but probably not dangerous to anyone but himself. Remember the man you saw sneaking around at Gammages that day? He went in the shed? That was probably Martin who knows the place like the back of his hand because he played there as a kid when he was home from school. I tend to forget the cottage and all that land belong to Joan Gimblet, too.'

The instant his feet hit the floor and he started to dress, Alex hopped from the bed and gathered her things for the shower. 'I'm coming, too,' she said. 'I'm really worried about Scoot and Kyle, though. What did Dan mean about them, about watching them closely?'

'He seemed to think telling us to do it was enough. I'm surprised he said as much as he did. It's going to be hard with those boys, knowing they're anxious about Sid but not being able to tell them he's at least safe for the moment.'

'Dan thinks Ellis could come to Folly again? Why would he?'

'That I don't know.' He weighed risking really

320

upsetting her. 'Don't overact, but it could be that Ellis killed Nicky and tried to pin it on Sid.'

'She was his wife,' Alex said quietly. 'Surely he wouldn't kill his wife to implicate another man.'

'Ellis has a history of violence toward her. They didn't like each other. If he was desperate enough and thought the other man posed a threat to his deal with Gary and Nicky happened to be handy, he could have killed her in a rage and then come up with the idea to pin it on Sid. Sid might seem as if he was replacing Ellis as Gary Podmore's main man. And I had another thought. Would Ellis take Kyle to keep Sid under control? If he took the kid and told Sid to do as he, Ellis, said, or else, that would probably be enough to have Sid running in any circles Ellis wanted.'

'I wish Sid had never taken the bait and decided to make extra money working for Podmore, not that he had to know it would all be crooked from the outset.' At the door, wrapped in her bathrobe, Alex stopped and looked at him. 'What could Dan mean by smuggling. How would Sid be smuggling? What would he smuggle?'

'Hop to,' Tony told her. 'I don't have any of the answers you want – and I want – but I need to make sure the boys are covered. I'll find out if the police are watching the school. And the cottage, come to that. I have to think they are. I should have checked with Dan. You can see the cottage from the bathroom window. Take a look and see if there's anyone stationed there. I'll deal with the school.'

* * *

321

'Anything you think we should agree on before going into the hall?' Alex said.

Tony drove slower than usual, a thoughtful expression on his face. 'Between you and me,' he said. 'I think it would be a really good idea if we didn't openly disagree on any point unless it's absolutely necessary.'

'Agreed. I feel better knowing the police are watching both the cottage and the school. Mum said Kyle wanted to go to school today but she told him Dan wouldn't like that and he didn't bring it up again. Dan seems to have a hold over both those boys. That, or they really admire him.'

'He's got a boy of his own. That could help with the way he talks to them,' Tony said.

She smiled a little. Tony had an explanation for everything. 'Here we are.' They turned at the parking lot in front of the parish hall. 'I don't like the idea that Ellis could show up at any moment. Martin doesn't really bother me. He's always seemed such a pussycat. More shy than anything. I should probably have made more of an effort to get to know him. He always looks as if he'd like to talk. But this Ellis is a nasty piece of work. Really dangerous.'

'Dan didn't explain anything about him but never forget what they say about the quiet people. He could be a case of deep, running waters for all we know.'

Inside the hall officers moved quickly, they also moved quietly, but Alex decided that was because they were too busy for chatter.

LeJuan Harding came in behind them, his handsome, usually cheerful face looking decidedly frosted. He passed Tony and Alex and went directly behind the screens.

'Not a happy man,' Alex said.

The detective constable emerged again, taking off his coat, and saw them. He frowned even deeper. 'Were you there when I came in?'

Alex said, 'Uh huh. You're very busy.'

At last he smiled. 'Take a pew. Dan and Bill said you would be coming and I should try to make clear what's been happening.'

'Sid's still in custody?' Alex asked, hoping he might have been allowed to leave but pretty certain he hadn't been.

'He is. At least he's safe. Those boys deserve better.'

Neither Alex nor Tony responded. Alex agreed but she didn't want to say so out loud when it seemed disloyal to Kyle and Scoot – and Sid until they knew exactly what had happened.

'We can hope Sid gets the benefit of extenuating circumstances,' LeJuan said. 'If he feared for his sons' safety he might feel forced to do as he was told. It seems likely his kids might have been used as leverage. The human trafficking is going to complicate things for him, big time.'

Alex said nothing.

'So Ellis is still on the run?' Tony said. 'Any sightings of him?'

LeJuan was reading phone messages from sticky notes on his desk. 'Looks as if they've got him. And he's doing his best to blame anyone and everyone for his troubles. Poor fool. All Gary Podmore's fault, including Sid supposedly murdering Ellis's wife and they've matched

Ellis's fingerprints to the envelope on the woman's body with drugs and money in it. And Sid was in Holland when that happened, or so they think. Ellis is also fingered for human deliveries – mostly young women. No wonder they've been protecting the money. It has to be huge. Shit, I hate this case.'

'Nasty,' Alex agreed, not wanting to interrupt the flow of information. 'What have they had you doing this morning?'

'Yorkshire. Went up last night to talk to the board of that school. Amblefield. The one where Paul Sutcliffe was head. I wouldn't send a coma-tose rabbit there. Did you know Martin Gimblet was a student there? And people wonder why he's an odd one.'

Alex made a noncommittal noise.

LeJuan was on a roll. 'Only one thing on those old geezers' minds at that school: keep any dirt off the reputation of our wonderful school. They'll get theirs. They're ever so sorry if it was Weston Bell who got beaten to a pulp and buried among some geo-thermal pipes. But even if it was him, it didn't happen anywhere near squeaky clean Amblefield. Nothing to do with them. Nothing to see there. *Tossers.*'

No wonder LeJuan was wound so tight. 'Rotten,' Alex said. 'But you think the dead kid was called Weston Bell and he was one of their boys?'

'They're not going to be thrilled if it was him,' LeJuan said, 'but their reaction to my questions makes me more sure than I was when I went there that there's something fishy – something a lot fishy – there.'

'Did they tell you anything about his family? Someone must have asked questions about him.'

'I'm working on that. Forensics says they'll be back to us in an hour or so. The kid's mouth was pretty messed up.' He gave Alex an apologetic wince. 'Sorry. Dental has taken longer than it should but I'm thinking that's what's coming.'

Tony caught Alex's eye. He frowned and shook his head slightly.

She could take a hint and shut up immediately.

Scuffing heels announced the arrival of Dan O'Reilly with Bill Lamb. They, Alex thought, looked quite chipper.

'To the sitting room,' Dan said. 'If there's ever another case around Folly, which, of course, there won't be, we put the sitting room together at the outset. Agreed?'

Tony raised one eyebrow and didn't look amused.

'Do you have everything signed, sealed and delivered then?' Alex asked. 'What will happen to Scoot and Kyle? Will Sid have to do time?'

'Can't say,' Dan said, 'but I don't want to see Kyle in a foster home. We're going to have to see what can be done about that. I wish Sid had gone to the authorities the moment he figured there was smuggling, and it was big, bad stuff.'

'We pretty much know about that.' Tony wanted to be careful LeJuan didn't get a tongue lashing for saying too much.

'Yeah. I didn't want to jeopardize the case by revealing things too soon,' Dan muttered, with enough grace to look sheepish.

LeJuan approached and gave a long note to

Bill who crossed his legs and was instantly engrossed. He slapped the paper down on his knee and laughed. 'Talk about thick,' he said, chuckling. 'Sid's motorcycle and Nicky's shoes were found hidden not so far from where her body was left. We already know that. Of course, Ellis said Sid did put them there after he killed her. He really should have checked that Sid wasn't hundreds of miles away.'

Dan looked at his partner with a mixture of irritation and confusion. 'Are you sure that's what you should be saying out loud?'

By then Bill had hung back his head to laugh even louder. 'Bloody criminals. Not a brain between most of them.'

Dan held up a hand. 'Hold your horses.'

'Ellis wouldn't have known the bike had been hidden where it was, or that the shoes had been put there too, unless he did it himself. After he took the shoes off her feet. How much did he hate the poor woman? Anyway, he walked right into it. I bet he's who Kyle saw from his bedroom window at the cottage.'

Alex looked at the rafters and Tony cleared his throat.

The laughter faded abruptly and Bill gave an eloquent shrug. 'They are working on the case with us, aren't they?' he said, nodding at Alex and Tony. 'They already knew all this, didn't they?'

'Of course we did,' Tony said drily. 'We were just about to tell you.'

Bill rubbed two fingers between his eyebrows and kept quiet.

'Does all this mean the case is closed?' Alex said. 'Apart from figuring out Scoot and Kyle's living arrangements? I think there'll be a good fight put up to keep them here in the village.'

'I think so, too,' Dan said. 'But have you forgotten the dead boy? I doubt if Ellis had anything to do with that.'

Forty-Eight

'If you think child protective services will go for it,' Tony said to his father. 'And I think it's terrific of you, Dad.'

'It isn't as if I haven't had a boy and his friends running in and out of my house before,' Doc said, smiling at Lily who was grinning in return. 'I've already let Dan O'Reilly know what I want to do and I think I qualify as an upstanding citizen with plenty of support to go to for advice if the boys turn into delinquents. Anyway, it may buy us time until we know exactly what's happening to Sid although I do think he'll have to do time. We just don't want Kyle dragged into the foster system out there and moved around, especially if Scoot can't be with him.'

They stood in Lily's little dining room watching Kyle play with Bogie and Katie in the back garden.

'Sid has to be a good father or the boys wouldn't have grown up to be so decent,' Alex said. 'They want to stay in Folly and we've got to make sure that happens.'

An insistent tapping came at the front door and Lily hurried to answer. The Burke sisters, with Radhika, stood on the doorstep but didn't have to be asked twice to come in. All three carried bags or boxes.

Radhika remained in the hall and asked to speak to Tony.

He joined her and peered into the small carrier she held in her arms. 'Oh,' was all he could think of to say.

She kept her voice down. 'This is why I wanted to talk to you before seeing Kyle. I thought it would be really nice for him to see Naruto. I'll take her back to the clinic afterward. She needs about another week before she's ready to go. Do you think this is going to work out, Tony? Will Kyle be able to keep the little one?'

He hesitated only a moment before making up his mind. 'It would be wonderful for him to see her. And if anyone puts up a roadblock to his having her, we'll just keep her as the clinic cat and Kyle can come there as often as he wants.'

She smiled and her so-dark eyes glistened. 'You are a very kind man. And if there should be a need, Naruto can come to me until Kyle can take over. I have already told Harriet and Mary that she is not available for them to adopt which has disappointed them greatly although I think they only made the request to pressure everyone into making sure the kitten goes to Kyle. They are most wily, those two ladies.'

'Come on,' Tony said. 'Alex, could you call Kyle in and ask him to put the dogs in the boys' bedroom until we can be sure how they will behave.'

Alex came quickly into the hall, took one peek into the carrier and nodded understanding. 'How super,' she said, almost giggling. 'Wait till he sees her.'

With Radhika hidden in the sitting room together with the Burke sisters, Alex helped Kyle take the dogs upstairs.

'They were having fun,' Kyle said on the way back down. 'They'll think they're being punished for something. Do we have to go out? What's happened?'

The strain on the boy's face made Tony think he must be thinking about Sid and expecting news. Doc and Lily were hovering in the dining room doorway and Tony pointed to the sitting room. 'Radhika came to see you. And Harriet and Mary Burke are with her, too. You're popular around here.'

Kyle went into the sitting room and looked at a cat cave made of gray wool with large colored felt dots sewn all over, and an opening for a lucky feline to crawl inside placed in front of Mary Burke. The sisters had dishes and a litter box and Kyle looked seriously at each one before going to his knees in front of the carrier Radhika had used to carry Naruto. He unzipped the mesh door carefully, reached in and took the little cat in both hands.

'So dear,' Alex said, smiling at Tony.

Kyle held the kitten on his cupped hands,

peered into her eyes and tickled her ears until she fell sideways in ecstasy.

'Radhika says she must go back to the clinic for a week. She's still very little.'

'Can't I have her with me?' Kyle said.

Tony didn't look at anyone when he said, 'Of course you can – if Lily doesn't mind. You're a very good vet in training.'

Forty-Nine

Alex walked from window to window in the bar and restaurant. Midnight and she couldn't sleep. Tony had finally drifted off almost an hour earlier and she had waited until she was sure of not waking him before dressing and coming down.

Across the High Street at Corner Cottage, all the lights were off. Alex visualized the boys asleep in their small room with the kitten in her cave, or on the bed with Kyle. The thought made her smile. Whatever happened, Scoot and Kyle would be looked after. Too many people in Folly cared about them to let the boys drift.

'Alex?'

Dan O'Reilly's voice startled her and she spun around. 'Yes?' she said, too loudly.

'Hush. Sorry. I didn't mean to shock you. You can't sleep either. The curse of the overactive mind.'

She held the neck of her quilted red gilet and

took deep breaths. 'Yes.' Being with him, on her own, always felt vaguely dangerous. 'There's so much going on. I know about all the answers, but I can't help thinking there's another shoe to drop.'

'Me too.' He came to stand beside her in front of a window seat in the bar. 'I'm expecting it. And it will come. You heard about Doc wanting to take in the Gammage boys?'

'Yes. It's perfect, especially with all the help he'd have.'

'I intend to work to make that come off.' He leaned to look out into a cold night with stars pricking a black sky and wind wailing softly through the leafless trees. 'You people are something else. You look after your own.'

She didn't want to get deeper into a philosophical discussion with him, not now.

'I hope to have my son with me for the next school term,' he said. 'I'm looking forward to it. I miss him.'

She held her breath an instant. 'Then I'm glad, I can't imagine being separated from my child.' She didn't add, 'if I still had one.'

'Alex, I want to say something that may make you feel uncomfortable, but it might be best out of the way.'

Her heart thudded. Why did he have to complicate things, now of all times?

'I know you're in love with Tony and he's in love with you. How you deal with that is nothing to do with me. But something stops the two of you from throwing your lives into a pot together.'

He was quiet but she didn't answer.

Soon he added, 'I just want you to know that if you ever decide you need a friend to talk to, someone who understands the hurdles of trying to be together with just one other person, I'd like to be that for you. I admire you. You're a survivor. And I'm . . .' He turned to look down into her face. 'I've been there and I'm a good listener.'

A slow breath escaped her as if she were saved from something she didn't want to face. 'Thank you. I'll remember that. I look forward to meeting your boy when he comes.'

Dan continued to look at her with rapt concentration she felt even in the gloom.

His phone gave a dull buzz and he took it from his pocket, looked at the readout and answered. 'Yes, LeJuan. What is it?'

She could hear the voice at the other end of the line but not what it said.

'This is what I want you to do,' Dan said. 'We need an ambulance but impress on them not to use any sirens. Get close but keep out of sight. I'll contact Bill – he's already there. Good. I'll see him up there – he can go with you. No one gets any closer. If there's a negotiator in the area, we'd like him in reserve, but nothing from him unless I say so. Above all, quiet. Listen, don't talk, don't give any orders – or advice. I'll be right there.'

Alex grabbed his arm as he switched off. 'What is it?'

'Tinsdale Tower. Potential jumper.' He fastened a hand behind her neck. 'No heroics. This joker wants to talk to you.'

* * *

Dan took his Lexus and Tony drove Alex. She had tried to leave him to sleep but he'd come instantly awake, dragged on jeans and jumper and raced with her to his Range Rover.

'Tinsdale Tower? You're sure?' He'd already asked the question more than once.

'Yes. Let's just get there.'

'I haven't been there since I was a kid. It's a good job it's easy to find.'

Alex rarely thought of how Folly-on-Weir got its name from the tower, built on a hill above the dimple where both she and Tony had their homes.

'We're to look for parked police and emergency vehicles. They'll be just off the road under the hill. They're waiting because I'm needed.'

'I don't like it,' Tony said, ducking, to peer into the darkness ahead. The Range Rover's lights made a bright swathe ahead but around them the darkness was absolute. 'What are you supposed to do?'

'I don't know. But whatever it is, I'll try.'

'Not if it puts you in danger.'

They had wound uphill, past the road leading to their own homes and turning higher toward the little-used track where the tower – the Tooth as the locals called the jagged stone building pointing skyward – sat in lonely solitude. Even the kids avoided the place since the stories of falling rocks and ghastly injuries – and the occasional haunting – were a vivid part of local lore.

'There?' Alex leaned forward to point at a collection of parked vehicles visible because of their light paint.

Tony drew in and turned off the engine and lights. The door was yanked open by Dan O'Reilly who said, 'Tony. Glad to see you. There may be nothing we can do but you and Alex follow us.'

The tower stood on a flat, rocky plateau barely bigger than its base. The rocks were mostly pieces of stone that had fallen from the tower, either alone over the years or with the help of someone fulfilling a dare.

Mostly quite still, figures stood in groups. Alex could make out their upturned faces and followed the direction of their eyes. The top of the tower, reached by interior steps that wound upward between two intervening floors to the very top which had once, although not in Alex's memory, had a roof. Without that roof the uppermost floor, surrounded by a broken, waist-high wall, stood open to the sky and the elements.

A movement up there stopped her breathing.

'You see him?' Dan whispered. 'His canvas jacket just shows. There!'

'I see him,' Alex said, her stomach meeting her diaphragm.

Tony stood behind the two of them. 'So do I. Is that . . . who is it?'

Alex thought she'd faint if it was Sid.

'Martin Gimblet,' Dan said quietly. 'He told us he's got a lot to say, but not until he's explained himself to you, Alex.'

A gulp broke free of her throat. 'Why me?'

'You're the only one who was ever nice to him. Didn't you realize that?'

334

'I hardly know him.' He was younger and she hadn't been aware of him until recently.

'That's not the way he sees it. Can you manage to speak to him over a loudhailer?'

'No,' Tony said emphatically. 'He's going to do what he's going to do. This is to make sure he's got the maximum attention for whatever it is. Alex can't have any responsibility for him.'

She knew what Tony was thinking and loved him for both his insight and for caring so much about her.

A group sigh sounded.

Martin hooked a leg over the wall and sat astride it.

'It could crumble, boss,' Bill said to Dan. 'There's a negotiator just arriving. Says he'd like to take the first shot talking him down.'

'Where's Alex?' Martin's voice was faint, taken by the wind.

She cupped her mouth. 'I'm here, Martin. Please come down and talk.'

He didn't answer.

'Wait,' Dan said.

Human shadows shifted at the edge of Alex's vision. She shivered but sweat broke out on her face and back. Her eyes misted and she blinked, scrubbed at her face.

Martin moved, bent over and seemed to hold his head.

'Where's the bloody negotiator?' Bill hissed through his teeth. 'We're losing him,'

Tony reached to grab Bill's shoulder and talk quietly in his ear. They huddled with Dan, all three keeping their voices very low.

For a moment Alex stood alone, looking up at the hunched shape on the exposed tower wall.

He wanted to talk to her – but he wasn't going to while there was an audience, she was sure of it.

Backing up, stepping smoothly, quietly down from the plateau, she doubled over and ran softly around the base of the mound, looking up only to see how far she'd gone. The entrance to the tower steps was on the far side and that was her aim.

Expecting to hear her name at any second, or to be grabbed by one of the men, she made it as far as she needed to go and climbed to the plateau again. The darkness was almost absolute but the tower entrance was still a denser black against everything else and she made a run for it.

Once inside, she waited, hoping her eyes would adjust, that she could at least find the base of the steps. From memory she saw how those steps curved around, through an opening into first one, then a second floor and finally at the top.

There was no handrail now, the original metal ring and rope grips having rotted away long ago.

The toe of her right trainer hit the side of the steps. She could vaguely see the outline of them now, spiraling up into ever deeper darkness.

Alex leaned against the wall and used her hands on the steps to steady her climb. She could not look outward toward the middle of the tower. That way lay nothing but a fall through dead air to rough stones below.

She didn't know, couldn't guess how long it took to reach the opening into the top level. Carefully, she stretched her head through and squinted around until she saw Martin, or the shape that was Martin, silhouetted against a gunmetal sky.

She took a deep breath and said, 'Martin, it's me, Alex. You wanted to talk to me.'

He straightened so abruptly and his shoulders swung so that she almost cried out, expecting him to fall.

'Alex,' he whispered. 'You're here?'

'Yes, Martin, of course I am. I'm going to sit on the floor by the wall on this side. Those steps are so scary.'

He gave what sounded like a choked sob. 'I put you in danger.'

'No,' she said, adding a dismissive note. 'I'm just not so good in the dark. Come and sit with me.'

He didn't answer.

And he didn't move.

Alex decided to wait until he did say something.

At last he said, 'I should have been stronger. It's almost all my fault. They have to get Paul. He ruined everything. He's a monster.'

'I think Paul's on his way back from the north,' she told him, trying for a conversational tone. 'Do you want to tell me anything?'

'I'm only going to tell you and no one else. That's because you matter to me. I want you to know what happened. I took Kyle but I didn't hurt him. I shouldn't have done it but I was going to blame it on Paul so he'd be caught and everything he's done would come out.'

A pain throbbed at Alex's right temple and she rubbed it. 'You brought Kyle back.' She couldn't believe what he was telling her. 'That was the right thing to do.'

'I used his father's van. I couldn't risk Mother's car. I don't have one – I lost my license for drunk driving. I took Kyle back because I couldn't risk Paul doing to him what he did to Weston Bell – and to me. Do you know, Paul told me what he'd done to Weston. And he thought he was so clever to go to the police and report Weston missing – to throw them off just in case some-thing went wrong later, he said. He never expected the body to be found, damn him. He told me about it all because he said I'm weak and pathetic and he liked to see me afraid and sick. And he said I'd never repeat what he told me because then it would all come out about me. Everyone would know what happened to me at Amblefield, how he . . . he used me, and I wouldn't be able to stand that.'

'Don't worry, Martin. You'll be safe. I'll make sure they listen to you.'

By now the negotiator should be talking. She feared the silence meant she'd been missed and the police were trying to intervene.

'May I come over by you. It would feel better to be near you up here.'

'Be careful,' he said softly. 'I don't want you hurt.'

On hands and knees, Alex crawled across the rough floor until she was beside his leg. He shifted to touch her and his fingers patted her hair.

A rattling, sudden and horrifying, shot against the outside wall; scree sliding free of the stone wall to cascade downward.

'Come off the wall,' she said, hearing a note of hysteria in her own voice. She breathed through her mouth. 'Please, Martin, come off the wall.'

'I can't. Don't you want to know what would all come out if I told my story?'

She only wanted to be back on the ground outside, standing beside Tony.

'Amblefield. Why did I have to go there? My mother thought it was good for me. Paul treated me as if I was special in front of the other boys and they hated me as much as he did. They punished me and he punished me, only he was worse. The humiliation tore away my confidence. I still feel his hands on me and hear him saying that if I told my mother he would say I was a liar and a pervert and everyone would find out. And then it got worse, and worse. He hated me because my mother loved me. He didn't want to share her and she was the only woman he could bear.'

He was breathless, gasping. And Alex wanted to be sick.

'Say something!' he cried.

'Martin, you're all right now. It will all be all right. Paul will be arrested, if he hasn't already been arrested. The police have been closing in on him, I'm sure.'

She heard a scrape and knew what it was. Someone was stealthily climbing the stairs.

'Did you hear that?' Martin said. 'If they don't go away, I'll jump and they'll never know it all. I want you to promise you won't tell what I've told you.'

'I'm on your side,' she told him.

'He only started with the other boys when I was gone,' he said, his voice breaking. 'And eventually, as it should have happened years earlier, the rumors started. He didn't retire, he left the school because it was his only chance to stay away from prosecution and the board at the school went along with it to save their stinking reputations. Weston Bell was his last victim. At the school, I mean. Paul thought he got away with everything but then Weston showed up.'

'Blackmail,' Alex murmured.

'Get away,' Martin yelled so abruptly she jumped and her heart took up a violent thud. 'I hear you. Come up any closer and there will be death. It will be your fault.'

Alex listened, but the scraping stopped.

'What did Weston want from Paul?' Alex asked. She hadn't intended to push for answers but that boy's broken body would stay in her mind.

'He wanted Paul to take him in. What family he had were overseas. They sent him to Amblefield and he was alone. Paul took everything Weston had, even his sense of self, and Weston came looking for Paul, hoping he'd want him as no one else did.'

'Paul didn't want him?' Alex said.

'Paul only wanted me,' Martin said. 'To do what he wanted forever. He taunted Weston with that and Weston threatened him. He promised